KILLER

a novel by

S T E P H E N   C A R P E N T E R

ISBN: 1482678888

ISBN-13: 9781482678888

CONTENTS

PAST IMPERFECT
Five Years Ago

PRESENT PROGRESSIVE
Five Years Later

PAST IMPERFECT

Five Years Ago

CHAPTER ONE

Most suicides leave notes. My Sara didn't.

Most women who kill themselves choose non-violent means. My Sara went to Chalet Sporting Goods in Pasadena and selected a Mossberg 12 gauge shotgun in matte black. She put it on her Visa, waited the requisite ten days, then picked up the gun from the store and drove back to our rented home in San Gabriel. Then, after smoking enough cigarettes to fill the Santa Anita Racetrack ashtray we bought at the swap meet, my Sara tied her short brown hair back, went into the backyard, kneeled on the grass, placed the gun muzzle under her chin, and reached down for the trigger. The police later figured she must have only barely reached it—my Sara stood 5'3" in gym socks—but reach it she did, and she blew the front half of her head into the bright blue cloudless Southern California sky.

CHAPTER TWO

Fifteen months later I woke up in a hospital. My hands were bound to the bed and two middle-aged men were telling me I was charged with murder.

For a few minutes my mind wouldn't work at all. I couldn't remember anything—who I was, where I was, how I got there, what had happened. It is a lonely thing to find yourself adrift, without a past. I lay there those first panicky moments, not moving, all of my energy focused on remembering, searching to find something to hold on to, anything to root me back into my life.

An image came to me—*Sara smiling up at me from the couch*—then I remembered her name, just before I remembered my own. And then I remembered the Unspeakable afternoon in San Gabriel when I came home and couldn't find her and I went to the back door and opened it and saw the gun on the ground and then I saw her lying on the grass and my desperation to remember suddenly became desperation to forget. I had been safe in my ignorance before the Unspeakable came to me, and now it took every ounce of will to resist the agony of memory and push it back to the place where memories live when they are unwanted. But memories don't always obey.

How long had it been since that day? A week? A month? Yesterday—?

"Richard Bell?" said one of the middle-aged men, his voice rising to let me know it was a question. I saw a badge on his belt and he fixed his baggy, boozy eyes on mine.

I shook my head, having just remembered my name.

"My name is Rhodes," I said, my voice an unrecognizable rasp. Shaking my head was a mistake. My bruised brain bounced around inside my skull and the dull ache revved to a chainsaw whine.

"We know that, Mr. Rhodes. Do you know a Richard Bell?"

I closed my eyes, afraid to remember anything more, afraid to think or move as the approaching thunderstorm of a hundred-year hangover threatened to flood my head if I tried too hard to do anything.

Who the hell was Richard Bell?

Boozy Eyes held out a mug shot from a laser printer that was low on toner. Richard Bell looked like a guy who would wind up murdered—swollen nose and deep, angry lines stamped into his face. A mean son of a bitch. A junkyard dog from *Cops*.

"I don't remember," I croaked.

"You don't remember what?" asked the other cop. He wore a blue necktie flecked with soft clouds, like a child's pajamas. *Happy Father's Day, Daddy!*

"I don't remember him from anywhere, no," I glanced up from the picture, my voice coming back, accompanied by random, spectacular lightning bolts of pain in my head.

"We found Mr. Bell in Highland Park this morning," Cloudy Necktie produced a glossy 8 x 10 crime scene photograph of Richard Bell, curled up in a trash dumpster like a sleeping baby. Richard Bell's throat had been cut so deeply that his head was only hanging onto his body because his stark white spinal cord was still intact. Someone had started cutting through the front of Richard Bell's throat and didn't stop until they had gotten almost completely through the vertebrae in his neck. One of his eyes was half-closed, the other eye was wide open and staring at a rotting head of lettuce in front of his face. I wondered if that head of lettuce was the last thing Richard Bell saw on earth. I wondered who would throw out an entire head of lettuce. Then the room began to spin.

"Your car was found near the body," Cloudy Necktie informed me. He showed me another glossy photograph: my car, parked near the dumpster, with blood all over the interior.

"That's impossible. Last night I was…"

Where the fuck was I last night? Where the fuck was I *right now?*

"Last night I was…" I began again, to prime the pump of memory, but all that came up was a flood of sour whiskey, which washed up out of me and all over Boozy Cop's shoes.

"Goddamnit!" The detective jumped back and looked like he was going to shoot me right there. Cloudy Necktie suppressed a smirk and held up the photograph of Richard Bell in the dumpster again.

"Last night…?" he prompted me.

Even if I hadn't been too busy throwing up to answer, I had seen enough *Law & Order* to know this was the point where I should probably shut up.

CHAPTER THREE

Getting arrested for murder and chained to a jail infirmary bed for a week is an incredibly effective way to begin your journey to sobriety. I hit the belly of the bottom the second night I spent cuffed to my cozy, rusting bed, sweating and shivering with *delirium tremens*. The cockroaches crawling over me were only the beginning—the trailer before the Feature. It occurred to me later that the roaches might not have been a hallucination. Lying awake the next night, I saw two rats scamper up under the covers of a comatose guy named Angel. Angel had tried to commit suicide by cop, but only managed to get shot in the shoulder—not enough to kill him, just enough to introduce a bullet fragment into his blood stream, which lodged in a blood vessel in his brain and turned him into a brussel sprout. The rats ate some part of Angel that I know only as a dark blood stain on the sheet between his legs as they rolled his body out the next day.

The real bottom came after the cockroaches, when my Sara appeared at my bedside with her head at a strange angle, revealing her stark white spinal cord. In her hands was a rotten head of lettuce, which she was offering me. She said my name and I cried out when I saw the look in her eyes—a look of infinite pain; of hollow, bottomless regret. She ran a cool hand over my hot forehead, down my wet cheek, then she let her hand fall across my neck.

Then angry lines formed between her eyes and around her mouth and Sara's face became the face of Richard Bell, and his hands tightened around my throat. I couldn't breathe, couldn't scream, and couldn't fight back, although I must have tried like hell. The next morning I awoke to find my left hand puffed up like a cartoonish purple balloon hand. The doctors told me I had broken two of my wrist bones trying to rip my arm from the cuff.

But alas, I was sober.

CHAPTER FOUR

My purple balloon hand saved my ass. The tiny fractures in my wrist bones became infected and extended my stay in the infirmary, which set my arraignment and trial back. The combination of my alcoholism and the negligence of the Los Angeles County Jail infirmary doctors led to avascular necrosis in my wrist bones and I was transferred to UCLA, where they rebuilt my wrist, replacing the dead bones and ligaments with chrome and plastic parts. And it was during that time that a local news station picked up the story of Richard Bell's murder. And Archie Bledsoe, God bless him, came forward with my alibi. Archie was the bartender at McDougal's the night Richard Bell met his last head of lettuce. I was dead drunk, as usual, and Archie had picked me up and ushered me into the alley, where I slept until the police found me early the next morning and brought me to the jail infirmary. I had no memory of any of this, but Archie swore to it. At the time of the murder I was where I always was—the corner booth in back, the darkest and farthest from the door, appearing nightly, ladies and gentlemen, *Mr. Jack Rhodes! Good evening, my invisible friends, and welcome to my slow, sad, painless death by alcohol. Listen, listen, and I will tell you my tragic tale of love and loss and limpid alabaster atomized into sky...*

The police pieced together that Richard Bell had rolled me in the alley, taken my wallet and keys and stolen my car and somehow wound up in Highland Park on his final dumpster dive. The cops had no reason to hold me, the case against me was dropped, and I was released.

So there I was, sober and free after a fifteen-month forgotten nightmare. Fifteen months since I had found my Sara and went crazy—panicked, sobbing crazy—that awful sunny afternoon in the backyard, trying to find her face.

Please God, let me see her face again… Please don't let this be real, it's not real…I only want to see her face again please God oh please…

Fifteen months since I found her; fifteen months of drinking in the morning, in the afternoon, and at night. Every night. Fifteen months of my life that are gone forever in memory. Fifteen months and I had finally awoken from my Jack Daniel's dream to find my shattered life still shattered, my heart still blazing with pain that I had doused all day, every day, for fifteen months. And now, without the booze to douse it, the horrible fire roared back and I did the only thing I could do to stop it; the only thing I could do to keep from reaching for sweet, bottled relief.

CHAPTER FIVE

———

I moved from our home in San Gabriel and took a tiny apartment in Pasadena and I began to write the same way I used to drink—every day, obsessively, without a pause or a break, except to go wash dishes at Delancey's for the dinner shift. There I rinsed the grease and the unwanted food off the plates and lost myself in the puzzle of my first book.

Before Sara's death I had tried my hand at all kinds of writing: short stories, spec screenplays, TV pilots, all with little success. Here and there I sold something—an article to *Rolling Stone* about B movies, and another to *Esquire*. I even wrote a true-crime book for a fly-by-night publisher about infamous serial killers—the only book I'd ever had published at the time. But always I kept coming back to the Great American Novel, as Sara and I called it, with as much sarcasm as we could muster. I had tried and failed at a few chapters, at last giving up and giving in to the need for money. The Great American Novel became the Reduced Expectation of simply sustaining some kind of a life as a writer. Sara taught kindergarten at a pricey private school in South Pasadena while I scrambled from agent to agent, magazine to magazine, never quite making enough to sustain our household on my own, but Sara's paycheck took up the slack and we were young, still in our twenties, and there would always be time…

Now with Sara gone and the constant, numbing flow of booze behind me, I wrote desperately to keep the demons and the memories away during the day, and at night I gripped the heavy stainless steel spray nozzle in the kitchen at Delancey's and washed the encrusted baked potatoes and cold rinds of steak fat off the plates and slowly loosened the knots in my head until I eventually untangled a promising story—or situation—for a series of novels that might just work.

And it did work. I wrote the first book in six months, titled it *Killer,* and sold it to Terrapin Publishing for the fabulous advance of $10,000 dollars. The hardcover sales took everyone by surprise—they couldn't keep it on the shelves. The order for the first printing of the paperback was 250,000 copies, and by then I was halfway through the second book in the series. My publishers even bought the rights to the true-crime book I had written about serial killers years before, and published a slick new edition.

When I used to do interviews, I was sometimes asked to explain the success of the *Killer* series, and I always said that I thought people just bought the hook: a meticulous serial killer masterminds a murder in every book, but we never meet him or hear him described. We only know him through his handiwork, as seen through the eyes of the determined young FBI agent, Katherine Kendall, who works desperately to solve each book's murder and prevent another. Katherine Kendall, *who stands 5'3" in gym socks*, never quite catches her killer, but she prevents the death of a young woman in each book, and in that way she defeats the killer in every book. And I sold a lot of books.

The kitchen staff at Delancey's gave me a drunken little party when *Killer* sold and I gave my notice. At the party I found myself wanting a drink for the first time in a year, so I left early. I went home and wanted a drink even more, so I decided it was time to move.

Which brings me to Vermont.

CHAPTER SIX

The point was to get as far away from California as possible. Away from the old drinking haunts; far, far away from the Unspeakable sunny afternoon in San Gabriel. I sat at home with an atlas the night after the Delancey's party and measured the distance from Los Angeles to the farthest point away in the U.S. The answer was Maine. But I remembered a few movie people I'd met and didn't much like who had summer homes in Maine, so I chose to avoid it. In the end, I met an editor at a publishing event who recommended an area in Vermont which she felt would be perfect for my desired seclusion.

So I left. Just like that. I gave everything away except Sara's things, which I put in storage, and got on a plane with a single bag in my hand and wound up looking at cabins and homes in rural Vermont with a divorced realtor in her sixties from New York who was determined to settle me *somewhere.*

A few weeks later I moved into a 2300 square-foot cabin on sixteen acres near Featherton, a tiny town in the middle of Vermont. The cabin was built by an orthodontist and his wife as a second home, but divorce forced them to sell the place before they moved in. It was a brand new cabin, built of split pine logs. It had a master bedroom, a smaller bedroom which I converted to a study, a spacious living room with a big fireplace, and a modern kitchen. It was quiet and secluded and I felt I could work there. The day after I moved in I drove my rental car to Burlington and bought a Ford F-150 pickup from a dealership. I drove my new pickup to Featherton and bought a chainsaw and other tools from Langtree Hardware. Virgil Langtree owned the hardware store in Featherton, as well as the grocery store and the gas station with the mini-mart. Virgil, who seemed at least a hundred years old, sold me wedges and chisels and guided me with Yankee parsimony in selecting tools to stock my cabin and the utility box in the back of my pickup. I learned a lot from old Virgil—how to cut down the dying pines on my property; how to notch the trunk at the appropriate height and depth. How to avoid kickback with the chainsaw, how to alternate sides when notching the trunk to make the tree fall where I wanted. I spent late afternoons and weekends splitting the logs into firewood and stacking them alongside the cabin. Eventually the cabin was surrounded by firewood and I gave up the chainsaw for an axe. Virgil showed me how to set wedges to split the wood. It was hard work, but it felt good to get up a sweat at the end of a day of writing. When I had more wood laid up than I could ever use I bought a table saw and built a large woodshed on the border of the woods that surrounded the cabin. I insulated a small section of the woodshed and hung drywall. I also hung a speed-bag and a heavy bag, and bought a bench and some free weights. When it was too cold outside to perspire, I worked the bags and the weights until I had sweat out the day's dose of caffeine and my muscles loosened and my breathing deepened and I forgot everything but the rhythm of the bags and the weights and the blood pounding through me.

I was alone but I wasn't lonely. The isolation and self-reliance were a balm. I took long walks through the woods at the end of the day, or whenever I got stuck on a writing problem. I discovered the ruins of an 18th century farmhouse on my property that had been razed a hundred years ago. I would wander around the ruins of the farmhouse, ruminating on my writing and looking absently for signs of the old structure. Sometimes I would find little artifacts; a brick, or an old nail. My bookshelves became littered with relics I found there. A three hundred year-old old bottle of Kill Devil rum sat empty on the window sill above my kitchen sink, catching the morning sun through its thick, bubbled, wavy blue-green glass.

So I spent the next five years in Featherton, Vermont, felling trees with my axe and my word processor, piling up firewood and filling paperback racks in airports and grocery stores everywhere. No one would ever confuse me with John Updike but I didn't care. I had wood to cut and books to write. Always, always books to write. Because the demons were always, always just around the corner.

———

PRESENT PROGRESSIVE
Five Years Later

CHAPTER ONE

I'm sitting at my desk, wondering if I should kill the cute sheriff with an axe or a claw hammer in the final chapter of my fourth book when there is a sharp knock at my front door. It sends my over-caffeinated heart into a sprint. No one ever knocks. Even the UPS guy leaves his packages at the mailbox out on the state highway to avoid the quarter-mile driveway I deliberately leave rutted and unpaved. The door itself is solid oak—*real* oak, two inches thick, with four heavy gauge steel hinges and three titanium deadbolts, one by the doorknob, one on top of the door, and one at the bottom of the door, installed by the orthodontist, a lifelong New Yorker.

I unlock the door and open it to find Claire Boyle, the local sheriff and inspiration for the doomed fictional sheriff whose nude body I was just about to hack to pieces on my word processor. I don't mention the coincidence to Claire.

"Morning, Jack," Claire gives me a prim Yankee smile; the same smile I get from all the locals. After five years, the good people of Featherton, VT. have come to regard me with cautious curiosity. In town they nod at me on the street, but they don't maintain eye contact for long. Claire has more reason than most to be cautious about me. Two years after I moved to Featherton, my barber Jezzie decided it was a sin and a shame that a local land-owning heterosexual man of marrying age was still single, so she set me up with Claire. I figured maybe enough time had passed since Sara, but after two awkward dates I told Claire it was too soon. I never called her again. And now, three years later, it's too late.

"Want some coffee?" I ask as Claire comes in. She glances at me nervously, turning her Smokey the Bear hat around and around, hand over hand, as if she were steering her Sheriff's Dept. SUV in a u-turn out of my cabin.

"No thanks. I, ah…just got a call from the Los Angeles Police." She looks at me to see if this means anything. It doesn't.

"They want to talk to you."

"About what?"

The Smokey the Bear hat turning hard right, right, right.

"Well, I didn't get much information from the detectives there, but I guess there was a homicide—a young woman—and they think maybe it was some kind of…copycat situation. From one of your books?" Her eyes flick up at mine for a second.

Shit. I have wondered occasionally about something like this—some random wack-job mimicking a gruesome murder from one of my books. I sit on the couch, hoping it's a mistake.

"What makes them think it has anything to do with my books?"

"Evidently the young woman was found in a, uh, manner that a victim in your book was found."

"Which book?"

She looks down. "I'm not sure…you know I haven't really read much of your work." Claire seems embarrassed. I remember her telling me she hadn't read any of my books on our first date, as if it mattered to me. She's too solid, too practical. Maybe even disapproving. She's a fourth-generation Congrega-. tionalist. Her ancestors wouldn't have messed around with me. They would have burned me at the stake for conjuring spirits, lickety-split.

"Okay. Sure. They can call me here at home."

"Actually, they want you to come to Los Angeles." She holds my gaze steadily.

"Why?"

"Like I said, they didn't give me much information."

"Well I need more information. Tell them they can call me and I'll help them any way I can."

"Look, Jack, I don't want trouble any more than you do, but they said it was important that I get you to cooperate."

Again the steady look. *What the fuck does that look mean?*

"Is there something you're not telling me, Claire?"

Round and round the hat goes. I wait, biding my time trying not to notice how she fills out her olive uniform, how the dark stripes on her slacks follow the curves of her thighs, the way she wears her holster just slightly lower around her hips than regulation probably dictates... *If she had worn her uniform on one of our dates things might have worked out differently...*

"It's not so much what they—" she begins. "They just said there were an awful lot of...consistencies with the murder scene and what was in your book."

She stands there, turning her hat and looking at me.

"That's it?"

"Pretty much. They were pretty tight-lipped."

I look out the window. The color is all but gone from the trees. Most of them are bare now, against a slate November sky. The ground is hard from the night frost and soon it will be covered with snow. I turn back to Claire, who is standing in the middle of the large braided rug on the living room floor. She looks out of place, the rug's pattern of brown and white rings encircling her. I suddenly realize this is the first time a woman has set foot in this cabin in three years. It's not a happy thought. The phone rings.

"Jack," the voice of Arnie Brandt, my agent. "Have you heard?"

"I have a member of Featherton's finest right here in my living room as we speak. What do you know about this, Arnie?"

"Well, I don't know what she's told you, but this detective, Marsh, I think his name is, called me from L.A. to track you down. We may have a problem."

Arnie never called unless he had something concrete to say—news which was either good or bad. He's using his "bad" voice.

"They won't tell me anything more," Arnie says. "They want you to come to L.A. so they can talk to you about it."

"So I'm told. What do you think?"

"I think we'd better get out in front of this. You're about to deliver and we don't need this kind of publicity. I think you should go and cooperate in every way you can before this gets a chance to hit the press."

And the shit hits the fan.

"Alright," I say finally. "I'll get the next flight I can. Have you talked to Joel?" I ask, meaning Joel Fisher, my lawyer in New York.

"Not yet. Obviously we need to keep him in the loop, but I don't think you need to bring him along to L.A., per se," Arnie says carefully. "Nobody at Terrapin knows yet, as far as I know. Just go and talk to the LAPD. That's all they want at this point."

I hang up, relieved to see Claire holding her hat still and giving me a wan smile. I look at her and shrug.

"Okay," I say.

THINGS PAST

It was his fifth birthday but he didn't know it. He didn't know his name; he didn't even know he was awake until he heard the Witch's voice. In the dark place it was sometimes hard to tell when you were asleep and when you were awake. But the sound of the Witch laughing with a man woke him. The light under the door shone into the dark place and, after endless hours of complete darkness, the faint light hurt his small eyes. He was too young to understand the sounds from the room outside the closet, but he had heard them many times—the Witch laughing and moaning and shouting vulgar things to different men over the wild, thrashing music. He didn't know the concept of "mother." He only knew the dark place and the sounds with the men and the abrupt, terrifying attacks from the Witch. He hated her and wished her dead.

He knew it was wrong to hate. At least, he knew others *thought it was wrong. But he couldn't understand that. He had been to Sunday school—a day care center at a local church—when his mother was briefly incarcerated. He had no other family anywhere; he had never been to kindergarten, never seen a doctor, only rarely been outdoors. So when Social Services found him they didn't know what to do with him. The people from Social Services were all the same: dull, officious, with their forms and clipboards and limited eye contact. No one said, "Your mother pleaded guilty to felony possession of methamphetamines and she's doing thirty days at the county jail." They simply said, "Your mother's at County," as though he would know what that meant. They had precious little time to spend on him, so Social Services took him to the day care at First Baptist and moved on to the next intractably messy and irresolvable case.*

From the moment he arrived at the day care he was stunned—overwhelmed—so much so that he couldn't speak for days. His young mind soaked up the sights and sounds, the songs, the picture books, the caring, compassionate women who ran the center—and the daylight. For the thirty days his mother was "at County," he was passed from family to family at night, and during the day he sat, entranced, and listened to the songs the other children sang and looked at the picture books of baby Jesus and Mary and the angels... and he loved it all so much that he cried often. The women thought he was sad but he didn't know how to explain that his tears were pure joy. He had never once told anyone about any feelings he had. He didn't know how. He knew, even at this young age, that he was different. He could see the tender feeling in the women at the center; he could tell they loved Jesus and wept for his suffering. But the bleeding wounds of Jesus excited him in a way he couldn't tell the women about. Even at this young age he knew he couldn't tell anyone about those feelings. Later he would come to understand the special feelings, and they would bring him power and pleasure in measure with the heaven that the dying Jesus promised. In my father's house are many mansions.

But on the brink of turning five, it was much simpler. He loved everything about the day care, but most of all he loved the stories. Daniel in the lion's den, Jonah in the belly of the whale, and his favorite—David and Goliath. He thought a lot about small David killing the brutal giant. He thought of it constantly and it comforted him.

Sometimes the families who took him in at night read fairy tales to their children. The happy-family children delighted in the stories and slept soundly after hearing them. But to him, the sorry young charge, the fragile charity case, the fairy tales loomed as large as the Bible stories, and he did not sleep. Because he had now learned about witches.

He thought one day he would tell stories to others. He could feel the budding urge to tell others about his life, his story, his Witch. He knew that his life had gone horribly wrong. He knew it when he saw the way the day care children lived with their families. They slept in beds, they were fed and clothed and loved. He felt the desperate need to be listened to, to be paid attention.

The women at the day care were surprised at how quickly he learned his letters and began to read. They encouraged the bright young boy when he printed his alphabet with his big red pencil, and then, soon, his name. He had a gift, they told him, and he nearly burst with pride and happiness, although he couldn't express his feelings. They thought he was shy. "Don't hide your light under a bushel," they told him. And it increased his longing to learn one day to tell his stories to someone—to anyone who would listen.

Then his mother was released from her prison and he was returned to his. But he was blessed with a miracle—a present from one of the women at the day care: the small figure of an angel. She was head and hands only, eight inches tall, pink lips and blue eyes against pure white porcelain, her perfect little hands pressed together in prayer. In the dark place her presence soothed him in the hours of his torment, the hours of crying, begging, screaming… He would look at the Angel in the half-light, the Witch's cluttered pile of filthy clothes his bed. The Angel looked down on him over her praying hands, head tilted slightly, Mona Lisa smile, her eyes china blue ovals of infinite compassion bordered by fine, dark lashes painted with delicate brush. He did love her. As much as he hated the Witch.

He pressed his hands to his ears to shut out the sound of the Witch and the man and the pounding music. But the sound wouldn't stop. Tears ran silently down his soft cheeks and he thought he would begin screaming—a thought which terrified him. Screaming meant the door would fly open and the light would blind him and then would come the hands of the Witch—sometimes open, sometimes closed, once holding a high-heeled shoe which left a bleeding dent in his temple. He bit his lip to keep from screaming. Bit down hard until he tasted the warm wet salt of blood.

And then, that night, on his fifth birthday, just when he could bear no more, another miracle—

The Witch sounds were drowned out by the Angel's voice.

He took his hands from his ears, astonished. The Angel had never made a sound before. But now he heard her clearly—her voice filled his ears, his head, his small heart.

He lay on the hard floor, mesmerized by the sound, as clear and sweet as a blackbird's song. She was singing to him—a song he had learned at the day care.

> Jesus loves me, this I know,
> For the Bible tells me so.
> Little ones to Him belong,
> They are weak but He is strong.

She sang softly as he wept and finally slept. He dreamed of being held in the arms of the Angel, held like the baby Jesus in the picture books, held and kissed and caressed.

Loved.

CHAPTER TWO

She is sitting across the aisle from me on the plane. Small and round, late fifties, Nieman Marcus from head to toe, and she is reading my last book, *Killer Unbound*. She is reading with the intensity I like to imagine everyone has when they pick up a book of mine at an airport, which is where most people pick up my books. We are halfway to Los Angeles and she is halfway through the book when she happens to glance up and see me watching her. I look away quickly, but not quickly enough. From the corner of my eye I see her check the back of the paperback, where my postage stamp-sized photo is sequestered between the bar code and ISBN number. I feel her look back at me. I wish I'd splurged on first class.

"Excuse me," she leans across the aisle toward me. Her wire-framed glasses are smudged at the edges with makeup and her breath is stale.

"I couldn't help but notice…" she holds up the book, indicating my photo, then pointing at me. "Are you Jack Rhodes? The author?"

"Yes," I smile politely.

"Oh my God," she says too loudly and presses the book against her breasts. "I don't believe it! I'm sitting here reading your book and there you are, right across the aisle from me!"

"Yep. Right here." *Please let there be turbulence. Oxygen masks dropping…screams from the galley…*

"I read *Killer* when it came out. Couldn't put it down. Then I read *Killer At Large,* and now *Killer Unbound…* Oh my God, I just love your books."

"Well, thank you very much." I press the button overhead for the flight attendant.

"I always wanted to write. I studied at LSU. Creative Writing. And I've always loved the way you have of pulling the reader into the story..."

"Thank you." I press the button overhead again. Not a flight attendant in sight. They have obviously taken the escape pod.

"I mean, just the way you follow the story...the way you..." she struggles to come up with *le mot juste*, "...the way you *seduce* the reader. It's *so* good."

"Thanks."

"Where do you come up with your ideas? I've tried to write...I mean, nothing at all like you—well, in a way maybe a little," she blushes slightly. "But I just can't imagine how you come up with so many characters and stories and... Where do you get your ideas?"

"They just come to me," I shrug. She gives me a blank look. This won't satisfy her. I pray for a lightning strike. *Ah, folks, we've just lost both engines and we're going to have to ditch in the Rockies so please stop talking to one another...*

"They just come to you? I can't imagine. All those characters and the *detail*... you just make it all up?"

"Pretty much."

She stares at me as if I were an ostrich in the aisle seat across from her.

"I can't imagine."

"It's not really that mysterious. The story just kind of...tells itself."

"I just can't imagine."

That's right. You can't. And I can. Big deal.

A flight attendant who resembles the seventh grade math teacher from Sara's school reaches over my head and turns off the service light.

"Is everything okay?" she asks.

"Just great. Could I get a pillow, please?"

"Certainly." She heads off to the secret pillow cache.

"I'm sorry, I know you want to sleep, but could I just ask you one favor?"

"Sure," I smile again. It's getting harder to smile.

"Could you sign my book?" A timid girl's giggle as she holds the book toward me. I take it from her and reach for the pen that's always in my pocket.

"To...?" I prompt her.

"Maryann," she says, blushing fiercely.

I sign her book and, feeling guilty for being a jerk, I make it a little extra personal. *Keep writing!* I hand it back and she reads it and the blush spreads from her cheeks and down her neck and for a moment I'm afraid she may explode and blow a hole in the fuselage, killing us all. The flight attendant returns with my pillow.

"Thank you."

I rest back against the pillow and close my eyes.

"Thank *you*," Maryann says.

"You're welcome," I say, and close my eyes and turn aside as Maryann returns to *Killer Unbound*.

Where do you get your ideas? It was the question that finally caused me to stop doing interviews and book signings. Arnie and my publishers were genuinely perplexed. It's the most common question for an author—an inevitable question. And most writers have a stock answer. Some even enjoy talking about their writing process. Some, in fact, will never shut up about it. But the question irritated me on a deep level. I don't know why. I once read a quote from George Bernard Shaw, who said that for him writing was like taking dictation. All he had to do was begin and the play wrote itself. I have no pretensions to the level of a Shaw, or anyone for that matter. I know who I am and what I write and I think it's pretty good for a white trash kid from West Covina who grew up without a father and a mother whom I barely knew—a mother who drank and drugged all day with one boyfriend after another. I don't believe in Muses or writer's block and I don't read reviews. But I understand what Shaw was saying. I simply sit down every day and write what is already in my head, waiting to be put down on paper. I don't know how it got there. I don't question or analyze it, I just write it down. At a book signing once, a flirtatious woman of a certain age asked me if I had a Muse and I said "Yeah, his name is Dave." She didn't laugh, but from then on I jokingly called my muse Dave. *Dave* told me to write this or that. *Dave* said kill her with a claw hammer. *Dave* would figure out how to get out of the building barricaded by the SWAT team.

Not that I didn't wonder at first where all the ideas came from. At first I had privately marveled at my facility to concoct each murderous scheme, each vicious, perfect killing, each elaborate plan to elude capture. It all came so easily, as if each story were already fully formed in my head and I was just taking dictation from some uncharted part of my subconscious. I didn't want to look too hard at that uncharted part—it was clouded with pain that would stop me in my tracks. My lapse in memory began before Sara's death, before the drinking. I remember virtually nothing from my early childhood, and I didn't care to conjure that time to consciousness. I've always had the profound feeling that some things are best left unexamined. My writing had kept me sane and sober for five years. It kept my restless mind busy with imaginary situations and problems of my own creation. I would never be lonely as long as my characters were speaking to me. I would never be bored as long as I could sit at my computer and slip into that peculiar trance where their voices were almost audible... Maybe this isn't normal or maybe it is. Maybe it doesn't matter. Maybe some rocks are best left unturned.

Fuck it. I turn my face into my pillow. Dave the Muse gets all the blame and none of the glory. Well, that's how it goes, *Dave*. Get your own goddamned publishing deal. And next time book me in first class.

CHAPTER THREE

I forgot my sunglasses. I close my eyes against the low, piercing November sun as my taxi curves around the long ramp to get on the 110 freeway. We are headed downtown, to LAPD headquarters at Parker Center. Once the sun is behind us I look ahead at downtown—a cluster of earthquake-safe skyscrapers against the San Gabriel mountains. I can see the foothills just above the neighborhood where Sara and I used to live.

Part of her lay in those foothills for a season, until the rains came. Maybe part of her still does.

My plan is to meet with the police, then rent a car from the rental agency two blocks from Parker Center. I will then drive to San Gabriel, to the storage facility where Sara's things have rested for five years. I will pick up the boxes I have already bought over the phone from the storage office, and I will pack Sara's things. There isn't much. Some books, some clothes, and odds and ends I couldn't bring myself to deal with when I left. I had asked Sara to marry me a year before she died, and she had begun collecting things—bridal magazines, honeymoon travel destinations clipped from magazines, and some photos of homes and gardens she liked. Sara was fiercely independent and I had teased her about becoming so domesticated so quickly. She would make a face at me and say, *"I am a girl, you know. Did you forget?"*

"Never," I would say, and then we would wind up making love. We did this so often that the bridal magazines and the travel magazines became props in our foreplay. She would come home with a new *Architectural Digest* and flash

it at me with a sly smile and say, *"Got some yuppie porn for ya."* We would ooh and ahh at the Craftsman bungalows and post-and-beam ceilings as if they were centerfolds and I would slowly remove her clothes…

I found the magazines after she died, stuffed in the back of her closet. She had saved them all.

How do you throw away things like that?

I look up at the foothills of the San Gabriel mountains again.

Why did you do it, Sara?

I force the question away, out of reflex. I know that, if I let it, the question will haunt me right back to thirst for my own oblivion. And yet, after all this time, I still feel selfish for wanting to go on living.

I have arranged with the storage people to have the boxes sent to me in Vermont, and I will decide what to do with them from there. I haven't been back to L.A. for five years and I don't want to come back again. The charge that appears on my Amex statement from the storage place is a monthly reminder of the final loose end, the last piece of a life that hangs unfinished. I have put this off long enough, and I am ready to face the ghosts in the small storage space—they are free to reside in my attic in Vermont, or to be given away, to whom I don't know. Sara's father abandoned them when she was a toddler. Sara had no siblings, and her mother, who never left Pittsburgh, retreated from life after Sara's death. She wants nothing to do with me and I don't blame her. But maybe she will accept these things of Sara's if I simply send them to her. I will decide later. For now it is enough to muster the wherewithal to take this one step. I will pack up Sara's things, then drive to the airport for a midnight flight and never return to this hateful city.

The cab barrels down the ramp and onto the clotted downtown streets. After a brief, lurching ride, we stop in front of Parker Center and I go inside. I am waved through metal detectors and wanded and when I tell the cop at the end of the security line who I'm supposed to see he directs me to the elevator. Third floor, Robbery-Homicide.

After writing four books about a serial killer I have had plenty of experience around cops and Homicide Divisions. I have bought drinks for uniform cops, veteran detectives, prosecutors, even a couple of FBI agents, and I have pried them with endless questions about the true-life secrets of their trade. I have met with them in their offices, shot with them at ranges, sparred with them at the gym, gone on ride-alongs—including a couple of roller-coaster nights in NYPD choppers. I have jumped out of cruisers and followed cops into dark alleys and tenements, ignoring their orders to stay back and pressing to the front to feel what they feel and see what they see, beyond the bravado and the hard shell of silence.

There was always some kind of unspoken test—in order to get closer access I would have to participate in something dangerous or horrifying. The things hidden from civilians are jealously guarded secrets by those on the front lines. Not because of procedure or rule, but simply because civilians are not in the club. Cops are a tight lot, and they routinely have difficult encounters with civilians in the course of duty—a problem they refer to as "the asshole factor." Civilians are unpredictable, emotional, abusive, and prone to prevarication. As a civilian, I would have to prove my mettle before I would be allowed in the club, even as a guest. I would have to tour morgues and see the week-old infant that had been cooked in a microwave. I would have to spend hours in a forensics lab watching them painstakingly match shattered jaws with shards of gunshot teeth. I would have to watch the skin peeled back from a dead grandmother to count exactly how many stab wounds there were, which organs they pierced, and which were the fatal wounds. I would have to watch for hours through one-way glass while ignorant, impoverished murderers were angered and manipulated and worn down by detectives until they confessed or gave it up on their best friends or family or feared enemies. I would have to sit through endless court-room proceedings, watching the professionals grind the wheels of their trade relentlessly, until the final verdict was reached. I have done all these things and never stepped back or flinched and have thus been allowed glimpses into What Really Goes On in order for we good citizens to feel safe—and for me to write my books with some sense of authenticity.

Despite all of this, after everything I've seen, I am still struck by the banal-ity of it all. This is why, when I get out on the third floor, I am disappointed—instead of finding a bustling hive of colorful TV detectives with .38's in shoulder holsters, I find an empty hallway. I walk down the hall, looking at the unmarked doors. Where are the cheap suits? The sullen perps? The sassy hookers?

I come upon a set of double doors and open them to find a warren of tiny offices. A guy in the first little office looks up from a computer screen.

"I'm looking for Detective Marsh," I say.

"Who are you?"

"Jack Rhodes, he's expecting me."

He punches a button on his phone, says my name to someone, then tilts his head toward the deep end of the maze of offices.

"At the end. On the left."

I follow the tilt of his head, past one deserted office after another, thinking *there is either a lot of crime today or none at all.* At the last office on the left, I find a fit guy in his forties with premature gray hair and—at last—a shoulder holster. He looks up as I stop at the door.

"Detective Marsh?" I extend my hand. "Jack Rhodes."

Marsh rises and shakes my hand. "Thanks for coming out, Mr. Rhodes. Can I get you anything?" He is already on the move, leading me out the door. I turn to follow, but before I leave I notice a dog-eared copy of *Killer* on the credenza behind his desk.

I follow Marsh back through the office rabbit-hole and out into the empty corridor. He walks down the corridor and stops and unlocks a door and opens it for me to enter ahead of him. The door has a small window at eye level which is reinforced with steel wire, and when it closes behind us I hear the bolt sliding back automatically, locking us in.

"Have a seat, Mr. Rhodes." Marsh indicates a metal chair at a metal table with a faux walnut top. There are two other chairs across the table. There is nothing else in the little room. No phone, no clock, not even a wastebasket.

Marsh takes one of the chairs across the table from me. He has a manila folder in his hand, which he places on the table between us. He pulls a piece of paper from the folder and reads it for a moment. His eyes are small and gray and his face is smooth and hairless, with a preternatural tan. The silence becomes uncomfortable.

"So how can I help you, Detective?"

Marsh sits back and looks at me. We both let the moment play out until he puts the piece of paper down and squares it carefully against his manila folder and decides to speak.

"Do you know a woman named Beverly Grace?" he asks.

The name is familiar. *But from where?*

"…No," I say. "I don't think so."

Marsh looks at me with what I realize is his poker face. His interrogation face.

"You sure?"

Then it hits me: Beverly Grace was the name I chose for the murder victim in my first book. *But I changed her name…*

"I'm sure," I say. "What's this about?"

Marsh leans back and laces his hands behind his head like he's shooting the breeze with his buddies: "They're building a bunch of condos out near Temescal Canyon, in the Palisades. Fucking developers just won't stop, you know," Marsh smiles, his eyes not leaving mine, looking for my response. "Four months ago, a backhoe digging the sewer lines dug up a woman's body."

Marsh reaches into the folder and takes out a photograph and slides it across the table to me: a nude, headless woman's body in a hole in the ground. What's left of her skin is shriveled around her bones like wrinkled, rotted brown wrapping paper and her arms end in handless stumps.

Jesus. That's how I killed the victim in the first book. Decapitated. Hands cut off…

I push the photo back across the table and Marsh is watching me. I know I am one of hundreds of people who have sat in this chair in this little room and looked across this table at this man with the small gray eyes. I am one of hundreds of suspects, victims, witnesses, snitches, bystanders, dead-ends, and liars of every stripe.

"Took forensics forever to figure out who the woman was. Then one of our Assistant DA's mentioned the case to his wife, who happens to be a big fan of yours, and she gave me your book. *Killer*, it's called?"

"That's right."

"In your book, the killer murders a woman with a similar name. Cuts off her head and her hands and buries her in Temescal Canyon, right?"

I feel the blood drain from my face. *I had forgotten that it was Temescal Canyon in the book. A shallow grave…*

Arnie was right. I don't need this.

"That's right," I tell him.

Marsh just sits there. He lets the silence fill the room again.

"So you think this is some kind of…elaborate copycat…" I begin, then I hear a key unlock the door and in walks my old friend, Cloudy Necktie. From the Infirmary. Five years older, and a much more somber necktie.

"I asked my associate to join us. You've met Detective Larson," Marsh says.

Larson looks at me and nods. I nod back, noticing a manila folder in his hand. Nobody says anything. I turn back to Marsh.

"So you think this is somebody copycatting the murder in my first book?" I intend it as a statement but it comes out as a question. I notice the small of my back becoming damp.

"Well, we just have some questions for you, Mr. Rhodes," Marsh says casually, tipping his chair back on its rear legs. *Just a couple of guys shootin' the shit.*

"Sure."

"In your book, a woman named Grace Beverly is decapitated, her hands are cut off, and she is buried in Temescal Canyon."

"That's right."

"Now we find a woman named Beverly Grace decapitated, hands cut off, buried in Temescal Canyon."

"I understand. So you think someone has used my book as a…to copycat the murder in the book."

Larson sits on the edge of the table too close to me, his arms crossed, facing me.

"Can I ask you something, Mr. Rhodes?" Larson's voice is harsher, raspier than I remember. "Where do you get your ideas? For your books."

Again that question.

"I make them up," I reply. The two detectives look at me, allowing the silence to swell.

"What's going on?" I ask. "Some nut decided to mimic a murder in one of my books. This is why you wanted me to come out here?" I look at both of them, getting irritated with the silent treatment.

Larson looks down at his shoes. I notice he wears no wedding ring. Maybe I was wrong about the Father's Day necktie. His jacket sleeve is stained at the cuff and there is a button hanging loose. Divorce is more likely.

"Your first book, *Killer,* was published in 2002?" Marsh asks me.

"That's right, in February." 2/2/02 was the day Arnie called to tell me the book was going to press, the date fixed forever in my memory.

"Beverly Grace was reported missing in 2001," Marsh says.

I stare at Marsh, trying to comprehend this. I can't.

"A year *before* your book came out," Larson helps me with the math.

"I don't understand," I say.

"We're a little confused about it, too," Marsh says. "That's why we wanted to talk to you. See if you had any ideas." Marsh rocks further back on two legs and laces his fingers behind his head again, looking at me steadily.

"I have no idea…" I shake my head. "There must be some mistake."

"Do you remember where you were or what you might have been doing back in the summer of 2001?" Larson asks.

"No. I don't."

"You were drinking a lot, weren't you?" Larson has a slight smirk now. I resist the urge to get up and twist his face into a different expression.

"At least, that's what we know from the file we have on your arrest," Larson adds, opening *his* manila folder. "The murder charge? Richard Bell?"

"Right," I say. "You charged me with a murder I didn't commit, I do remember that."

"And the juvie arrest, in West Covina," Larson says, reading my file. "Assault and battery on one Carlos Vasquez, age 19. Wanna tell us about that?"

"I grew up in a bad neighborhood. I blame the schools."

"You put a gangbanger in the hospital."

"And this is the thanks I get."

"So you're a badass," Larson gives me the hard stare. In a weird way it calms me down. Guys like Larson are easy. Their only weapon is fear.

"I don't like bullies," I say.

"That why you broke Vasquez's jaw?"

"The only way to quell a bully is to thrash him," I say.

Larson glares at me, his face getting pink. He reads from my file again. "Third place Golden Gloves regional welterweight…"

"Second place. If you're gonna intimidate me with expunged juvie records, at least get your facts right."

Larson's jaw muscles start flexing. He wants to hit me so bad *I* can taste it.

"Alright, take it easy," Marsh lets his chair down on all four legs and leans toward me, his elbows on the table, his steady stare unchanged. Guys like Marsh are harder to deal with. They don't rattle. They don't try to intimidate. If Marsh boxed he'd be an out-fighter, keeping his distance, controlling the pace of the match and methodically wearing his opponent down.

"Let's take it a step at a time," Marsh says. "You published your book in February of '02. But you obviously wrote it before then."

"Of course."

"When did you write it?"

"A year or so before. I don't remember the exact date I finished."

"Do you remember when you submitted the manuscript to a publisher? Did you give it to a friend before then, or an agent? Another writer, maybe?" Marsh asks.

"My agent read it and he submitted it to several publishers. If you want names and exact dates you'll have to ask him. Or my attorney," I add, just to say the word aloud in the room. "But I finished it in the spring."

"In 2001?" Marsh asks.

"Yes."

Marsh nods slightly. Then we go back to the silence. I'm starting to feel claustrophobic.

"Was your book based on any…personal experience?" Larson asks.

"Of course not. It's fiction."

"We recognize that," Marsh says affably. "We just have a set of unusual circumstances here and we're covering all the bases."

"You said she was reported missing in 2001," I say.

"Right," Marsh says.

"Was that when she was killed?" I ask.

"Hard to say," Marsh admits. "Forensics is still breaking it down."

"Well, all I can tell you is I wrote the book and sent it off to my agent sometime in the spring of 2001 and it was published in February '02 and that's it," I say. My shirt is sticking to my back and I want out of this little room with these two men. "Is that it? Because I have some other business in town I need to deal with before I go back to Vermont."

They glance at each other.

"We're just trying to put together a time line," Marsh has left the crime scene photo turned toward me so I can look at it: a headless, handless corpse these men have to account for. A real woman who had family and friends and boyfriends, a young woman living her life until…

Then Marsh does something I have seen detectives do before. He slips out another photograph: an 8x10 of Beverly Grace, alive and happy. He places it right next to the police photo of her decayed, mutilated corpse so I can see them side by side.

I open my mouth to tell them I know this trick. I have the words already formed in my head: *I know what you're trying to do, Detective, but it won't work on me because I don't know this woman—*

And then it hits me.

I *do* know her.

The photograph—the happy one—the high school yearbook photo…

I know this picture.

The back of my neck chills as I look at Beverly Grace's smiling face before me. *I know this girl—class of '97. Long, straight hair. A brunette with large, sweet eyes and a soft, oval, pretty face and that black turtleneck sweater with the delicate gold cross hanging around her neck on a gold chain as fine as angel hair…*

The room constricts and I can't focus on anything but that picture…that face that I know, even though I have never seen it.

But I *have* seen it.

My heart shifts into high gear and needles of panic prickle up and down my arms and legs. I look at the detectives and I can tell they see the hot flush on my skin. They have become still, watching me. I have to get out of here.

I stand up.

"If you want to talk to me any more about this I think you should call my lawyer in New York," I say.

They stare at me like I'm Charles Manson. I turn to the door and wait. My hands are shaking.

"Mr. Rhodes," Marsh begins—

"We're done," I cut him off. "Either let me out of here now or get my lawyer," I say the magic words.

Finally Larson gets up and unlocks the door and I am free. I walk down the empty corridor as fast as I can without running, my heart hammering in my chest.

"We'll be in touch, Mr. Rhodes," Marsh calls after me as I head down the empty corridor.

THINGS PAST

The first thing he noticed when he awoke was that, for the first time, he could no lon-ger stretch out fully on the floor of the closet. He was eight years old now and he knew it. He knew because that's what the Witch told Social Services when they came and made him start school. He had begun first grade at age eight. He was older than the other children but he was small and frail for his age, and incapable of social interaction. He was given an IQ test his first week of school and the teachers were astonished. He scored 168—higher than any student they had ever seen—but he only lasted another six weeks before he was expelled. He had written a story about cutting the head off a girl in his class who had refused to talk to him. He liked the girl because she looked like the Angel, with her blue eyes and pale skin. But when he finally mustered the courage to speak to her she ignored him and he became enraged. He knew he couldn't hurt her or he would be in trouble and the Witch would beat him. So he wrote about cutting her head off and found himself in trouble anyway. And the Witch burned him with cigarettes and beat him with an extension cord until his back was striped with bright red blood.

He had come to accept the beatings in silence, his eyes dry and vacant. Any form of attention was a relief compared to the closet. He couldn't bear the isolation, tossed into the dark place like the soiled laundry that made his bed. That's what enraged him about the girl at school. She didn't mock him or lash out at him—she ignored him.

The second thing he noticed when he woke was a new feeling. He had dreamt of being held naked in the arms of the Angel and as he came awake he found himself with his first erection. He explored himself in the darkness, looking up at the Angel. He whispered things to the Angel—sweet things of childlike longing—and she responded in kind. He had spoken with her many times since she sang to him that first time, on his fifth birthday. He loved her so. She listened. She responded. Now the feeling became more intense, and he knew he could never, ever live without her.

CHAPTER FOUR

Sara runs before me, laughing, her yellow sundress wet with surf. I chase her along the jagged line between sea and sand. It is getting dark and we have wandered along the beach for hours and we have no idea where we are but we don't care. We are young and in love and we will never know fear or pain or loss because we will always be together and we will live forever.

★★★

I am standing on the beach, staring at the fading pink glow over the cobalt Pacific. My shoes are submerged in sand and I realize I have been standing here, staring at the setting sun, for a long time. I look at my watch. Only 5:40 and the sun is a memory. I have abandoned my plan to go to the storage place. When I fled Parker Center I walked quickly—ran, really—to the car rental agency. I gave them my Amex, they gave me a Ford Escort, and I drove down Third Street to get on the freeway.

But I passed the 110 East to San Gabriel and found myself getting on the Santa Monica freeway and driving west—toward the water, to the edge of the continent, where I drove down the California Incline to Pacific Coast Highway, which I took north until I reached Will Rogers State Beach and I parked the car and got out and stood in the sand in front of my car and stared at Sara's ghost…gripped by a memory, lost in a memory that I didn't even know I had until this moment.

The cool, steady ocean breeze has dried the sweat from my shirt and I am breathing again. But my face is wet. I realize I have been crying.

What the hell happened back there? I fled Parker Center like a felon. My heart pounding, I simply fled. Something in me had been awoken; some deep, forbidden button was pressed. I shut down and got out and drove—no way I could face Sara's things now. So I drove west, toward…what?

The airport. That must be it. In the back of my mind there must have been the thought that I could take an earlier flight. Get the hell out of L.A. Yes. But the California Incline only goes one way, and I wound up driving north along Pacific Coast Highway until I came to Will Rogers Beach and the sudden memory of Sara called to me like a siren. A memory from long before the Unspeakable…

"It's ridiculous," Sara would say. *"We live in L.A. and we never go to the beach."* I had finally relented and we made a day of it…and half a night…

I shake it off. Get in the car. Maybe there will be an earlier flight. I drive to the exit from the parking lot. I look right, then I look left, and then I see the traffic light, far ahead north—

Temescal Canyon.

I stop the car in the middle of my right turn onto Pacific Coast Highway. Then, suddenly, I turn the car left, toward Temescal.

I have never liked being afraid and I have learned that anger can trump fear and now I am angry.

CHAPTER FIVE

The Escort's headlights illuminate the dusty row of eucalyptus trees that line the parking lot in Temescal Canyon Park. I stop the car near the end of the lot, where the darkness starts, and I get out.

It's warmer here than at the beach. The pavement and dirt and brush hang onto the heat longer than the wet sand. The air is still and saturated with the dry fragrance of eucalyptus and sun-baked sage. I walk toward the darkness at the edge of the parking lot. I don't know where I'm going and yet, as I approach the edge of the paved lot I somehow know there will be the entrance to a trail... and there it is.

How did I know?

I take the trail, my focus hard ahead of me. I have no idea where I am going, but the landmarks along the way are sudden reminders of...*what?*

The cinderblock meeting-house. The tombstone-sized granite slab with the park's donor's names on a bronze plaque...

I have never been here but as I climb up the trail, dusty sage bushes brushing my legs, I recognize little things—the boulder with graffiti, the railroad ties embedded as steps where the trail becomes treacherously steep.

And then I come to it: the small plateau—the clearing where Killer buried Grace Beverly in the book.

But I invented this small plateau.

Sara and I drove past this park, when we went to the beach that day. We were driving back, it was late at night, and I noticed the sign that said Temescal Canyon. I liked the name—liked the music of it, and I told her and she liked it too and I reached for it later when I was writing the first book. But I've never set foot here. I am certain of it. As certain as I am of anything…

I walk ahead, refusing the fear growing inside me. I walk toward the site where I buried poor young Grace Beverly in my imagination years ago.

As I come closer I am briefly calmed. There is no crime scene tape, nothing to show that the police have ever been here. *Nothing to see here, folks…*

And then I see it.

Twenty feet ahead of me, illuminated only by the thumbnail moon over the ridge, is a gash in the ground, partly overgrown now. I know this wound in the earth. I created it. This is the shallow grave where I buried Grace Beverly in *Killer*.

My heart swelling into my throat, I approach the ragged rectangular hole in the dirt. *What the hell am I looking for?*

I should run.

But I can't. I can only move toward the shallow grave on stiff legs, straining my eyes in the colorless moonlight to see inside the grave's shadow. I come upon it and stop well back, afraid of stumbling in. I lean over the edge of the grave and look inside and see only a black void.

Suddenly, a flash of stark white and a pair of wild eyes snarl up at me from the darkness of the grave and then a scuffling spray of dirt shoots against my legs as something climbs up and out of the ground and rips a hole in the surrounding brush as it tears off into the night.

I stagger back, terrified, and stare after the Thing that has leapt from the grave and I realize I have seen coyotes, a large one followed by a smaller one—a mother and pup, disturbed in their sleep, scrambled by an intruder up and out of their safe hole in the warm desert earth.

I turn and run back down the trail, my heart released from the sudden freeze of fear and now pounding so hard I think that something inside me might break or burst.

I make it back to the parking lot and stop. I try to breathe. I look around and force myself to calm down and I close my eyes and then open them again. My gaze falls upon the row of picnic tables near the cinderblock meeting-house.

Something else…something else is here. Near the tables…

At the end of the row of picnic tables. The olive tree…the dark hollow part inside…

I can almost hear a voice urging me on to it. A low, sonorous voice with the sound of a smile behind it.

Like a sleepwalker, I move toward the olive tree. As I come closer I can see that it looks diseased; half of it grows with hale greenery, the other half is clearly dying, no leaf or bud on any branch, and between the two halves of this sad, doomed tree is an oval opening. A dark, hollow place that—once again—I somehow knew would be here.

Come closer, I hear the deep, sonorous voice say. *Look inside.*

I see only darkness and I move my head around to catch the moonlight— and I see a faint sparkle inside the hole in the tree. I clamp my jaw shut tight to fight back the fear and I reach inside and grab a handful of something damp and cold and stringy. Like reaching into a freshly carved jack 'o lantern.

I pull my hand out and I am holding a clump of mottled bark and grime. But in the middle of the clump is something—I shake it off and once again the sudden recognition of my own imagined horror washes over me.

I am holding a hair clip—a large, cheap, plastic thing, bedecked with purple glass beads—and I recognize it as the clip that I described Grace Beverly wearing to hold her hair back in the book. The clip that Killer adjusted to hold her hair out of the way when he applied to the knife across her neck…

Attached to the hair clip is what I can tell now is a clump of hair, and dangling at the end of the tangle of hair is a dark, papery shred of what I realize is scalp. A small insect crawls around the patch of dried skin.

I make a shuddering, involuntary sound and stuff the thing back into the tree and run to the car and fumble with the keys like a teenager in a slasher movie and get inside and start the engine and drive like hell out of there.

CHAPTER SIX

I drive down the freeway, my mind racing: *I have never been there. I have never hurt anyone, ever. I could never do a thing like…no matter how out of my mind with booze and…I could never do it…never do that…never, ever…*

I realize I am saying this aloud. I've been saying it, over and over, for most of the drive to the airport. I look down and see that I'm going ninety miles an hour. I slow down suddenly and nearly miss the exit to LAX.

How did I know?

I leave the car where I'm supposed to for the rental pickup, then take the shuttle to the terminal. More than enough time to make my flight. More than enough. I cling to my small carry-on as I get off the shuttle and get in the endless series of lines to find my gate, my plane, my escape.

I don't care how drunk or out of my mind with grief and pain… Never. Never.

I get through the airport lines, avoiding the eyes of every cop and security officer I pass. There is a heart-stopping moment when the chrome alloy parts in my repaired wrist set off the metal detector, but they let me through and I take the escalator to the departure gates and find my gate and sit down in the closest chair near me. It feels like I haven't breathed for hours. I sit back and place my small bag on the stained carpet at my feet and relax my grip. I force myself to breathe, letting the panic subside. And it does. After a few moments the racing thoughts drift into the background and I slowly become more aware of my surroundings.

I look up at the gate. The sign above the empty desk reads *Newark 11:58 – On Time.*

Thank God. I look at my watch. 9:10. Two hours until we board, then the flight, then connect to Burlington and then home...

I just have to calm down. Stop my mind from running. Calm down.

Never. I could never...

I have to think clearly. There *has* to be an explanation. She was taken...kidnapped, but she wasn't killed until after the book... *Forensics is still breaking that down,* Marsh had said.

But how could I have known those things? The grave, the hair clip...

I try to remember the details of the murder from the book but I can't. Five years and three books later and the details are gone.

I turn, looking for a newsstand, and I see one at the end of the terminal. I get up and hurry toward it—then slow down as I pass a security camera pointed at me. I duck my head and continue to the store.

In the store I go to the back, toward the magazines—*yes.* A long row of shelves with paperbacks. I turn my head to read the authors' names, going alphabetically to find...there, on the bottom shelf, I recognize the cover for the paperback edition of *Killer.*

I grab the book and thumb through it as I kneel on the floor. I haven't looked at my first book in years and I am surprised at how little I recognize. I flip through it, trying to find a sequence describing the crime scene but I can't find one.

Frustrated, I get up and go to the cashier and buy the damned thing. I also buy a copy of the New York Times to wrap around it, hiding my photo. Then I walk back to my gate, past the security cameras, and I sit down and begin to read.

CHAPTER SEVEN

Katherine Kendall stood over the shallow grave. The crime scene unit's banks of 2,000 watt floodlights filled the grave with a harsh, shadowless glare. Grace Beverly's body had been removed by the coroner's people hours ago, and already Katherine knew her boss was right to send her out here.

It was Killer. Katherine was certain. Decapitation between the sixth and seventh cervical vertebrae, amputation of the hands at the radiocarpal joint—all of it done with a rubber-handled knife at least 10" long with moderate serration. All of the cutting done premortem.

FBI Behavioral Science called him Killer because they had nothing else to call him. He hadn't murdered enough to be given a clever nickname—at least not that they knew of—and the news media hadn't connected the murders. FBI kept the bit about the heads and the hands out of the news, to filter out the scores of nutcases and attention-seekers who routinely call to confess to crimes they didn't commit.

After three murders in three different states they knew only the barest facts—the general profile of the victims, the cause of death, the weapon, the method of disposal, and little else. After the facts there was the reasoned speculation: he was a white male, 30's or 40's, average height and weight; he was strong, he was smart, he was cool-headed, and he was meticulous. Katherine had seen all manner of crime scene photographs of other murder victims' graves, but this was the first time Katherine, in her rookie year as an FBI Special Agent, had seen Killer's handiwork up close and in person.

The most telling thing, she thought, was the pattern of footprints around the grave. It was always the same. Not the prints themselves—Killer changed his shoes for each murder, using different sized shoes. It was the pattern of the footprints that revealed him to her. She could tell from the footprints that he had walked around the grave for a long time, looking down at Grace Beverly before he began dumping dirt on her. All of the other footprints—approaching the scene, carrying the body, then leaving—showed an economy of action. His movements were direct and certain; he knew exactly what he was doing and where he was going and there were no false starts, there was no backtracking. Except for the burial itself. And then, at each gravesite, he would move around the grave many times, walking around and around it several times…

To what purpose?

Katherine imagined him, pacing around the grave. She could see from the angle of the footprints that he was looking down at her—all of the footprints pointed toward the grave, with a slightly deeper indentation at the front of the foot, suggesting his head was tilted down. It seemed to have the feeling of ritual. There was something almost elegiac about it.

Or was he simply gloating? Admiring his work.

A warm Santa Ana wind blew Katherine's short brown hair across her face. She thought of Grace Beverly in her final moments when he took the knife to her—and the projection of sheer terror made Katherine stop her mind instantly, as she had been trained. She tucked her hair behind her ear and knelt carefully at the gravesite and examined each footprint closely, focusing on the job to chase away the Darkness that was palpable in places like this. Since her training began she had been on site at eleven separate murder scenes. They could drag out a million floodlights and the Darkness would still be there, hovering around the place of death. Katherine didn't believe in ghosts, but she believed in monsters. Because she had seen firsthand what monsters do.

CHAPTER EIGHT

Dawn is breaking over New York City as we make our approach at Newark. I have finished *Killer,* reading a few passages several times. I close my eyes, exhaustion catching up with me.

There was nothing in the book about the hair clip or the olive tree. I remember why now. In my first draft Killer put Grace Beverly's head and hands in the tree, with her hands in a praying position. But Judith Price, my editor, had scratched the sequence out with her blue pencil. "Too much information!" she had scrawled in the margins. It gave her the creeps. I told her that was the point, but I didn't put up much of a fight. It was, after all, my first book, and it was far too long. I had to cut something. So I took it out.

The wheels bump on the runway and I am propelled forward as the pilot deploys the thrust reversers. I feel tired and drained by fear and confusion.

The passage about Katherine Kendall's visit to the crime scene at Temescal Canyon was hauntingly exact, but there were a few odd discrepancies. The parking lot was gravel, not paved, the cinderblock meeting house was on the other side of the creek, and the grave was much higher up on the ridge. Like Beverly Grace's name, which I simply reversed to Grace Beverly, there was a strange kind of reversal to certain things. They were flipped, as though reflected in a mirror.

I sit staring ahead, my mind and body numb. I am hungry and tired and I can't think. I get up and follow my fellow passengers off the plane as everyone takes out their cell phones and calls the office, calls home, calls their ride, calls someone.

I come out of the gate and into the airport and I go to the window and stare out at the morning over the city. It's clear and cold here. I could feel sharp drafts of frigid air from the gaps between the jet way and the body of the plane when I got off. I turn away from the window and find a monitor listing my connection to Burlington. It's on time. I have an hour.

It's not possible. Unless someone read the manuscript and…

But who?

I can't think and I can't *stop* thinking. I take out my cell phone and dial.

"It's Jack Rhodes for Joel." I wait a moment, then I hear Joel Fisher, my lawyer, in his car.

"Jack? Where are you?"

"Just arrived at Newark."

"You don't sound good. How'd it go in L.A?"

"Badly," I say. "I have to talk to you right away. I was on my way back to Vermont but I just changed my mind. I'm coming to your office right now."

"Okay…" I hear him try to hide the surprise in his voice. "Can it wait until lunch? My morning is kind of crazy–"

"Joel," I interrupt. "I'm in trouble."

CHAPTER NINE

Fisher, Bloom & Caruthers occupies the top two floors of a sleek mid-century building in Midtown. The lobby of the firm has been redone to exacting minimalist standards: a large, open space with a polished concrete floor, dark wood reception desk, and hospital white walls featuring artless paintings of extraordinary value.

I sit on the hard black leather couch across from the reception desk, waiting for Joel. I can't stop thinking about the book. Beyond the panic, despite the worry and fear about my situation, my writer's ego is alive and well. I was pulled into the book right away. And although I occasionally winced at a cliché or a metaphor that was stretched beyond usefulness, I was proud of how far my characters had come in my recent books, in contrast to their wooden antecedents.

But the most striking thing was the character of Katherine Kendall. I was shocked to see what a completely transparent cipher she was for Sara. Katherine's character brought fusillades of deep, forgotten memories of Sara back to me—her morning routine; showering, blowing her hair dry vigorously, standing in front of her closet in her bare feet, grabbing clothes and pulling them on, then applying a minimum of makeup, all of it done as quickly as possible, with open impatience. Like Sara, Katherine resented the fact that her appearance *mattered* as much as it did. She knew she was attractive, and she knew that any attention she paid to her appearance would have an unfairly meaningful effect on her professional life. And yet, despite their practical approach to the feminine rituals of beauty, both Sara and Katherine were keenly aware of their need to be attractive to men, and their feelings about that were infinitely complex and ambivalent. Like anyone, they needed to feel wanted, and to be loved.

The more I read, the more it became apparent that I had fallen in love with Katherine for the same reasons I had fallen in love with Sara—so much so that I had to take breaks during the reading or I knew I would begin to cry in my window seat on the plane. I had no idea when I was writing that I was simply conjuring Sara in the guise of Katherine. It's obvious to me now—embarrassing, even. How *couldn't* people have seen it? How could *I* not have seen it? I remember feeling that writing the book was an escape—a diversion into an utterly different world, with people of my own creation; the private fantasy I could retreat to and obsess over to remove my focus from my own pain. But it wasn't removed at all. It was all *about* the pain.

"Jack?" Joel striding across the lobby, his hand extended. I get up and shake his hand and see sudden concern in his eyes. I realize I must look like hell.

"Jesus," he says softly. "Come on back."

I follow him back to his office and he lets me in and closes the door. I collapse on his couch, an overstuffed velvet piece of furniture in a warm, paneled room. Good old Joel; late fifties, wife and kids in picture frames on his oak desk. I have only been here a few times, all of them good times—signing deals, occasionally meeting to talk about a negotiation. Joel was useful as the hammer to bring in when Arnie's loyalties between client and publisher had reached their understandable limits. Joel had been good to me, and I to him. But this time everything is different.

I look at Joel: he is a product of serious weightlifting. Big and thick, with a receding hairline that he mitigates by keeping his dark hair extremely short. Joel is an imposing figure, and I know he cultivates that image—bullying anyone who decides to play rough, and rattled by nothing. He presses a button on his phone.

"Dara, bring us coffee and water and… What do you want to eat, Jack?"

"Nothing, I'm fine."

"Some fruit from D&D, right away, okay?"

He clicks off and comes over and sits in the Morris chair across from me.

"I asked an associate to join us. Nicki Feldman. She was with the Manhattan DA's office for four years. You'll like her, she's a tough cookie," Joel smiles.

"I didn't know you guys had a criminal attorney here."

Joel's smile broadens and he shrugs. "Our clients get into trouble once in a while, like anyone else. Nicki has the advantage of having been on the other side. She had a ninety-nine percent conviction rate as a prosecutor."

"What's her record as a defense attorney?" I ask.

"Even better," Joel says. "So far, not one of our clients has ever set foot in a criminal court."

There is a quick knock and Joel's door is opened by a woman who ducks her head in.

"Hi," she says.

Joel and I get up.

"Jack, this is Nicki Feldman, I was just telling you about her."

Nicki Feldman comes in and shakes my hand. She is pretty, with wide, bright blue eyes and short, tousled blonde hair, dressed in a tailored black jacket and skirt.

"It's nice to meet you, I'm a big fan of your work," she says, smiling. I thank her, but guess that her compliment is more courtesy than anything else. We all sit down.

"So," Joel says again.

"So," I say. And then I tell them the story, from the beginning. Everything. I never understood people who lie to their lawyers or their doctors. What's the point of lying when the meter's running and they can never tell?

It takes a surprisingly long time to tell it all. Joel shifts in his chair a little but Nicki Feldman sits absolutely still, her eyes wide and unblinking. Finally, I get to the end of it.

"Wow," Joel says, and runs his hand through his short hair.

Nicki is staring at me, eyes wide, her brow furrowed. I don't think she has blinked for ten minutes. She sits forward and speaks to me.

"The hair clip," she says. "It wasn't in the book?"

"No," I say. "That's why I'm here. I have to tell them about it...."

"Tell who?"

"The police. It's evidence."

"Is it?"

"Of course," I say. "Isn't it a crime to withhold evidence?"

"Yes," she says. "But what makes you think the hair clip is evidence?"

"Are you serious?" I say. "I knew it was there."

"How?" she asks.

"I told you, I don't *know* how."

"Did you know this woman? Beverly Grace?"

"No."

"And your discovery of this hair clip was based on what?"

"I just knew it would be there. I—wrote it that way."

"So you have no actual knowledge of the crime, you just had a vague feeling based on something you imagined years ago and then wrote in a book."

I don't have an answer. A tiny smile comes to her; she knows she is winning the argument. The smile softens her sharp blue eyes—a disarming technique that must serve her well with clients and witnesses. It also makes me want to know more about her. I look down and notice there are bits of sagebrush still clinging to my khakis and my gray socks, the tiny taupe buds covered with fine, silvery hairs.

"That's all true, but shouldn't the police be told about what I found?" I say.

"Yes. But you also have the right not to incriminate yourself. The truth is, you don't know *how* you know about the hair clip, you don't know anything material about the circumstances of the actual homicide, and you're willing to believe you're guilty of anything at this point," she says.

"I told you what I know."

"I understand how upset and confused you are. This is very unusual, to say the least. But we need to know more before we start calling the police about hair clips right this second. We'll tell them. But I want to know a few things first. Especially about the chain of custody of your manuscript, and some more details about the case. Is it alright if I call this Detective Marsh, and your agent?"

"Sure. Anything. This whole thing has me..." I shake my head, unable to complete the thought. I rub my eyes. I am too tired to think clearly.

"Mr. Rhodes, have you ever heard the story of the guilty man and the innocent man in jail overnight for the same crime?"

"No."

"Two men are arrested for the same murder," she says. "One of them sleeps soundly in jail after he is arrested, the other one is up pacing and worrying all night. Which one is guilty? The sleeper or the worrier?" she asks.

"I give up," I say.

"The sleeper is the guilty one. He's tired of running. He can relax now, he's been caught. The game is up, the nightmare is over. The innocent man is the one who's up all night, worrying and pacing, because for him the nightmare of being an innocent man charged with murder is just beginning."

"So what's the moral of the story, Ms. Feldman?" I ask politely.

"The point is, you look like a guy who's been up all night worrying. You look like you haven't slept for a week. In fact, you look like shit." She smiles again, more warmly.

"Thank you," I say, returning the smile.

"You're welcome. And you can call me Nicki."

CHAPTER TEN

Joel arranges for a car to take me to the airport while I make small talk with Nicki. At the same time, Joel's assistant books me on an evening flight to Burlington and packs a lunch for me. They send me home like a sick schoolboy and by the time the sun is setting I am taking off on a commuter jet for Vermont.

At the Burlington airport I find my truck in the parking lot where I left it. I get in and head southeast to my place. Flakes of dry snow swirl around in the truck's headlights, and I catch glimpses of snow on the north sides of the trees and in the hollows of the hard ground. It's a two hour drive to my place and I pull into my rutted driveway just as I am about to lose my battle to stay awake.

I unlock my front door and enter the cabin, which is dark and freezing. I drop my things inside the door and turn on the lights and turn up the thermostat and hear the pilot light flick to life and the gas begin to hiss. A moment later I feel the rush of dry heat on the back of my neck. I undress and shower and pull on a pair of sweatpants and a long-sleeved t-shirt and go to the polished pine counter that separates the kitchen from the living room. I stand at the counter and eat the lunch Joel's assistant prepared for me. I turn on the little TV on the counter to distract myself but I am quickly bored by the repetition of the news channels and I turn it off. Despite Nicki's assurances, my nerves are still jangling from the trip.

How could I have known those things? The things I saw at Temescal Canyon?

I can see the doorway to my office from the counter and I go to the office as I chew on a cold chicken leg seasoned with rosemary.

In the office, I stare at my books.

If I knew those things at Temescal, what about other things? From the following books? A murder in each book...

I reach for a copy of my second book, *Killer At Large,* an advance copy from Terrapin, signed on the cover page by my editor, Judith Price: *Thanks for keeping me awake nights! XO, J.P.*

I sit at my desk and open the book and start to read. It is a little more recognizable than *Killer,* but not much. After a few pages I feel my limbs getting heavy with fatigue, and I wash up and take the book to bed with me.

At eleven p.m. I realize I have read the fourth page of the book three times and I can no longer stay awake. I close the book and put it on the nightstand and turn off the light and turn into my pillow and in less than a minute I am sleeping like a guilty man.

THINGS PAST

*By age thirteen he had begun to seek the refuge of the closet on his own. The Witch was
gone more often than not now—sometimes to County, sometimes off with men for days,
weeks. He had learned to care for himself in the filthy little house by the freeway. He could
have slept on the couch when the Witch was gone, but he didn't—and he couldn't even
conceive of sleeping in her bed.*

*He liked the closet now. He was far too big now to sleep on the pile of clothes, even
when curled in a fetal position. So he had fashioned a method of piling and folding the
grimy couch cushions on the closet floor and against one wall. His head was supported at
a comfortable angle so he could gaze at the Angel without even lifting his eyes, his knees
raised and propped up by a cushion he had folded into a V and duct-taped to the floor.
He would lie there, naked—always naked—and talk and listen and, in the darkness, he
would forget the world, forget himself, and go with the Angel to the places from the picture
books. Cradled in her arms, touching and being touched, her perfect blue eyes twin North
Stars guiding him toward indescribable bliss. The dark place had become Heaven. Because
he had made it so.*

*He never went to school any more. Social Services had forgotten him years ago. He
had fallen through every crack of every city, county, state, and federal bureaucracy. Officially,
he existed only in a few early school records, in fits and starts. He had no birth certificate,
no Social Security number, no medical or dental records.*

*He had learned to take care of himself quite well as the Witch's absences increased
in length and frequency. He had grown. He had left the house many times and gotten
daylight and fresh air. And with the Witch gone, he got regular meals. He taught himself*

to become an expert shoplifter. He had a natural cunning, which was sharpened by years of maneuvering around the Witch—to bathe, to eat, to move around the house without disturbing her and drawing her wrath. He started by stealing small amounts of produce—anything without a tag or bar code that would set off the security alarms that flanked the automatic doors at the large Ralph's supermarket six blocks from the house. Then he figured out how to remove the tags and bar codes of other merchandise with a small pair of nail clippers. People were so stupid. So trusting. So easily confused and misdirected. Cattle. The hoofed beasts of the field. A few drops of cooking oil discretely dripped on the floor in front of the busy deli counter, near a towering pyramid of soda or beer or other merchandise, and all he had to do was wait until some bovine shopper would slip and knock over the stacked merchandise and send the security guard, clerks, and managers running to help, to apologize, to clean up. Twice he had walked out during the confusion, pushing a shopping cart brimming with his favorite foods.

He never went hungry. His limbs grew longer and heavier, his mind sharper still. He cut his own hair. He bathed carefully every day, when the Witch wasn't there, of course. He had no need for companionship, other than the Angel. He never watched television or listened to music. He had stolen a paperback Bible from the book rack at the supermarket. A King James version, just like from the day care. It didn't have pictures, but he had outgrown the picture books. Besides, the pictures he created with the Angel were far better.

So while other gangly thirteen year-olds were listening to music or playing video games or dating or doing homework, he read his Bible—read it deeply, constantly. He still loved the day care stories, especially David and Goliath, but lately he had become fascinated with the New Testament, particularly the book of Acts, in which Paul had his conversion on the road to Damascus.

It was the blinding light that first caught his attention; the blinding, brilliant light which struck down Paul—Saul, as he was called before his conversion. The blinding light—like the light which burst from the door when the Witch attacked him. After the Witch attacks he would lie on the closet floor, beaten, sometimes bleeding, and he could see nothing until his eyes adjusted once again to the dark closet, and the porcelain face of the Angel would slowly form, hovering above him, nothing else visible; alone, head and hands, head and hands, serene, compassionate, loving, listening, touching…

Then came the day of his own conversion. And the transubstantiation of the Witch.

The blinding light that led to his own conversion was the direct summer sun that exploded into the dark closet when the Witch threw open the door. He had been in a special new place with the Angel, a place based on a picture he saw on a gift card at Ralph's. The picture was a crude, tiny reproduction of a Corot pastoral, featuring a lone woman *seated near a shallow slough in which three cows meandered under a thumbnail moon. He pictured himself at the water's edge, in the arms of his Angel, and then the light struck him blind and the Witch found him there, naked, tumescence in his moving hand, gazing at the Angel.*

He turned away from the light and the assault he knew was coming, but all he heard were vulgar words and then—horribly—the sound of shattering porcelain, and he knew right away what the Witch had done.

He knew, even before he turned and saw the shards of pure white porcelain, head and hands, now shattered on the floor near him, and the Witch began to kick him with the sharp heels of her knee-high boots.

The next thing he heard was a shriek—not from the Witch, but from his own throat. A strange new sound; part deep and guttural, part a small boy's scream, as he lunged from the closet and toppled her and sat atop her and beat her with his fists until she lay motionless.

And yet he beat her still.

CHAPTER ELEVEN

I startle awake with the unmistakable sense that there has been a loud noise in my bedroom. I lie still in the dark for a moment. I can't remember the sound, but I have the inexplicable conviction that it was loud and very close. I lie listening to the soft tick of the clock on my nightstand. A faint wind rises, brushing the branches of a pine against my bedroom window.

I get up and head down the hall. I leave the lights off, remembering Lt. Foley, a retired NYPD detective who once told me in his thick Bronx snarl, the humid scent of scotch on his breath, *"The last thing you wanna do is turn the lights on if there's an intruder. You know your place—they don't. The dark gives you an advantage."*

I think a raccoon on the roof is more likely than an intruder, but nevertheless I go to my office and grab *The Dangerous Summer* from the top shelf of the bookcase by the door. I pull the book cover off the small wooden box I built in my woodshed. Inside the small pine box is the stainless steel Smith & Wesson .45 with the rubber grip that I keep there. I bought the gun after encountering a bear one night while I was taking out the trash. The guy at the gun shop suggested a shotgun but I want nothing to do with shotguns. So I bought the .45, which my cop pals tell me will kill pretty much anything if used with the proper ammunition, decent aim, and a persistent lack of empathy. I have hollow-cavity rounds, my aim is decent, and if it's between me and the bear, the bear's going down.

I grab the gun and head back down the hall. No bears in the living room. I peer out the window at the trash containers outside. Sealed shut and upright.

No animals. I look at the clock on the fireplace mantle: 4:45. I debate putting on coffee and starting work, but I'm still too tired. I head back to bed and I'm about to put the gun back in the bookcase when the floorboard under my foot pops loudly.

That was it.

That was the sound that woke me. No question. I stand there for a moment.

Relax. The cabin was freezing. You turned the furnace on and the floorboards expanded with the heat and made a noise. Nothing mysterious.

Thank you, Mr. Science.

I half-smile at myself and decide to forget about it. I head back to bed, but stick the gun under the mattress where I can reach it. Just in case.

CHAPTER TWELVE

Six hours later I wake from a series of disconnected dreams. I sense there was something important about them so I try to remember but the harder I chase them the faster they slip away.

I get up, see that it's almost eleven, and go make coffee. Frost covers the cabin windows. I can see only that it's dim and gray outside. I turn the phones on and check the voicemail. Nicki Feldman's office has called twice. I call her back and leave a message, then hang up and pull a large Circulon skillet from the cabinet beneath the phone. I turn the flame on low under the skillet, then drop a dollop of butter into it. As the butter melts, I crack four eggs into the skillet, splash in a little milk, and sprinkle in some shaved cheddar cheese. I turn the heat up and scramble the eggs while they cook.

Sara had disdained my scrambled eggs method, although she liked the results. She thought I should mix the eggs and milk in a bowl, then dump the contents into a pre-heated skillet. We had an old Teflon skillet which had begun to peel, and she didn't like the idea of the eggs sloshing around in it too long, absorbing exotic polymers. She was probably right.

"I just like doing it this way," I say as I stir the eggs, which are beginning to form tiny islands of solid mass in the Circulon skillet.

When I moved to the cabin, after I had bought my hardware, I had everything for the *outside* of the cabin, but the inside was as empty as a church on Saturday night. I didn't even have a fork. So I drove to Burlington, went to Macy's at the mall, and at the housewares desk I found a young man tying a ribbon on a box for a woman. He had neat, short brown hair, with a cowlick that was faintly frosted blonde. He wore a pale blue Brooks Brothers shirt, dark wool slacks, and black Kenneth Cole loafers. His socks and belt were exactly the same shade of dark cerulean. He finished the ribbon and turned to me.

"Hi, I just moved here and I need some things," I said, and handed him a two-page list of items on yellow legal paper. He stared at the list. His nametag said "Jonathan."

"You need all this?" he said, his eyebrows raised.

"Yes," I said. "Do you carry all of it?"

"I'm pretty sure we do..." Jonathan said, scanning the list. "I'll have to check furnishings for the bed and the sofa and the rugs. They'll have to be delivered if they're not in stock."

"That's fine."

"Okay, well...guess we'd better get started," Jonathan said, then came around from behind he cash register.

"If you don't mind, you can go ahead and pick it all out and ring it up. I'll be in electronics," I said.

Jonathan blinked at me. "You want me to pick out all your stuff?"

"If that's okay."

"It's fine with me, but what if I pick out something you don't like?"

"I'm sure whatever you pick out will be fine. It's a pine cabin. The floors and walls are pine, with a medium brown finish. The kitchen is modern with stainless steel appliances and brown granite countertops. The bathroom tile is white with navy trim."

"What about price?"

"Just use your best judgment. I'll be back in a couple of hours."

"...Okay," Jonathan said, then started writing down my description of the cabin.

I went to the electronics section and sat down and watched the Oakland Raiders hammer the Kansas City Chiefs 32-0. When the game was over I returned to housewares and found Jonathan running the cash register, which was spitting out a paper receipt that spilled onto the floor like Rapunzel's hair. Jonathan was surrounded by boxes of merchandise.

"Perfect timing," he said. "Just finished."

I gave him my Amex but he insisted on at least showing me the items he chose. They were all perfect. He rang it up, I pulled my truck around to the loading dock, then drove my new household home, wondering why the Chiefs hadn't had a consistent offense since Joe Montana.

When the eggs are done, I spoon them onto a Macy's Cellar dinner plate. The plate is white with a navy border that perfectly compliments the brown granite countertop. I grab a Macy's Cellar dinner fork from the silverware drawer, and I am savoring the first bite when the phone rings. I pick it up and Nicki says "Good morning."

"Morning," I say.

"Get some sleep?" she asks.

"Yes, thank you." I take another bite of scrambled eggs.

"Turns out LAPD was less than forthcoming with you," Nicki says. "Temescal Canyon Park was renovated in the summer of 2001. They started construction a week after Beverly Grace was reported missing. The park was closed for two months and a security guard was posted there while the heavy equipment was on site. A fence was put up with a locked gate and it was inaccessible all summer. Which means they've pinpointed the week she was killed. It had to have been just before they started construction."

"Why didn't they just say so?" I ask.

"Because they wanted to see how much *you* would tell *them*."

"Okay," I realize she's right. "But how do they know she wasn't killed and buried after the construction?"

"According to the forensic bug guys, she was buried in the spring. They can tell from the decay of the maggot eggs in her—" Nicki stops herself. "Just take my word for it, okay? I'm eating lunch at my desk. What it boils down to now is we have to account for your whereabouts during the last week of April, 2001 and once we do that we're in the clear. Any thoughts?"

"Not a one. Like I told you, I don't remember a thing after Sara died until I sobered up fifteen months later."

"Nothing at all? For fifteen months?"

"I remember being at her funeral and waking up the next day on someone's couch. After that it's only vague impressions....random, nonsensical things."

"Would you be willing to talk to a forensic psychiatrist about that? He's an expert in memory recovery. He's helped me out more than once with witnesses who had fuzzy memories."

I take another bite of breakfast.

"Let me think about it," I say.

"It might be important later, if we can't find any other way to account for your whereabouts."

"I understand," I say. "It's just not a period in my life that I relish looking at very hard."

"Okay, but I think you should consider it," she says.

"So does this mean we're telling them about the hair clip?" I ask, to change the subject.

"Enough with the hair clip. Let's find out first where you were that last week of April '01. Unless you want to tell them about the hair clip so you can get extradited back to L.A. on a murder charge."

"Not really on my agenda," I say.

"Don't blame you. Okay, I'm going to need as much from you as I can get: credit card, ATM, phones, anything that might show a record of your whereabouts."

"It's not like I have much in the way of records from then. I was drunk pretty much all the time."

"Would you sign a release for the bank and the phone company to authorize my access to your information?"

"Sure."

"While we're on the subject of your bank we might as well talk about my fee. I have one investigator on this full-time already, as well as me. It could get expensive real fast."

"I understand."

"I need twenty thousand just to start."

"Just let Joel know. He can arrange whatever you need with my accountant."

"So it's not about the money, then," she says.

"What isn't?"

"Your reluctance to talk to my forensic shrink."

"No, it's not about the money. I just don't want to go there unless I have to."

"You may have to."

"Let me know when that time comes," I say.

"It may come sooner than later, unless we get lucky. By the way, does the name Gregory Dontis mean anything to you?"

"No. Who is he?"

"He was your editor's assistant when Arnie Brandt first sent your manuscript to Terrapin Publishing."

"What about him?"

"He's the only one who read your original manuscript that we haven't located. He's also the only one with a criminal record."

"What'd he do?"

"Assault with a deadly weapon, six years ago."

"Sounds pretty serious."

"It could mean he threatened somebody with a cocktail umbrella, for all we know. The case was pleaded down to a misdemeanor. We're waiting on the paperwork."

"You work fast," I say, impressed. "That's a lot of information in a day and a half."

"You should see me during a trial," she says.

"I hope I never do."

After I hang up I pour myself a cup of coffee and sit at the kitchen table and wonder why I don't want to talk to the shrink. I think of the low voice I heard at Temescal Canyon and wonder if it's because I'm afraid that I am going crazy.

No, not crazy. I don't want to talk to the shrink because I don't want to remember anything. People always talk about how hard it can be to remember things—where they left their keys, or the name of an acquaintance—but no one ever talks about how much effort we put into forgetting. I am exhausted from the effort to forget. To forget the sunny afternoon in San Gabriel, of course, but it's more than that. The thought of sitting with a shrink, delving into my child-hood memories, of which there are virtually none, fills me with dread. Who knows what would be dredged up? There are things that have to be forgotten if you want to go on living.

My coffee is cool enough to drink now and I take a sip. I feel a chill in the room and I turn and see that the kitchen door is standing wide open.

CHAPTER THIRTEEN

I can understand forgetting to *lock* the back door, but forgetting to *close* it? Especially since I don't remember checking it last night before going to bed. Which means the last time I checked the door would have been before I left for Los Angeles. And I certainly wouldn't have left it standing wide open when I was on my way out of town.

Would I?

It *was* awfully cold in here when I got home last night...

I examine the door. Nothing broken or scratched. The lock works, and it doesn't have any of the telltale tiny scratches around the keyhole from being picked. But I'm not a locksmith, what the hell do I know?

Do crazy people know it when they start to go crazy?

Of course not, that's what makes them crazy.

Right?

Enough of this bullshit. I close the kitchen door and lock the deadbolt and drink my coffee and rinse the dishes and put them in the dishwasher. I go put on a pair of jeans which are stained with tiny spots of oil I put in my two-stroke chainsaw engine. I pull on a Cal State sweatshirt that is so old the lettering has flaked off completely, leaving it far more comfortable. Then I put on wool socks and a pair of Vans and now I can go to work. Work will solve everything. And work goes better if you put on pants and a shirt. And shoes make all the difference. Show me a barefoot writer and I'll show you a rank amateur.

Ten minutes later I'm at my desk, waiting for my computer to boot. My screen comes to life and I open the file that contains the fourth book, which I have titled *Killer Unmasked.*

Arnie and the people at Terrapin loved the concept and the title for the fourth book, in which we finally reveal the identity of Killer and he meets Katherine Kendall face to face. Only "we" are having a bit of trouble with that revelation. I have managed to keep Killer's identity obscured from readers—and from my very smart editors—for one good reason: I don't know myself.

Actually, that's not completely true. It's not that I don't *know* who he is, the truth is I'm reluctant to reveal him because the gimmick of keeping Killer's identity hidden has served me well. Whenever there was a shaky story point or an implausible scene that I wanted for dramatic purposes I would simply chalk it up to Killer's mystique. We don't know *how* he does certain things, Katherine Kendall can only *surmise.* And alas, even the intrepid Katherine is not always right.

But after three books the gimmick is starting to feel tired and it is time to progress the series and unmask the monster to my heroine and I am hesitating. From here on it will be harder. It may even mean the series is drawing to a close. And it's too late to back out now. Terrapin has already leaked word that the soon-to-be-published *Killer Unmasked* will *"reveal the true identity of Killer once and for all!"* as the advance promotion has promised. The waiting lists for the book are double what they usually are.

So I have stuck myself with a problem and now I must solve it. I have put it off until the end of the book and now, of course, anything will seem anticlimactic. I sit staring at the screen and I realize I have been asking the wrong question. It's not a matter of *how* to reveal him—the real question is, *Does it matter?*

The most terrifying thing on earth is the human imagination. Consult the horrors of history and you will trace each horror back to the Big Idea someone thought up and then put into action. And when you conjure a monster for a book, it is not only your imagination at work, it is the *reader's* imagination that will focus the finest details of your monster. If the reader wants to picture the killer as their eighth-grade math teacher or their ex-husband it's best to let them—they'll do it anyway. But if you spend chapter after chapter detailing every single aspect of your monster's appearance and personality you run the risk of drowning the reader's images with yours, and you will wind up with a list of characteristics instead of a character. But now I am rationalizing and I know it.

I pick up a pencil and roll it between my palms, thinking. How do I have my cake and eat it too? Until now I have enjoyed the luxury of writing a human monster with as few details as possible, leaving Killer as a nameless free-floating malevolence bedeviling Katherine Kendall. But now the piper must be paid.

Katherine has a vague physical description of him—deliberately vague. He is the overlooked man in the crowd: average height and weight, medium brown hair, small brown eyes obscured behind rectangular wire-framed glasses. But the vague, average quality of his appearance isn't just a dodge on my part. His non-descript appearance is inherent to his madness. This is where I am with the book now, and Katherine Kendall is about to spell out the rest for me. I put the pencil down and begin to type notes on Killer's personality that have been rattling around in my brain for years; notes that will become the shape and sense of the final chapter in the book, in Katherine's voice, as she writes her final report:

"All of Killer's victims had, in random encounters, ignored him or not acknowledged him in some way, and this is the fuel that sets his molten rage to flame. The key to his pathology is the volatile mix of two opposing and compelling forces: his innate grandiosity, and the fact that from a very young age he was treated quite literally as though he didn't exist. For Killer, any kind of neglect, avoidance, or inadvertent inattention can spell a death sentence. There was never a consistent male figure in his life, thus woe betide the young woman who pays him no heed."

I read the note I just made, then I add:

"But despite his average appearance he does have one distinct quality: his voice. Low, sonorous, with a hint of a smile behind it…"

I stop, my hands frozen above the keyboard.

The voice.

Jesus.

How could I not have realized that?

It hasn't occurred to me until this moment that the voice I imagined at Temescal was the same voice I have imagined right here, for five years, as the voice of Killer. I must have been so panicked…

Of course. The association between Killer and whoever had done that poor girl in had been made in my head.

Low, laconic, almost lazy, with that audible smile…

I stare blindly out the window at the gray sky, my mind returning to the events of the last twenty-four hours.

I shake it off and return to the computer. But I lose concentration quickly, and find I am staring at the Documents icon beckoning me from the bottom of the screen. I click on it and I can see at a glance all of the files containing all four of the *Killer* books. Each book about one murder. I look at the file for *Killer At Large,* the second book, which I began reading last night.

If I knew those things from the first book, what about the other murders, from the other books...?

I select the file that contains the drafts of my second book, *Killer At Large,* and once again, I begin to read.

CHAPTER FOURTEEN

St. Stephen, Missouri, was incorporated in 1846 as a last supply point before travelers crossed the Missouri River on their way to the West. The town's only claims to fame were the two banks that Jesse James robbed, and the typesetting machine that Mark Twain invented there and lost a fortune trying to peddle. Shannon Belson had probably learned these facts in school, but as a bright, pretty, 20 year-old woman at the dawn of the 21st century she doubtless had little occasion to recall them.

Katherine looked down at the remains of Shannon Belson in her shallow grave and let her mind play over the facts of Shannon Belson's life and death. Killer had stayed true to his M.O., walking around the grave before finishing it. A DNA sample would reach the lab in a matter of hours for positive ID, since Shannon's head and hands were missing, but Katherine wasn't waiting to hear from Quantico. Katherine knew the minute she saw the yearbook photo of Shannon. She fit the victim profile to a T: age, size, the long, silky hair, and the manner of death and disposal. Killer was nothing if not consistent in his predilections.

But this time something was different. They had found Shannon buried in the woods beside an overgrown cemetery next to the Calvary Assembly of God Chapel on the outskirts of St. Stephen, near a ravaged asphalt rural route that wound through the hills along the muddy Missouri river.

What significance was the proximity to the church? Was it merely convenience to the road? Or was it something more? And the cemetery…?

Katherine pulled her North Face jacket close and looked up from the shallow grave. She looked at the abandoned church that was just visible through the trees, a hundred feet away. Here and there she could see a few headstones in the church cemetery, which bordered the thick woods.

Katherine walked out of the woods and among the headstones. The names on the grave markers had a musty old-west feel: Seamus Galloway, Christian son of Victor and Marybell Galloway… Susannah Lorraine Buford, Beloved Mother of Three, 1842-1903… Samuel Clay, Deacon of Calvary Assembly of God, 1876-1933…

Here and there Katherine saw a flat stone with only a surname and the dates marking the birth and death of the grave's inhabitant. A surprising number of them were children; their simple, square grave markers little monuments to unimaginable grief, obscured by stoic words engraved in stone that had softened with the patina of age and forgotten pain.

Nothing but ghosts here, Katherine thought to herself, and she zipped her collar up tight and headed back to Shannon Belson's final resting place and went to work.

CHAPTER FIFTEEN

I stop reading after I've read the name *Shannon Belson* for the fourth time. It is haunting me.

I click on my browser at the bottom of the screen and I am online. I type in "Shannon Belson St. Stephen Missouri" and get garbage. I try several variations on the name and finally I type Sharon Belson and I am prompted: *DID YOU MEAN "SHARON BELTON?"* I click on "Sharon Belton" and my screen fills with horror.

The first thing I see is an image of Sharon Belton and my breath catches because here she is: a pretty young woman with long, silky hair and brown almond eyes and oval face, smiling for her senior picture. And once again I feel the prickly hot panic that comes with the recognition of her face.

I know this picture, just like I knew Beverly Grace's picture. I have seen it.

But where?

The picture is from an item in the St. Stephen *News* from October 5, 2003:

Sharon Belton, a graduate of St. Stephen High School, has been identified as the woman found buried in a shallow grave off Rt. 90 last Saturday, according to Buck County Sheriff Ansel Cord. The Sheriff's Department discovered the body when two boys came upon the shallow grave near the woods next to Rt. 90. Missouri State police and Buck County Sheriff's officials are asking anyone with any information that might be relevant to the case to contact them…

I read the rest of the article with my fingers pressed against my temples.

Sharon Belton was reported missing on August 14, 2002, *two years before Killer At Large was published.* I scroll down to the bottom of the page and see another, smaller photograph.

I stand up and stare at the picture, my fingers pressed against my now-throbbing temples.

The small photograph is a grainy shot taken by a local news photographer. It is blurry and indistinct, showing mostly the backs of Sheriff's deputies and police. But I can clearly see the shallow grave in the foreground, and in the middle distance I see a few headstones from the church cemetery, and beyond that is the ramshackle frame of the church itself—an abandoned structure, its windows boarded up, its steeple slanted, eaves sagging under the weight of time, and in front of the church is a weathered sign which reads *"Calvary Assembly of God Chapel."*

Just as I had invented it.

I stand there for a long time, frozen, my mind reeling.

I do not know this poor young woman. I do not know this grave, this church…

And yet, again, I must know them.

I pick up the phone on my desk.

Call Joel—or Nicki…

And say what?

I can already hear Nicki's reaction. *You saw a picture online and now you want to take her on, too?*

I put the phone down. I walk out of my office and into the living room and stare out the window at the gathering gloom of an early winter evening.

I have to do something.

I go back to my desk and pick up the phone and call the airlines and ask for the next flight to Kansas City.

THINGS PAST

He stopped beating the Witch when his body and his rage had been exhausted. She was dead—long dead—and now he sat next to the Witch's body on the floor, numb, his breathing hard. When he got his strength back, he crawled over to the smashed Angel on the floor. He tried for a few minutes to put her back together but it was hopeless. A hundred tiny pieces of porcelain that could never be put back together again. He wept. His hands were bloody from the Witch, and from his torn knuckles. When his tears subsided, he got up and washed his hands clean in the kitchen, then returned to the pile of porcelain shards and picked each one up and examined it for something, anything he could take with him.

And then, another miracle. In the pile of shattered porcelain he found two perfect, china blue pieces.

The eyes of the Angel.

The porcelain ovals had chipped off perfectly. He held her eyes in his palm and looked into them and, as he did, he realized what he had to do.

He went to the kitchen and found a bread knife—long, with a serrated blade. He carried the knife back to the Witch and began to cut.

An hour or so of messy work, then he carried the head and hands to the kitchen and placed them in the dish drainer in the sink.

After the blood had drained, the careful work began. He took the porcelain eyes of the Angel and, with infinite care, he tucked them under the lids of the Witch's eyes. Then he went to the bathroom and dug through the Witch's cluttered drawers of cosmetics and returned to the kitchen. He covered the bruises and lacerations with makeup, the swollen lips with a faint coat of pink lipstick, and, finally, a meticulous application of mascara to replicate the fine lashes. He brushed the hair into a proper facsimile of the Angel's, then placed the hands together in prayer in front of the face. It took a while to figure out how to keep them in place, but the careful placement of tiny rolls of duct tape between the palms eventually did the trick. He stepped back, drew the curtains to darken the kitchen, and looked at his work. With the blood drained, the skin was properly pale, if still somewhat swollen. But it wasn't right yet. It looked like a doll—the china blue eyes staring up at nothing.

He carefully placed the head and hands on a bread board and carried them to the closet, where he put them on the shelf, exactly where the Angel had been. He drew all the blinds in the bedroom, tucked blankets into the cracks where the sun shone through, then he climbed into the closet and closed the door and closed his eyes.

He waited, eyes closed, breathless with anticipation. Please, please, come back, let this work...

Then he opened his eyes. Only darkness.

Then, slowly, the pale face of the Angel came into view, hovering in the darkness. She was reborn.

Tears ran down his face as the Angel began to speak to him once again. Like David, he had slain the giant, but far more, far better—he had transformed the Witch into the Angel.

He stayed in the closet with her for three days. He lost all track of time as they went to special new places—places he never dreamed of—places where the Angel praised his new power and exalted him and filled him with unimaginable pleasure.

★★★

On the evening of the fifth day he stayed up until three a.m., then took what was left of the Witch from the house in a duffel bag one of the men had left. He put it in a shopping cart he had dumped in a ravine, and rolled it to a vacant lot he had passed many times on the way to Ralph's. He had dug the shallow hole the night before, so all he had to do was dump it in and cover it with dirt.

On the sixth day he stole a taxidermy book from the local library, along with a textbook on police procedure. He read the taxidermy book in one day, and all night that night he worked carefully, meticulously, on his new Angel. A plan was forming. It had been forming since he first looked at the china blue ovals in his hand. He would take his Angel in a small piece of soft luggage lined with plastic wrap inside, and he would leave this place forever. There was a truck stop a mile or so away. He would go there with his Angel and catch a ride with a trucker, paying him, if necessary, from the cash he found in the Witch's purse. He would forget this place—the Witch was already fading from memory. He was focused entirely on his new life, on his plans. So much to do…

And on the seventh day he rested.

CHAPTER SIXTEEN

St. Stephen, Missouri, has been slowly dying for a century. Its population peaked one hundred years ago, at around eighty thousand souls. Since then its youth had been sucked away by the industrial revolution, wars, and Eisenhower's highways. Now its population is less than half its peak and its roads and buildings are aging gracelessly. *Going the way of the buggy-whip*, I think as I drive up Rt. 90 and St. Stephen first comes into view.

It is just after 2:00 a.m. and the clear Gibbous moon is slanting its half-light across the prairie landscape surrounding the town. All I know about St. Stephen is what I have learned while researching it for *Killer At Large.* I never bothered to come here. And as I enter the dark little town on the deserted main drag I think, *Who would?*

After reading about Sharon Belton's murder I booked the next flight I could get from Burlington to Boston and then to Kansas City, paying full fare, and once in Kansas City I picked up my rental car and now here I am, fourteen hours later, pulling into St. Stephen on the dark, lonely highway.

I have no map of the town, no idea where I'm going, but I know the church is on Route 90, so I proceed through the town, past the hair salons and gas stations and ratty bars, all the way through the main drag in two minutes and then I'm back in the darkness and the road gets rougher and I see a sign that tells me I'm on Rt. 90. I slow down, looking left and right as I continue north, past mile after mile of rusted barbed-wire fence and the barren hollows of a place no one wants to be.

I nearly pass right by it, but out of the corner of my eye I catch a glimpse of the canted steeple of Calvary Assembly of God Chapel and I stop in the middle of the road. I look back over my shoulder and there it is.

I back up slowly, watching the church come into view. It is even more dilapidated than I had imagined or the newspaper photos had revealed. There is a rutted gravel drive leading up beside the church and I turn the steering wheel toward it and the tires of my rental car crunch up the rough, rocky rise as I approach the broken-down sanctuary. I park in the church lot, which is clotted with generations of tall weeds and trash.

How long since anyone worshipped here?

I get out of the car and the cold bites at my throat. I tug my coat tight around me and walk over to the sign on the dirt lawn in front of the church, just to be sure I am at the right place, even though I know I am.

Calvary Ass of Go ape, the sign reads in ready-to-apply plastic letters, the victim of time and bored kids. I look up at the church. It is a gothic horror in its own right: a sagging prairie chapel with a broken-back roof and two large, peaked openings—former stained glass windows—now empty, arched black frames flanking the front doors, staring out at nothing like the eyes of the dead. The smaller windows along the side of the church are boarded up, and the coat of white paint is fighting a losing battle with the elements to protect the weathered gray clapboard underneath.

I walk around the side of the church, looking for the cemetery, and after a minute I see it in the moonlight. I walk to it. It is smaller than I had thought it would be, thirty or forty foot square by my guess, its borders ragged and unclear in the shadows near the woods. I glance down at the headstones and recognize none of the names. The mossy grave markers are cold and silent; they tell me nothing except that once there were living people here and now they are rotting beneath my feet. I clench my teeth and move on, toward the woods that border the dark side of the graveyard.

The woods are thick and black as tar. The trees seem ancient, their bare branches claw at the clear winter stars. I step into the brush, edging my way into the shadows until I see a shaft of weak moonlight ahead, illuminating a small clearing, deeper inside the woods. I move toward it, my heart already gearing up for what I might find.

I duck and dodge and stumble through the bramble and spider webs and tree roots and finally stand up straight and see what I have been looking for:

a rectangular hole in the forest floor. I turn back and see the church, over the headstones, the same angle the photographer took for the *News*.

This is it.

I look down at Sharon Belton's grave. This time my recognition of the grave is less shocking than that of Beverly Grace's grave at Temescal. I have already seen the photograph of this place, and my own imaginings of it have blurred with the photograph and I don't know where one leaves off and the other begins. But the sight and smell of the woods are real, the dirt beneath my feet is cold and hard.

Now what, dumbshit?

I walk around the grave, looking down at it. I have come all this way and I realize I have no idea what to do next. What is here for me?

Something out of the corner of my eye causes me to look up. Movement. My own shadow, probably. I ball my fists in my coat pockets.

What the hell am I doing here?

I look down at the grave and realize Sharon Belton must have thought the same thing as the end came for her.

I linger for a moment out of some misplaced sense of propriety, then I shift my feet to head back to the car, and the next thing I see is a flash of brilliant, blinding white light and the world and its sights and sounds and smells gives way to nothingness.

CHAPTER SEVENTEEN

I dream of something choking me. I fight but it pushes deeper into my mouth and as I wake I taste mold and soil and I try to open my eyes but they are pushed down by something. Dirt in my eyes. I cough and sneeze and try to reach up to clear whatever is choking me but my arms are held down by something. I feel dirt in my hands and now I realize that I am buried.

I struggle harder, panic pushing my arms and legs up, pushing against the avalanche of soil that is suffocating me. I am drowning in dirt. My lungs are on fire and I tuck my chin down to find a pocket of air and I suck the pocket empty and then dive up, choking and coughing, lifting my arms with every ounce of strength I have. I smell earth and damp and I feel something crawl across my left eye and I yell and spit and plow through an endless mass of grit and my right hand finds a space to move in and I twist and scratch my hand up until I feel cold air on my index finger and it gives me hope. I hold my breath and push the pressing avalanche away; now with one hand, now with the other, and I realize I have forgotten my legs and I kick and squall and claw my way up until both hands feel the cold air and I turn my hands back toward my suffocating mouth and I dig and throw dirt away and finally I can lift my head and my left eye opens and I can see the Gibbous moon and it spurs me to fight upward until my face is clear and I can breathe again and I suck the cold air into my aching lungs with the greedy passion of the living.

CHAPTER EIGHTEEN

I sit panting in my erstwhile grave, half-covered in damp dirt, grateful and terrified, my heart banging my ribs like a caged madman. I look around quickly, fearful, and see nothing but trees towering over me in stillness. My hungry breathing is the only sound. I crawl out of the pit and scramble to my feet, my voice making sounds I've never heard before.

I turn, looking around for whoever has done this to me and see no one. I look back down at the hole I climbed out of, my lungs still sucking the precious cold. It is Sharon Belton's grave.

I run off, back through these horrible woods, staggering through slashing brush and branch and out into the open moonlight, where I stumble over a headstone and fall and then get up and run to my car, heaving and mewling like a beaten animal.

I find my keys in my filth-covered jeans and unlock the door and get inside and start the car and tear off, spraying gravel and thanking God that Sharon Belton's grave hadn't become my own.

I roar back the way I came, down Rt. 90, gripping the steering wheel hard to keep my hands from shaking. Dirt and grit filter down from my hair and into my eyes.

"Hunhh! Hunhh!"

I shake the dirt out wildly, shuddering and sneezing and coughing up clots of soil and snot and nearly driving off the road. I right the car and wipe my sleeve across my face and think only primitive thoughts of getting away, getting out, getting back to bright lights and cities and airports and daytime and comforting furniture and pretty lawyers in clean suits with charming smiles and fresh fruit and coffee waiting to nourish and soothe and save me.

CHAPTER NINETEEN

Fuck.

I am back at McDougal's bar in Pasadena. In my dark booth in the corner, farthest from the door, and I am drunk.

Fuck fuck FUCK. Jesus God, what have I done? Five years of riding the wagon and now I've fallen off and fallen hard and I have really fucked up. Fucked up, drunk off my ass like the fucking drunken loser that I am. I look around. How the hell did I wind up here of all places? How long have I been here? How did I get here? I try to remember but my head is pounding and my mind is full of wet fog.

He comes to me with a fifth of Jack and two fresh glasses. He places the bottle and the glasses in front of me, then turns to the jukebox. He puts money in it and selects a song. The low, slow pulse of the bass guitar and the smoky, bluesy chords play from the jukebox:

> *Jesus just left Chicago and he's bound for New Orleans,*
> *Well now, Jesus just left Chicago and he's bound for New Orleans,*
> *Workin' from one end to the other and all points in between...*

He slides into the booth across from me in the dark. Who the hell is this? I try to think clearly but I can't. I can barely hold my head up. I can't see his eyes, only my own face distorted twice—reversed—once in each lens of his rectangular wire-framed glasses. The bar is quiet, and his deep, soft voice is pitched so low that I feel it resonate in my chest.

I listen.

"*Used to play this song all the time when I was hauling machine parts out of Chicago,*" he says.

I nod sloppily to the music, the slow Texas shuffle...

"*So you're a writer?*" he asks. *His face is solemn, but his voice has a hint of a smile behind it.*

"*Nn,*" I nod, a bobble-head drunk.

He opens the bottle and pours my glass full and the aroma fills my senses.

"*Well I've got a story for you, Doc,*" he says.

CHAPTER TWENTY

"Sir?"

A woman's voice.

"Sir."

I force my dry eyes open, the light sending a shot of pain through my head. A flight attendant, blonde with dark roots, glaring at me impatiently.

"Are you alright?"

I nod slightly, my head pounding.

"We're in Boston and you'll have to deplane."

I look around, remembering where I am. The plane is empty and quiet. I rise unsteadily, gritting my teeth against the pain in my skull.

"Are you sure you're alright?"

"Yeah."

I'm not hung over. I didn't get drunk. It was only a guilt-dream. I was attacked... buried...

Right?

I slide out from between the seats and reach for my small bag in the open overhead compartment above my seat.

"Did you want those?" She points to the seat-back pocket in front of my seat.

I look at where she's pointing and see two little bottles of Jack Daniel's tucked into the seat-back pocket, their tiny necks sticking above the elastic seam on the pocket, both bottles topped with brown whiskey and their seals intact. She leans over and pulls the bottles from the pocket and holds them out to me.

"No," I say.

"You sure?"

"Yes."

"Hang on." She puts the bottles in her pocket, then reaches into another pocket for a wad of small bills and starts to count out money for me.

"Did I—order any other drinks?" I ask.

"Nope. Just these, but then you fell asleep."

She holds out ten dollars.

"Keep it."

"Oh, no, here—" She holds the money out.

"Please." I hold my palm up. "Thank you," I say to her, and then turn and get off the plane.

Thank God. Thank you, God, I think as I get off the plane and head into Logan airport. I have had guilty drunk-dreams before but this was the most vivid. I pause to let the pounding subside in my head. I reach up and touch the bandage over my brow. It is damp and hot to the touch. I see blood on my fingers.

I go to the restroom and my reflection forces me back a step, from shock. My face is milk white and my eyes are red slits sunk in sallow hollows beneath filthy, coagulated hair. The Band-Aid I bought at the Kansas City airport is soaked through with blood. I didn't even realize I was cut until I had driven halfway back to Kansas City and a trickle of blood dripped into my eye. I don't remember being hit—I only remember the blinding light.

I had washed up at the airport in Kansas City the best I could, then wrapped some ice in a napkin and held it there until the bleeding stopped, but I guess it started again. I peel the blood-soaked Band-Aid off, wincing when I see the deep, open split in my brow. I may need stitches but not here, not now. My flight to Burlington connects in an hour and I will stop at the ER at the university hospital on the way home.

I wash up and dab the cut clean and put a towel against the wound until the bleeding stops and then I take the small packet of Band-Aids from my pocket and apply two fresh ones and go find my gate and sit there and think.

What in the name of God is happening?

I take out my phone and dial my voicemail. Four messages: *"Jack? It's Nicki. Call me right away, please."* The next one, again from Nicki: *"Jack, where are you? It's very important that you call me immediately. I'm at the office but here's my cell..."* A similar message from Joel, and one from Arnie.

Now what?

I sit there, wondering what to do. Everything in me resists the idea of calling them. I am certain it is bad news.

They call boarding time for my flight and I get up and I am the first in line to get on the flight to Burlington and get the hell out of here.

CHAPTER TWENTY-ONE

I drive away from Burlington International Airport in my truck and head for the University of Vermont hospital. I reach it in a few minutes and pull into the parking lot beside the ER.

I go inside and give my information to the registry nurse and she gives me a chemical ice pack for my head and I sit in the waiting room. I take out my phone and look at Nicki's number. I don't want to hear what she has to tell me, but how long can I put it off? I snap the phone shut and put it in my pocket and distract myself with the television hanging from the ceiling in a corner of the waiting area. The TV is tuned to a daytime talk show featuring the show's hosts, all women, interviewing transsexuals about their difficulties maintaining meaningful long-term relationships. I take out my phone again and look at Nicki's number. I try to gather my scattered thoughts and, in my dizzy, light-headed state, I find those thoughts focusing on Nicki. But not as my attorney. As a woman. I don't want to call her because I'm afraid of what she has to tell me. But I *want* to call her just to talk to her, to hear her voice. I wonder if I could have a meaningful long-term relationship with her. I listen to the advice from the women on the talk show, but none of it seems to apply. "Love is love, no matter who you are," one of the hosts tells one of the transsexuals, who is crying. *Love is a sickness full of woes, all remedies refusing.* The TV cuts to a commercial for floor wax. I close my eyes. *Love beareth all things, believeth all things, hopeth all things, endureth all things...*

I feel my pulse rising inexorably. I can't stop it. Panic needles again, up and down my arms and legs, more than before, more than I can remember…

The door opens to the waiting area and a short, round nurse calls my name and I get up and follow her back to an exam room, where I sit on the paper-covered examination table. Flecks of grave soil drop off my clothes and onto the white paper and I brush them off. I look up and see myself in a small mirror on the wall and once again I am taken aback by my wretched appearance. My face is colorless and my breathing is shallow and realize I am probably in shock. Maybe I have a concussion. I look dead. Hell, for all I know I *am* dead. That would answer a lot of questions—if I were lost in purgatory like some doomed character in a bad horror movie.

The door to the exam room opens and a young doctor breezes in. Thirty at most, with thick, jet-black hair and the brusque manner of every ER physician except George Clooney.

"Hello," he says, without looking up from the information I filled out for the registry nurse.

"Hello," I say. He kicks his rolling metal stool over between his legs and sits squarely in front of me and looks at my brow.

"Let's have a look." He snaps on a pair of latex gloves and swabs something across my Band-Aids and peels them off.

"Nasty cut," he says, and looks closer. "Got some infection. How'd you get this?"

Oh, I was just nosing around a murder victim's shallow grave at two a.m. and this blinding light struck me down like Saul on the road to Damascus and next thing I knew I was buried alive. At least I think I'm alive…you might want to check my vitals just to make sure, Doc…

Doc.

Killer liked to call people that. And in the dream…what was that the guy had said…? *"I've got a story for you, Doc."*

I have had dreams about Killer before—obscure, haunting dreams—but this dream was different. I actually believed this was really happening…it had the *feel* of something that really happened…

The doctor presses a wad of gauze against my eyes and I can feel him squirt Betadine over the wound. It stings like hell. He sops up the drips of Betadine then pulls the gauze away and I see the needle.

"Little stick now," he says, as he raises a syringe toward my face, its long needle moving up to my eye and over it, to my brow, and my shoulders tense as he sticks the needle right into the wound. I grit my teeth as the needle penetrates.

I'll give you a 'little stick,' you little prick. Why don't you just tell the truth? "I'm *gonna stick a needle right into your deep, bleeding wound and it's gonna hurt like a motherfucker.*"

I can see his gloved hand pushing the plunger down slowly, filling my wound with lidocaine, and I wait for the numbness and it comes and I realize how much it had been hurting me and now I feel warm fuzzy feelings for my friend the doctor whom I now like *ever* so much.

"I walked into a door," I answer his question belatedly.

I feel him look at me as he cleans the wound deeper. He doesn't say anything, just proceeds to treat me.

I flash on a long-buried memory of being treated in an ER while I was drinking. I had found myself in a downtown L.A. emergency room in the middle of the night, coming off a howling bender with a bad cut on the back of my head. I had no idea how or where I got the injury but I told the doctor I fell, and the doctor's silence was the same silence I feel now from the doctor who is quickly applying a series of butterfly bandages to my brow. I know I present like a drunk or an addict—having fallen down and hurt myself, looking like I slept in an alley. Or in a grave…

"Okay," he says, finishing already. "Here," he hands me a few aluminum sample packets of Polysporin and then snaps his gloves off. "Put some of this on there tonight and every day until you run out and if you see any redness or swelling you need to get it taken care of. The bandages will come off on their own in about a week," he says this slowly and clearly, as though he were talking to a five year-old. To him I am a stumbling drunk, or some kind of problematic person that he doesn't want coming back here.

"Thanks," I say, and get off the table as he writes something on my chart.

"Take care," he says, without looking at me, and then walks out.

CHAPTER TWENTY-TWO

I steer my truck homeward, running my mind over everything. I am confused and in trouble but somehow I feel okay. Maybe it's the lidocaine, but I feel calmer as I near my cabin. I feel my strength and confidence returning as I crest the last hill before my driveway and I am thinking of calling Nicki the moment I get home and then I see Claire Boyle's Sheriff's Dept. SUV parked near the front of my driveway, pulled off onto the shoulder of the rutted drive. As I come closer I see no one in the vehicle so I drive on by without slowing down.

Time to call Nicki.

I pick up the phone and dial, watching my driving carefully.

"Jack Rhodes returning Nicki's call," I say to Nicki's assistant.

I wait for what seems forever and then Nicki's voice in my ear.

"Jack? Where the hell have you been?"

"I'll tell you later. What's up?"

"We have a problem. Where are you?"

"Vermont."

"Have you been home?"

"Not yet. Tell me what's going on."

"LAPD is about to release your name as a person of interest in the Beverly Grace murder."

Jesus. "What exactly does that mean?" I ask.

"Legally, absolutely nothing. It's their way of leveraging you to cooperate without formally charging you or calling you a suspect."

"What does 'cooperate' mean?"

"They want you to come back to L.A. so they can talk to you again."

"Shit."

"I've been putting them off, hoping I could come up with something on your whereabouts in April '01 but I've come up with zip. But if you come back to New York I may be able to get them to compromise on a meeting here, with me present, at the Manhattan DA's office. You ended the interview abruptly in L.A. and I think they're mainly concerned that you've made a run for it, since no one has been able to locate you. Where were you?"

"Long story. I'd rather not go into it on the phone."

"Can you meet me here?"

I hesitate.

"Jack, this guy Marsh at LAPD is no dummy. He went back to the scene, at Temescal, and he saw fresh tracks, which he assumes are yours. He's not gonna let go. If they find the hair clip and it has your prints on it…"

"I know."

"He has a real bug up his ass about you. He's reading all your books now. Jack, please tell me where you are. Are you headed home? Because LAPD has asked the Sheriff's office there to go to your place and wait for you there."

"I'm on the road, but I'm not home."

"Jack, listen to me. Don't go home. You need to come to New York right now. We can talk to the LAPD here, and I'll be right there with you the whole time. If you want, we can talk to my forensic shrink before the meeting, as a last ditch effort to get you to remember where you were that last week of April '01. I've already talked to him and he's willing to help."

I hesitate again.

"Jack, I know you don't want to look back at that period of your life but you may have to if we're going to get you out of this," she says.

"What about that lead?" I say. "My editor's assistant, Dontis…assault with a cocktail umbrella?"

"Gregory Dontis. We haven't been able to find him. My investigator has checked everywhere—police, employment records, DMV, IRS…every place we can think of."

"Coroner?" I ask.

"…I'm not sure, hold on," she says. I hear papers shuffling, then she comes back. "It's not in my investigator's notes. But he did check police records."

"Your investigator didn't check the coroner for a missing person? Who is this investigator?"

"A junior associate here."

"Coroners and police don't always exchange information," I say.

"I know. I'll call there myself as soon as I get off the phone with you. Jack, don't change the subject. Come to New York."

"Alright," I say. "I can be there tonight."

"When?"

"Late. I'll call your cell."

"Why all the mystery? What the hell is going on?"

"I wish I knew."

"Look, Jack, don't fuck with me, okay? I'm your lawyer and I'm here to help you and I *will* help you any way I can but you've got to be straight with me."

"I'll call you when I get to New York and I'll tell you everything I know."

"Promise?"

"I promise," I look at my watch. "I'll be there by nine o'clock tonight."

"I'll be waiting," she says.

CHAPTER TWENTY-THREE

It is 9:17 when I cross the George Washington Bridge. I call Nicki's cell and she answers on the second ring.

"Hello?"

"I'm here."

"Where is here?"

"Heading toward Midtown." "It's too late to meet at the office. Why don't you come to the Mirabelle Hotel, it's on 56th. They have a restaurant that's open late and you can stay there tonight. I've already booked a room for you, if that's okay."

"That's fine."

"I spoke with Dr. Abrams. He said he can see you tomorrow morning, first thing. His office is three blocks from the hotel. Sound okay?"

"Okay. What about the coroner?"

"I talked to a friend there. She's checking as we speak. I'll be at the Mirabelle in fifteen minutes. In the restaurant."

"I'm not exactly dressed for anything upscale," I say, thinking of my filthy clothes. "I mean, I look like hell."

"That's okay, it's dark."

CHAPTER TWENTY-FOUR

"Holy shit, you weren't kidding," Nicki says as she sees me approach her table in the restaurant off the lobby of the Mirabelle Hotel. She stares at my filthy clothes. Then she sees the bandages on my brow and her concern turns to alarm. "What the hell happened?"

I sit across from her and before I can begin to tell her a waiter approaches. Nicki orders something small and healthy and then gets me to agree to a steak and potato and vegetables.

"You need to eat, you look like death."

I smile and tell her she's not far from the truth and then I tell her what happened in St. Stephen. Our food arrives just as I finish and she doesn't even notice. She sits and stares at me, astonished. After the waiter leaves she leans forward.

"This person—whoever assaulted you—did you see him? Do you know him from anywhere?"

"I didn't see him," I realize how hungry I am and I start eating. "He must know something…how else could he have been there? And I had this dream…"

"What dream?"

"From when I was drinking. I dreamed about a man…" I trail off, the dream is gone from memory.

"What do you remember about him?"

I shake my head. "Nothing…I don't know…"

She watches me eat, her brows knitted as she works the problem in her mind.

"It doesn't make any sense, does it?" I say.

"No, it doesn't. But there has to be an answer." Her eyes dart back and forth quickly as she works the problem. "Jack, these women—the pictures. Are you sure you never knew them? Never met them?"

"Yes, I'm sure. I didn't know them. But the pictures… I knew the pictures. I know it sounds crazy…""Finish your dinner and get a good night's sleep. I'll call Dr. Abrams and we'll meet with him first thing in the morning."

I nod.

"We'll figure this out, Jack. There has to be an explanation."

"What if the explanation is that I'm crazy?"

"You're not crazy."

"What makes you so sure?"

"That cut over your eye didn't come from your imagination," she says. "There has to be some explanation."

"Why?"

"Because," she says. "There always is."

She takes a piece of paper from her little black Kate Spade handbag. "By the way, you were right about checking with the coroner's office. Gregory Dontis died in May '01." She looks at me. "Good call," she says.

"How'd he die?"

"Shot with a .22 caliber automatic."

"How come his name didn't show up in the police reports?" I ask.

"He wasn't identified until after the initial investigation. He was a John Doe until the suspects were charged," she says. "My investigator only asked the police for the initial reports, so his name didn't appear."

"I think you need a new investigator," I say.

Nicki takes a sip of her wine.

"I think you're right," she admits.

"Who killed him?"

She looks at her notes. "Buenavestario Funiccilatierro."

"Say what?"

She slides the paper over to me.

"AKA Bennie Fun," she says. "You were right about checking with the coroner, but it still doesn't help us. Dontis is dead and his killer's been at Sing Sing ever since. It's a dead end."

"Who's this Salvatore Funiccilatierro?" I ask, reading the notes.

"Sallie Fun. Bennie's brother," Nicki says. "The brothers ran a small-time sports book and Dontis got behind on the vig, so they showed up at his apartment one night to collect and it got out of hand and Dontis wound up shot in the back of the head and dumped in a ravine off the New Jersey turnpike. Both brothers were charged, and the DA's office flipped Sallie."

"Sallie still live in Jersey City?" I ask, looking at the address scrawled under Sallie's name.

"Why?" she asks.

"If Dontis had the manuscript at his apartment, the brothers show up and kill him, then maybe grab some of his stuff on the way out. Bennie goes up for murder and Sallie's left with Dontis's stuff, including the manuscript. Maybe Sallie reads the manuscript and gets ideas."

"That's why I'm giving this information to the police, when the time is right," Nicki says.

"You mean after your skilled junior associate shakes him down?"

"When the time is right," she says.

"I know people who could check Sallie out."

"Who?"

"Cops, FBI, people I've used as technical advisors for the books."

"I don't think it's a good idea for you to give any information to the police or FBI right now, no matter how tight you are with them," she says.

"Maybe." I look at Sallie's address on the piece of paper. Nicki watches me, her eyes steady and serious. The corners of her mouth turn down.

"You're not thinking of going there to talk to him yourself," she says.

"Who, me?"

She puts her hand on mine and looks right through me, her eyes clear and hard. I can imagine her using those eyes to penetrate some poor soul in cross-examination.

"Promise me you won't do anything stupid," she says.

I look at her.

"I promise," I say.

CHAPTER TWENTY-FIVE

Two hours later I'm sitting in my truck, halfway down the block from Sallie Fun's apartment building. My truck is equidistant between the two feeble streetlights on the block, where the shadows are deepest. My rearview mirror and both side mirrors are adjusted so I can watch the apartment and also see anyone coming up behind me without turning my head. I keep a steady scan going: apartment, left side mirror, rearview, right mirror... After sitting stakeout with NYPD Homicide countless times I've picked up the basics. All I need are some stale donuts and lukewarm coffee.

I glance around the street. It's not far from the tidy, leafy streets of the Heights, but the gentrification that began in the 1980's has passed over this particular neighborhood. Graffiti and trash are everywhere, and there are no people out for a stroll on the dark sidewalks. The buildings that line the street are old and ragged. Next to my truck is a parking meter that has been smashed open. I look at my watch. 12:25.

I have no idea what Sallie Fun looks like, and I have even less of an idea what I'll do if I see him. Maybe he'll be carrying a shovel. Or a dog-eared copy of *Killer*. Or maybe I'm wasting my time. But at least I'm doing something.

I lean back against the headrest. If Sallie had the manuscript before *Killer* went to press, he could have killed Beverly Grace. Far-fetched, but conceivable. But it still wouldn't explain who killed Sharon Belton. I run my hand through my hair, trying to think. Specks of dirt fall onto my shirt. Grave dandruff. I could be showered and shaved and tucked between the crisp sheets of my king-sized bed at the Mirabelle, eating a shrimp sandwich from room service and watching pay-per-view, but I'd still be thinking the same thoughts. Might as well be thinking them here. Nicki wouldn't approve, but so far I haven't done anything stupid.

I look at the apartment, at the left mirror, the rearview, the right mirror…

I liked it when Nicki put her hand on mine. I'm sure it was a purely professional gesture of concern, but it was nice to feel the tactile care of a woman. She wears no wedding ring. A boyfriend is likely, given how attractive she is, but from what I've seen she works long hours and she seems like she'd be choosy about the men in her life. There is a self-sufficiency about her. She has been friendly and frank with me but there is something guarded beneath it. There could be any number of reasons for that. I'm a client, of course, and possibly a serial killer. There's that. But I have a feeling there's something else. Maybe she picked up that I'm attracted to her but I'm not her type. Maybe she's found the perfect guy and she can think of nothing but him night and day. Maybe she prefers women. Maybe she's Amish. Probably she's overwhelmed by my animal magnetism and grave-scent. I try to think about other things, but for the first time in a long time I seem to be preoccupied with a woman.

"Progress," I say.

A male figure lopes down the street toward me, toward Sallie's apartment. When he passes under a streetlight I get a good look: thirties, dark hair, small dark eyes, advanced male pattern baldness. He is wearing Air Jordans, Fila sweatpants, and a NY Giants jacket.

"Welcome to 1989," I say.

He climbs the steps to Sallie's building and enters. I wait until I see a light come on in a third story window. I count the number of windows from the corner of the building to the lighted window, then get out of the truck.

I cross the street to the building and step into the shadows of the doorway and scan down the list of tenants by the buzzers for the lobby door. *S. Funaculaterri* is misspelled and listed as residing in 3D. The lock on the lobby door is broken so I open the door and go inside.

The lobby is cramped, the walls painted and repainted so many times that the surface is rippled and buckled over the tectonic plates of old paint. The floor is filthy and there is a rusted bicycle frame leaning against one wall, minus both wheels. Next to the bike, a stained twin mattress sags against the wall. When I walk past the mattress I smell urine and something like soiled baby diapers.

Somewhere upstairs a stereo is playing. I can't hear the music, but the thump of the bass rattles the metal bike frame. I walk past the ancient elevator and take the stairs to the third floor.

The lights are out in the third floor hallway. I stop and let my eyes adjust to the darkness. The door across from me has plastic characters nailed to the center panel, plated in peeling faux brass: 3A. I move down the hall until I reach 3D. I stop and look at the door. The trim around the jamb was painted without being taped and brush marks slop over the trim and onto the wall haphazardly.

Now what? I could turn around and go back to my hotel and my imaginary shrimp sandwich. And then what? Wait until morning for another interview with Detective Marsh sitting across from me with his manila folder and his small gray eyes? And Det. Larson smirking at me...

I knock. A few moments pass, then I hear someone moving inside the apartment.

"Who is it?" a man's voice from inside, close to the door.

"Sam Spade," I say.

"Who?"

"Philip Marlowe," I say.

"Don't know you. Get lost."

"C'mon, Sallie, it's me. Open up."

The door opens a few inches. Sallie Fun glares at me from under his caveman brow. He has shed the Giants jacket, allowing full view of his puffy steroid muscles, which pack his white wife-beater like the cream filling in a Twinkie. He's short, and wears a gold necklace with some kind of medallion on it. Another victim of *The Sopranos*.

"Fuck do you want?" he says. His voice is high and nasal. His right hand is holding the edge of the door and his left arm is down at his side, his hand hidden behind his back.

"Just want to talk," I say.

"'Bout what?" he glares.

"Gregory Dontis."

Sallie takes a moment to absorb this. It seems like it might take Sallie a long time to absorb anything.

"You a cop?"

"No, I'm an international best-selling author," I say.

"Fuck off," Sallie says, and starts to close the door. I stick my foot in the way to stop it.

"Get your foot outta my door, fucko," Sallie says, giving me his tough-guy glare.

"Fucko?" I say.

Sallie pulls a small pistol from behind his back and points it at my face.

"You don't wanna fuck with me, jerkoff. Get the fuck outta here."

"You say 'fuck' a lot," I say. "Can I assume you're not much of a reader?"

Sallie pulls the slide back on the gun, jacking a round into the chamber. He narrows his small eyes at me, as if his gun has spoken for him. At least the gun didn't say "fuck."

"Don't think I won't do it," he says.

His finger curls tighter around the trigger. I believe him. It was probably Sallie who shot Gregory Dontis, then ratted his brother out for it. He seems like that kind of guy—tweaked on steroids and God knows what else. Maybe this wasn't such a good idea.

"Turn your ass around and get the fuck outta here," he says.

"I can't do that," I say, thinking of Nicki telling me Gregory Dontis was shot in the back of the head.

"You *will* do that," Sallie says.

"No, I won't," I say, now remembering an NYPD weapons trainer yelling at a green Academy cadet over the gunfire at an outdoor range: *"Arrest procedure 101: never, EVER turn your back on an armed suspect."*

"Yes you will," Sallie says. "Turn around and walk away, shit-stain."

"I can't do that, Sallie," I say. "I promised someone I wouldn't do anything stupid. And it would be stupid to turn my back on a twitchy little wannabe gangster with a pimp gun aimed at me and a round in the chamber. Toss the gun under the bed over there and we'll talk."

"You don't know who you're dealing with, man," Sallie says, his hand starting to tremble, his high voice rising higher.

"Put the gun down and I'll go."

"Fuck you," he says.

We stand there for a moment. It would be a Mexican standoff except I don't have a gun. I hear a small child fussing from one of the apartments down the hall. I look at the barrel of the gun in my face. A Ruger .22 automatic.

"Look, I just want to talk to you about *that*," I point to a corner of the room behind Sallie.

He turns to look and I kick the door hard, spinning him halfway around. I grab his gun-hand and ram my head into his chest and slam him down to the floor of the apartment. I pin his gun-hand to the floor with my right hand, and put my left knee on his right elbow and grind my right knee into his stomach with all my weight.

"Ooph," he says.

I reach down with my left hand and grab his testicles through his Fila sweats and squeeze as hard as I can.

"Ahh!" Sallie says.

"Drop the gun and I'll give you your balls back, Sallie," I say.

"Fuck you, motherfucker—" he grunts.

He squirms and I yank his testicles down as hard as I can and he screams.

"You ought to lay off the 'roids, Sallie. Your nuts are like raisins," I say.

Sallie struggles to raise his gun but can't. The gun goes off, popping a small hole in the tweeter of a stereo speaker across the single-room apartment. Sallie fires again, the slug hitting the ceiling.

I pull even harder on Sallie's testicles. Sallie makes a sound like a cat being tortured. His breath smells worse than the mattress in the lobby. I glance around the room. A sagging bookcase against the wall holds a cheap stereo, some CD's, a copy of *Club* magazine, a picture book about bodybuilding, and a pair of hand exercisers intended to make your forearms look like Popeye's. This is definitely not a guy who would read a manuscript and meticulously craft a copycat murder. I look down at him and see fear in his eyes. I start to feel sorry for him, then I stop the feeling right away.

"Tell you what, Sallie. Reach down with your little finger and release the magazine and let it fall on the floor. Then I'll let go of your raisins."

He glares up at me ferociously. I twist his testicles and he howls.

"You can release the clip on that Ruger with one hand. I've done it and so can you. If your hands are strong enough, that is," I say.

Sallie grits his teeth. Tears run back from his eyes and into his ears. He slides his little finger down and presses the release button on the gun butt and the magazine falls out onto the floor.

"Alright," I say, then I let go of his testicles and hit him in the face with a left cross as hard as I can. He makes an abrupt rasping sound and a cut opens on his cheekbone and blood starts running down his face, following the trail of tears into his ear.

I pick up the gun and the magazine and get up.

"Ever read a manuscript called *Killer*?" I ask.

"I don't know what the fuck you're talking about," he whines, curled in a ball on the floor.

"Didn't think so," I say. Then I tuck the gun into the back of my waistband and put the magazine in my pocket and walk out, closing the door quietly behind me.

CHAPTER TWENTY-SIX

The adrenaline hits me after I get back to the Mirabelle and take a long shower and I notice my hand shaking while I shave. I rinse the remnants of shaving cream from my face and look in the mirror and see a drop of blood ooze out from under the bandages on my brow, loosened by the hot water.

I find a packet of Polysporin from the Burlington ER in my shaving kit and take a Q-tip from the chrome dispenser on the vanity and I'm about to treat the cut when there is a quick, sharp knock at my door.

I move to the bathroom doorway and wait for a beat. I glance at the clock on the nightstand. 2:50 a.m. Another, louder knock, and the adrenaline peaks.

I open the drawer of the nightstand and slip Sallie Fun's Ruger into the pocket of my hotel bathrobe. I keep my finger on the trigger and lean beside the door jamb.

"Who is it?"

I hear a small, exasperated sigh and Nicki muttering "Thank God."

"Nicki," she says, louder.

I open the door and here she is—sneakers, jeans, and a white sweatshirt with a hood that falls over the back of her blonde glove-leather jacket. She is furious.

"You went there, didn't you," she says flatly. A statement, not a question. I'm still rushing with adrenaline, so I say something stupid.

"Usually, when a woman knocks on my door in the middle of the night she greets me with a little more decorum."

Her blue eyes shoot through me. This is the first time I've seen her in casual attire and she seems smaller; more like the petite, tomboyish girl she must have been. A different look, but no less captivating. 5'3" in sneakers and lovely. But boy, is she pissed.

"What happened?" she demands.

I open the door and step back and she comes in. I close the door and sit on the edge of the bed and take a couple of deep breaths to let my heartbeat downshift toward a more normal pace.

"I went home," she says, standing over me like a scolding schoolmarm—except schoolmarms don't wear tight jeans and fitted leather jackets. None that I know of, anyway.

"I went to bed but I couldn't sleep," she says. "I just *knew* you went to Jersey City. I called your room half a dozen times and then I decided to—"

She stops short when she sees the butt of the gun sticking up out of my bathrobe pocket.

"Jesus, Jack—*tell me what happened*," she says.

I put the gun back in the nightstand drawer and return to sit on the bed and Nicki sits beside me and glares as I tell her about my adventure with Sallie Fun. She listens, shaking her head with disapproval, then disbelief, and her eyes grow sharper still with anger.

"What were you thinking?" she says, after I finish. "What the hell is wrong with you? You promised me…"

I nod. "I'm sorry," I say.

"Don't ever lie to me again. Don't ever break a promise to me. Don't ever do anything like that again, do you understand me?"

I nod again. I find it hard to look her in the eye.

"So *reckless*. You could've been…" she says, and then she stops herself. She gets up and goes to the mini bar and takes out a tiny bottle of Skye vodka and twists the top off and dumps all of it into a cut crystal whiskey glass and drinks half of it in one gulp. She turns and looks at me.

"It's my job to defend you and to protect you. And I can't do my job if you go off and do idiotic things like this. Now I want you to promise me—and mean it this time—that you won't ever do anything like this again, and you will do as I say, as long as I'm your attorney."

"I promise," I say, looking steadily into her eyes now, to show her how sincere I am. Her eyes dart back and forth as she looks into mine, reading me for any sign of guile. After a long moment she sighs and takes another drink—a small sip this time.

"What is it?" I say.

"What's what?"

"This isn't just about you protecting me as my attorney," I say. The tunnel-vision from the adrenaline is gone, and I'm more interested in her reaction to my errant behavior than I am in playing the tough guy.

"What is it?" I say again.

She looks down. Takes another delicate sip of her drink.

"Look, I'm sorry," I say. "But I'm here and Sallie was a dead end and it's over. It's okay."

"It's *not* okay," she says, looking down into her glass. She starts to say more, then changes her mind, and cuts the conversation short.

"I just feel like now I can't trust you. And I need to know that I can," she says into her glass. "I need to know that you won't do something stupid like this again."

"I told you, I won't," I say.

She glances up from her drink at me. She notices the loose bandages on my brow, then puts down her glass and heads into the bathroom and comes back with a couple of Q-tips and leans close to me and dabs the blood away, her face close to mine. I can smell the faint, sweet scent of her—a delicate blend of skin cream, soap, shampoo, the fresh spice of vodka under her breath. I feel a stirring deep inside me that I haven't felt for a long, long time.

Then she stands up, heads to the bathroom, and tosses the Q-Tips into the wastebasket, then dumps the rest of the vodka down the sink. She puts the glass back on the sideboard and looks at me.

"Get some sleep," she says, and turns to go. I get up and walk her to the door and reach over her shoulder to release the safety clasp on the jamb. A brief breath of her scent again, and without looking at me she says, "I'll see you in the morning." And then she leaves.

I take off the hotel robe and hang it on the hook on the back of the bathroom door. I slide between the crisp sheets of my king-sized bed and turn off the lamp on the nightstand and lie back on the pillow and close my eyes.

There was something more to her reaction than just professional concern. Some raw nerve had been scraped. She was angry, yes, but there seemed to be something more—something behind the anger that she wouldn't talk about.

I try to imagine what nerve I had touched in her, but the adrenaline has drained me and I suddenly feel very tired. My muscles loosen and my breathing deepens and then I drift off in the darkness, along with the last traces I can sense of her.

THINGS PAST

─────

He was fifteen but he had grown tall and strong for his age, so when he told people he was eighteen no one batted an eye. It had been two years since he had left the Witch buried in the vacant lot—and in memory—and caught a ride with a trucker, just as he had planned.

The trucker took him all the way to West Virginia, where he got a job in a small town, washing dishes at a truck stop whose owners weren't choosy about things like child labor laws or immigration status—or health codes or minimum wage, for that matter. The owners, a mean, petty old couple, let him stay in a shed at the edge of the parking lot in exchange for a cut of his meager pay. The shed was no longer used, and barely bigger than a closet, but that suited him fine. He liked the tiny, windowless space. He plugged the holes in the rotted wood walls to keep out the light, and he was free to love his Angel or read his Bible in the twelve hours a day he wasn't washing the greasy dishes in the truck stop kitchen.

But by age fifteen he had become increasingly restless and discontent. Over two years' time, the Angel was deteriorating badly. No matter how dark he made the shed, it took more and more effort to keep the Angel looking right.

The skin was the problem. His first efforts at taxidermy had been clumsy and rushed, his thirteen year-old hands stitching ragged seams behind the hairline and the jaw. And since the book he had read was about animals it didn't take human skin into account. He stole an embalming textbook from a library while on an errand to Charleston but it was too late. No matter what he tried—makeup, putty, clay, wax—it was impossible to replicate the fine porcelain skin of the Angel. Even on the darkest moonless nights he couldn't help but be distracted by the sagging, shapeless, mottled features that had once been so clear and perfect. He had carefully pulled up the planks of the wooden floor of the shed and dug a small hole where he kept the Angel while he was at work. The damp earth only accelerated her decay, and soon he could no longer summon the Angel's voice at all.

Thus deprived, he became angry at the smallest things, although he kept his anger—and all feelings—bottled up inside. The other workers in the kitchen had long since given up trying to make conversation with him, which was fine, but it only increased his isolation, his desperate need to be paid attention. He didn't care to listen to the mindless kitchen blather about sports or women or their fucking cheap-ass bosses, anyway. He didn't want to listen, he wanted to be heard. But not by the crude, ignorant kitchen staff—by his Angel, who was crumbling before his eyes.

So he lost himself in his Bible, and began to branch out in his reading—to the worlds of Poe, Doyle, and a dozen or more mystery writers. They engrossed him and took his mind off his discontent in the hours when he was able. But eventually the books weren't enough, either. His life was a story in itself, greater than all the books in the world, greater, even, than his Bible.

And then, as he had found before in his young life, just when he was at his most desperate, a miracle arrived.

Caitlin, her name was, a pretty high school senior who took a waitress job at the truck stop after he'd been there two years. And the moment he saw her, his breath caught in his fifteen year-old throat.

She was his Angel—her skin perfect pale porcelain, her face the same Mona Lisa oval. Her hair and eyes were the wrong color but those could be changed. Even if he didn't transform her as he had the Witch, hair could be dyed, and he had read that some people wore colored contact lenses. Maybe, at the age of fifteen, he had found someone who could be with him. Really with him. The idea of sharing his stories and going to special places with a living, breathing Angel was a thrilling prospect—thrilling to the point of terror. He had never been with a girl; never really even considered it a possibility. Until now.

Caitlin was popular at the truck stop right from the start—full of laughter and vulgar talk with the kitchen crew and the truckers who flirted with her. She was stupid and common but he didn't care. Once she came to know how special and powerful he was, she would be his.

So one night, when the kitchen staff took a cigarette break in the parking lot, he made his first, fumbling effort to talk to the girl Caitlin.

And she looked right through him like he didn't exist, then flicked her cigarette away, turned her back on him, and walked away without a word.

He watched her go and the rage came boiling up from the pit of his stomach with such ferocity that he nearly vomited.

To her, he was nothing. He could see it in her face the moment he spoke. It was clear from her blank stare that she had never noticed him, never thought of him. She probably didn't even know his name. To her, he was just the weird, quiet kid who lived in the rat-hole out back and sweated over the steaming dishes in the grimiest, noisiest part of the kitchen; his sparse adolescent beard patched with acne from the greasy steam bath of the dishwashing tub. He was less than an appliance to her. Less than an insect.

After that night, her daily laughter and flirting sent him into a dizzy, spiraling rage that became harder and harder to hold back.

So he began to plan. He figured it would take about three months to prepare and to do it right. He started by reading more books. True crime stories, more mystery novels, books about police investigation—and he studied the techniques described in them. Then he waited. Watched. Learned her habits, her routine. Since no one paid him any attention, no one noticed him watching.

When he was ready, he broke into the local mortuary and stole some embalming supplies, taking only what he absolutely needed, leaving no trace of his burglary. He found a place to dig, an empty field not far from an antebellum graveyard—now a tourist site, of all things—on the outskirts of town, near the interstate. He dug carefully, first cutting and carefully lifting away the layer of topsoil, keeping the wild growth of weeds intact so he could seamlessly conceal the grave afterward.

He followed the waxing and waning of the moon in the local paper and then, when she finished her late shift on a new-moon Thursday night, he came up behind her as she passed his shed on the way to her car, and he hit her once behind her right ear with a heavy, padded steel pipe, rendering her unconscious but also un-bloodied and unmarked. He carried her five yards to his shed, where he had split open and spread plastic trash bags around carefully. He covered her mouth with several bands of duct tape to mute the screams, and removed the head and hands with a large serrated butcher's knife he borrowed from the kitchen. He did his embalming work on the head and hands, dyed the hair, and placed the china blue ovals under the eyelids. He applied makeup—very little, since it was young and already resembled the Angel. Then he wrapped the body in the trash bags and drove it in the truck stop's battered delivery van to the gravesite and buried it, topping the grave with the top layer of soil and thick weeds with meticulous care. Then he returned to his shed, and his new Angel.

She was perfect.

The rage and the restless discontent were gone, and soon also was the decayed former Angel—the transformed Witch—which he cut into small pieces and destroyed, night by night, piece by piece, in the heavy industrial garbage disposer in the kitchen.

The new Angel's voice was clear and sweet once more. Once more he was listened to, once more he was loved, and once more he was at peace. Peace that passes understanding. She brought his ecstatic feeling to new heights.

Even though physically she was new, she was still the same Angel—the one who had soothed him since he was five years old. The only one who knew everything about him. The only one who loved him and praised him and recognized his extraordinary power.

He would have to leave West Virginia soon, but not too soon. He waited until the searches and the public prayer vigils ended (if only they knew!). And when the locals started speculating that the pretty, flirtatious Caitlin Stubbs had simply run off with a trucker, he knew it was time to leave.

But while he waited, there came another, surprisingly powerful source of immense pleasure as a result of his transformation of the girl. It happened four days after he changed her. He was heading into the convenience store across the highway from the truck stop when he saw it: his Angel's picture on the front page of the local newspaper, inside a vending machine. Trembling with excitement, he dropped a quarter into the machine's slot and took two copies of the paper and returned to his shed and read and re-read the article about the missing girl Caitlin.

His pride and power swelled up in him as never before. His story was being told—being read by hundreds, maybe thousands of people. Of course, no one knew it was his story, but it was enough just to see the barest facts about the story in print. And the picture of her…of his Angel. It was HE who put that picture there. His work was immortalized, and it filled him with a delighted grandeur almost as enthralling as the Angel herself.

Day after day, he bought the papers and followed the stories and read every word dozens of times. He saw the reporter's byline on each article and thought about calling him, but of course he knew that was idiotic. Nevertheless, he indulged in the thrilling fantasy of talking to him over and over. He hated that some of the facts were omitted from the articles—some were even outright wrong. There was, of course, no mention of the grave, since no one had found it. And there were vague, titillating allusions to a possible sexual assault, which offended him. He wanted his story told right. He could set the record straight, he could tell his whole story…he had to. But he had no one but the Angel to tell it to. And, of course, she already knew.

Over time, the news articles went from the front page to the second, and then reduced to a sprinkling of occasional small items in the back of the paper. Finally, when the articles *ceased altogether and things went back to normal in the small town, he bought a fake driver's license from a Mexican trucker who trafficked in such things. He quit his job at the truck stop, caught a ride with an old rigger from the Midwest—his heavy, soft suitcase in hand—and rode all the way to Kansas City with his new Angel and his first published stories.*

According to the license in his pocket he was now twenty. And when the Mexican asked what name he wanted on the license he didn't hesitate. He chose the name of the hero of his favorite Bible story: the brave young leader of the Israelites—the righteous ruler, the warrior-poet, the bold lover—the boy who killed the giant, then cut off the giant's head to prove his victory, and was made king.

CHAPTER TWENTY-SEVEN

I wake the morning after beating Sallie Fun and find a note under my hotel door from the front desk. There is a package waiting for me. I call to have it sent up, along with breakfast. I wash up and when I come out of the bathroom someone knocks on my door. I put on the hotel robe and a waiter pushes a breakfast cart in and hands me a box. I open it and find slacks and a shirt, still with the tags on, and a note from Nicki: *"Guessed at your size, hope it's ok. Here's Dr. Abrams' address. He'll meet us at ten-thirty a.m."*

I eat my breakfast and cut the plastic tags off the clothes with the bread knife from the room service cart. Nicki's good taste extends to men's clothes as well as women's: gray Zegna slacks and a sky blue Paul Smith shirt with a combined price tag that's half my mortgage. I put the clothes on and look in the mirror. I look a lot better.

I leave the hotel and walk three blocks to the address Nicki gave me and ride up to the fifth floor and find a door marked *Dr. B. Abrams, M.D."* I enter and find Nicki in the waiting room.

"*Much* better," she smiles when she sees me in my new clothes.

"Yeah, I clean up good."

She is back in her lawyer uniform—tailored black jacket, cream-colored silk blouse, and conservative black skirt. We say nothing about last night, but I feel the deep stirring again and I know that something has changed in me. The ground has shifted under my feet and some safe center of gravity seems to be slipping away.

"I get the sizes right?"

"Perfect," I say. "Thanks."

"Don't thank me, thank Barney's for opening at nine-thirty on a weekday."

"I'll thank them when I take them back. These clothes cost more than Miley Cyrus tickets."

"Shut up," she smiles.

The inner office door opens and a receptionist says Nicki's name and we follow her back to the office inside.

Dr. Benjamin Abrams rises to greet us when we walk in. He is early sixties, with sparse gray hair combed back, wearing a cable-knit cardigan sweater. His eyes appraise me right away without distance or judgment. He looks me in the eye when he shakes my hand and gestures for Nicki and me to sit.

"I appreciate your meeting us on short notice, Dr. Abrams," Nicki says.

"Of course," Abrams says. "You said it was urgent."

Nicki turns to me. "Jack, I've brought Dr. Abrams up to speed on everything except the conversation we had last night. If you'd like, you can go ahead and talk to him with me here or I can wait out in the waiting room while you tell him the rest."

I shrug. "I don't mind, either way…"

"I think it would be best if Jack and I were to talk alone. Would you mind?" Abrams says to Nicki.

"Absolutely not," Nicki says, and she gets up and turns to me. "I'll be right outside."

"Okay," I say, and watch her leave.

Abrams looks at me and smiles. "So, I hear you're having some troubles."

I nod and, once again, I tell my strange story, starting with Sheriff Claire Boyle's knock at my door. Abrams listens, nodding occasionally, his eyes never leaving mine for long, and then he sits very still as I sum it up with the events at St. Stephen.

"Nicki told me we would be trying to work on some things you've forgotten. From five years ago, I think she said?"

"Yes. I was drinking heavily for over a year, after the death of my fiancée."

"How did she die?" he asks.

"She shot herself. I found her."

Abrams closes his eyes for a second and lifts his head in a slight nod, absorbing this. I have never been in therapy, but now I have a better understanding of its appeal. Here is a man—an understanding, avuncular man listening to me spell out a deeply painful event, and I feel comforted and encouraged to tell him about it because I know he can never tell anyone. He knows little or nothing about me, except what I am telling him. He has no preconceptions, no axe to grind, his job is only to help me.

I talk about finding Sara, and about the fifteen months of drinking that followed, and my lack of memory from that time. He is quiet for a moment after I finish.

"There are a lot of misconceptions about memory," he says. "We have this idea that our memories are like files in a computer, waiting to be accessed whenever we need them, but it doesn't work like that. Far from it. Memories are constructed, in much the same way we construct fantasies—in our imaginations. You're an imaginative fellow, a writer, and I'm sure you're already aware of the connection between your own memories and the books you write."

"Yes I am," I say.

"Memories come to us as distorted versions of what we've experienced. Two people can observe the same event and an hour later retell it in completely different ways. They're not lying, it's just that their imaginations are reconstructing events differently, and their imaginations are affected by anything and everything—suggestion, fantasy, trauma, their own desires to shape them.

"In your case alcoholism played a part in your amnesia, without question. But that alone doesn't explain your lack of recall. You show no signs of Korsakoff's syndrome—amnesia due to alcoholism. People with Korsakoff's are completely unaware of their memory defect, and they show no sign of concern or worry about it, and that doesn't appear to be the case here, am I right?"

"You couldn't be more right."

"With the exception of some rare brain disorders, a completely amnesiac episode is very unusual. And it's almost always the result of trauma, either physical or emotional. And it's clear that your fiancée's suicide was an extreme emotional trauma."

"Yes."

"What about physical trauma? Head injury?"

"Yes…" I say, thinking of the memory of that night in the downtown L.A. emergency room. "I did have a head injury, while I was drinking. I don't remember anything about it, though."

"Nicki said it was important for us to focus on this period in April '01, when there is some question as to your whereabouts?"

"Yes, but I don't think we're going to get anywhere with that."

"Why not?"

"Because I don't remember anything from that time. I wouldn't even know where to start."

"Well why don't we start with the last thing you do remember from that time."

"The last thing I remember is waking up on someone's couch the day after Sara's—my fiancée's—funeral."

"Were you intoxicated at the time?"

"I had been—before and after the funeral."

"What's the next thing you remember?"

"Waking up in a jail infirmary, fifteen months later."

"Nothing in between? Nothing at all?"

"Vague things…drinking in a bar, mostly…"

"Tell me about the bar."

"McDougal's. A dive in Pasadena, on a side street off Colorado Boulevard."

"What did it look like?"

"Dark. Dingy. Never very crowded. I liked that about it. I used to sit in a dark corner and just drink all the time."

"By yourself?"

I pause. "Yes…I thought so…but…" I trail off, unsure.

"But what?" he prompts me.

"I used to think that I just sat there alone, drinking. Talking to myself. Holding court with…imaginary people who would listen to my story about Sara."

"You say you used to think that?"

"Well, now I think it's possible I spoke with someone. A man. I had a dream about talking with him at the bar."

"What comes to your mind when you think of him?"

"Only vague impressions…his voice, his glasses…"

"What about his glasses?"

I shake my head. "Plain, rectangular glasses…kind of cheap. Silver wire frames. And I could see myself in his glasses so I could never quite see his eyes."

"What else besides his glasses?"

I think for a moment about his voice, and something else comes to me.

"His hands," I say.

"What about his hands?"

"They were rough, calloused. I could see the calluses."

"You saw his hands while you were sitting at the bar with him?"

"Not at the bar. In a booth, near the back."

"You sat with him in the booth."

"Yes."

"What else about his hands?"

His hands...pouring me drinks. Reaching in his pockets...

"He had things...things he showed me...."

"What kind of things?"

"I don't know..."

"Take your time."

Things he took from his pocket...or wallet? Holding them out. Placing them on the table...

"I'm sorry, I can't place it..."

"That's okay. What else do you remember about him? You said you remembered his voice."

"Yes. He had a deep voice."

"Do you remember what he said? What you talked about with him?"

I think of the dream, trying to remember what he said to me.

"Try to think of everything you can about the bar, the booth," Abrams prompts me. "What did it smell like?"

"Booze. Stale cigarette smoke."

"What were you drinking?"

"Jack Daniel's on the rocks."

"And his voice...you said he had a deep voice. What words was he saying?"

I lean back and close my eyes, trying to sort memory from dream.

"Think about his hands," Dr. Abrams says.

His hands... *Opening the bottle...pouring my glass full...*

And now I am back there, in that corner booth—

"I've got a story for you, Doc," he says.

"Yeah?"

"Yeah. You study writing at school?"

"Cal State," I try not to slur the words, to uphold the proud mien of my scholarship.

"That's right, you told me. Where you met Sara, right?"

"Thasright."

"She a writer?"

"Nope. Well, she wanned to be, kinda. But she was a teacher. We liked to read to each other…"

"That's nice. You really loved her, didn't you?"

"Love… Loved… Yeah. I loved her…"

"She must have been special."

"Don' talk about her, a'right?" I look at my face in his glasses. Mirrors reflecting my own face, but flipped, reversed…

★★★

My throat is tight and my eyes burn with hot tears.

"Can we stop?" I ask Dr. Abrams.

"Sure," he says. "Take all the time you want."

How many people have cried here, in this office, with this gentle, avuncular man?

"I talked to him about her—about Sara."

"What did you talk about?"

"He was—he seemed interested in her—in hearing about her. No one else would listen for very long…"

"But he listened."

"Yes."

"What did you tell him about her?"

"Everything. Her life…how she…"

"You talked to him about her suicide?"

"Yes."

"What did you tell him about it?"

"That I didn't know why…I didn't… I thought I must have done something…or *not* done something. She didn't leave a note or… I don't know why to this day… It was totally out of the blue…"

"She hadn't been depressed or ill?"

"No. She had a bout with depression before we met. She told me about it. She was on meds for a couple of years, but she stopped taking them when we started making plans to get married. She said she was truly happy for the first time in her life. That's what I don't understand. She said she didn't need the meds anymore and she seemed fine…"

"So this fellow in the bar, he listened to you."

"Yeah, he listened."

Now I remember something else. "He told me *I* was a good listener. That's why he told me things."

"What kinds of things?"

I rub my eyes.

"Do you want to stop?" he asks me.

"No…it's just that I haven't thought about this before… I can't remember any more."

"Take your time."

I sit quietly and think.

Nothing. I shake my head at Abrams.

"It's gone," I say.

"Let's go back to St. Stephen. The person who assaulted you. Did you get any kind of look at him?"

"No. I heard a sound and turned and he hit me with something and I was knocked out before I saw him."

"You didn't struggle with him at all?"

"No."

Abrams glances down at my left hand. My knuckles are scraped raw from where I punched Sallie Fun last night. I fold my hands, reflexively hiding the wounds on my knuckles. Abrams is quiet.

"That's from something else," I say.

Abrams doesn't speak or move. The silence in the room piles up and then, once again, I tell my tale about Sallie.

"Most people wouldn't have the physical courage to defend themselves like that," Abrams says.

I shrug. "I grew up in a bad neighborhood," I say.

"Even people from bad neighborhoods," he says.

"I don't like bullies. And I don't like being afraid."

"Who bullied you? Back in the neighborhood." Abrams asks.

"Guy named Vasquez. When I was a kid I used to go to a park near my house to read…to get out of the house when my mom was drinking or drugging. Vasquez and his friends would chase me off if they found me there. One day I got tired of running."

"What did you do?"

"Vasquez came up to me with his crew and said, 'This ain't a liberry.'"

"What did you say?"

"I looked up at him and said, '*library*'. "

A smile flickers across Abrams' face. "And how did he respond to that?" he asks.

"He beat the hell out of me. Broke my nose. The next day I went to a gym in the neighborhood where a trainer taught boxing and mixed martial arts. I fought Golden Gloves for a couple of years."

"Did you ever see this Vasquez fellow again?"

"Yes. He confronted me a year or so later and I broke his jaw."

"How'd you feel about that?" Abrams asks.

I think for a second. "Like I had completed something," I say. "It felt good not to be afraid."

"You say you boxed for two years. Why did you stop?"

"I was competing for a regional championship. I was ahead on points but the guy wouldn't go down. I kept beating on him and...all of a sudden I felt sorry for him. I hesitated and he clocked me. Knocked me out for the first time. I never fought again."

"You want to talk more about that?" Abrams asks.

"Not really," I say.

Abrams is quiet again. He shifts in his chair. "This association with your books and the murders...what can you tell me about that?"

"Not much, really. As far as I know there *is* no association. That's what's so frustrating. I can't understand how I knew those things... It doesn't make any sense."

"Memory and imagination are like two sides of the same coin," Abrams says. "Have you ever heard of a phenomena called cryptomnesia?"

"No."

"Jung wrote a fair bit about it. It's a kind of unconscious plagiarism. There are many cases of authors and composers who wrote things they believed were completely original, only to find that they had read or heard them from another source, from an earlier time in their lives. Helen Keller was accused of plagiarism when she wrote *The Frost King*, which turned out to be a fairy tale that had been read to her as a child. Cryptomnesia was even referenced as a mitigating factor in the lawsuit against George Harrison over the song *My Sweet Lord*. The melody was virtually identical to a song Harrison had heard years earlier, but forgotten. And more recently there was a famous case involving a young woman living here in New York—an artist. She was hit on the head and sexually assaulted. She disappeared and was found two years later, in Dallas. She had completely forgotten what had happened to her, but in those two years she painted dozens of vivid pictures of her assault, without any idea that what she was painting was actually a memory of a real event. Her paintings were even used to identify and convict her attacker. And although she slowly remembered more about the events surrounding the assault, to this day she still has no memory of the event she painted so vividly."

CHAPTER TWENTY-EIGHT

When I leave Abrams's office I find Nicki sitting on the edge of the corduroy sofa in the waiting room, arguing with someone on her cell.

"You are threatening to ruin a man's reputation based on evidence I have yet to hear," she says, then gives me a look and rolls her eyes. "Well if it's all coming from your boss maybe you should have him call me and we'll work something out. Mr. Rhodes is here with me right now, I'm looking at him as we speak. He hasn't run off, as you were so worried about, and you have yet to give me a good reason why he should come back out to L.A. after he's already come there and cooperated and told you everything he knows," she says. Then she stands up straight, holding the phone at her ear and listening, her eyes flashing bright with anger.

"Fine," she says. "*Please* have him call me. Give him my number and we'll work it out. Mr. Rhodes is anxious to help in any way he can." She hangs up and throws the phone in her little black handbag like it was something that washed up out of a storm drain.

"Asshole," she says. "Let's get out of here." She opens the office door and we go to the elevator and we don't say anything until it arrives.

In the elevator she says, "Did you get anywhere?" I shake my head.

"Not really. Some things came to me, but nothing about April '01."

We get out in the lobby and we're on the street when she turns to me.

"The DA is gonna call me today and give me the final word on whether your name will be released as a person of interest. Detective Marsh has a forensic team at Temescal right now. I have to be honest with you, Jack, it doesn't look good. You have things you told Dr. Abrams that I know are confidential but what you tell me is confidential, too. I need to know what you told him. Even if you think it isn't important. Even if it's painful or embarrassing. You can't shock me or make me think less of you. But I can help you more if you tell me what you told him."

"Okay," I say.

"You want to go back to the office?"

"Not really," I say.

She looks up and down the street quickly. "Do you mind if we go to a bar?" she asks.

"No, it's alright."

I follow Nicki as she jaywalks across the street with the brazen expertise unique to New Yorkers. We enter a small, dark place and sit at the copper-topped bar. We both order Cokes and I tell her everything I told Abrams.

She looks at me after I've finished, her eyes darting back and forth as her mind runs over all of it. She thinks quietly for a long time.

"I need a cigarette," she says finally.

We get up. "Be right back," Nicki calls to the bartender, who nods.

We go outside, to a bodega two doors down, and Nicki pays a dollar for a single cigarette from the loosey box and I grab a pack of matches.

We step outside and I light a match but the match blows out in the November wind funneling down the Manhattan canyon. I step closer to shield her from the wind that's blowing her short, tousled hair across her face. She tosses her head to keep her hair out of her eyes and I realize this is the closest we've been, next to each other, with the exception of last night's brief moment. I am close enough to take her in my arms and for an instant I imagine that some part of her would welcome it. *Isn't it pretty to think so?* She takes my hands in hers and cups them around the match, letting the flame grow. Her hands are soft and warm. She leans closer still and lowers her head, the tip of her cigarette in the flame, and she lights it and inhales. She turns away from me and exhales a tiny tornado of white smoke that whips away in the stiff wind.

"I don't smoke," she says.

"I don't care," I say. We stand there like that, me shielding her from the wind. I can feel her warmth and our eyes meet for a moment when she inhales again, the tip of her cigarette glowing orange.

And then the match blows out and I toss it away and step back from her. She takes another drag, then she looks at me funny. "You said the bar—where you talked to this man—you said it smelled like cigarette smoke."

"Yeah."

"You can't smoke in a bar in California. I mean, not even back then, right?"

"That's right," I realize, as the smoke from Nicki's cigarette sparks something in my mind. "It wasn't smoke in the bar that I remember…it was the smell of it on someone…on *him.*"

"He smelled like cigarette smoke?"

"Yeah," I say, remembering now. "He reeked of it."

And then more comes, a rush of pictures and smells and sounds that gather themselves into a single memory.

"We went outside," I say. "We went outside because he couldn't smoke in the bar. We went—we got in his van and went somewhere—"

Nicki's cell rings. She looks at the caller ID and answers.

"Hey," she says into the phone. "Okay, let me talk to him." She looks at me and I can tell from her eyes who it is: the DA from LA.

I turn away from her, returning to the stream of images that were on the verge of becoming memories…

We went out of the bar and stood there like Nicki and I are standing now, me shielding the wind from him while he lit his cigarette with his silver Zippo.

"Let's go, I want to show you something, Doc."

I follow him and we get into his van and drive…

I am distracted by Nicki's voice as it rises with impatience and then she hangs up and looks at me.

"They found the hair clip," she says.

I look at her and feel a knot begin to tighten in my stomach. A hard gust of wind nearly knocks me off balance, making me lean toward her.

She crushes the cigarette out with the toe of her black patent leather pump.

"I have to go back to the office," she says. "Go to the hotel and wait for me. I have to arrange for a meeting at the DA's office here, tomorrow morning."

"LAPD is coming here tomorrow morning?" I ask.

Her eyes soften at me. "Not LAPD," she says gently. "FBI. Marsh and his team found the hair clip last night and just got a match on your prints from your previous arrest. They were holding out until they got the results from the prints," she says. "You should be prepared to be arrested tomorrow morning. I'm sorry, Jack."

I feel weakness in my knees and the grinding knot tightens in my gut.

"I'll arrange with Joel and your accountant for bond, but we can't expect there will be an opportunity for you to post because they'll call you a flight risk. You'll be taken back to L.A."

I turn from her, rubbing my hand across my forehead. *Shit. Shit...*

She comes close to me, her hand on my arm, and looks right into me.

"Jack. I'll go to L.A., I'll be on the plane with you and I won't leave you, okay?"

I nod.

"We'll get through this."

I nod again, but I don't believe her.

"I'm sorry, but I have to get back to the office right now to prepare for tomorrow."

"Go," I say.

"Just go back to the hotel and wait, okay? I'll call you as soon as I know anything."

I nod again and she turns to look for a cab and then she changes her mind and comes back to me. She puts her hand on my arm again and looks at me. Her face has softened but her eyes are clear and direct.

"Listen to me, Jack. I have never said this to a client before, ever—but I know you're innocent. And I *will* get you out of this."

I look at her and my throat tightens and all I can do is nod again. She holds my gaze for a moment, then she leans forward with a quick movement and touches her lips at my cheek for an instant, then turns and waves at a cab, which stops for her. She gets in the cab and it weaves into traffic and is gone.

I stand there, the November wind blowing my collar up. I turn back to the bar and go inside and sit at the counter. The bartender comes over, a stout middle-aged woman with a nametag—*Madeleine.*

"Jack Daniel's on the rocks," I say.

CHAPTER TWENTY-NINE

First, the cold glass weighting my hand to stillness. I am trembling from the Manhattan wind and the chill of fear that is seeping deeper inside me by the second.

Then, the soft sound of ice cubes against glass, muted by liquid. *Music.*

Then I raise the glass—the sharp, heady sour mash and burnt Tennessee oak mingling in my nostrils…

…along with the dank, sweet-smelling McDougal's and its dirty floor and the bowl of stale Spanish peanuts on our table that no one ever eats…

Then, the taste—

As I tilt the cold glass against my lips to steady it and the brown liquid slips over my tongue with the old familiar sting that makes me shudder with the strong shock of alcohol after all these years and the whiskey burning down my throat, into the pit of my stomach, where the burn becomes a warm glow that radiates up and into my chest and out to the tips of my fingers, taking me back to the booth and to him and his glasses and his low, deep voice and his—

—his *pictures.*

CHAPTER THIRTY

Took a jump though Mississippi, well, muddy water turned to wine
Took a jump though Mississippi, muddy water turned to wine
Then out to California through the forests and the pines,
Ahh take me with you, Jesus!

"*I want to tell you about a girl I know.*" *he says in his calm, low voice, over ZZ Top on the jukebox. From his shirt pocket he takes a picture. He doesn't show it to me at first, but I see the picture reflected in his glasses—but flipped, reversed.*

"*Wha's her name?*" *I ask, looking at her picture in his glasses.*

"*Beverly.*"

"*Pretty,*" *I say.*

"*Oh, she's an Angel,*" *I hear the smile behind his voice as he turns the photo around and shows me Beverly Grace, smiling in her senior picture. "My Angel," he says, the smile gone from his voice now.*

The smile comes and goes…

I take another sip of whiskey, no sting this time, my tongue anesthetized by the first sip—now it is only warmth that spreads down my throat and out from my middle and deeper, further up my spine and into my head and opening doors that haven't been opened in years, into rooms and hallways and then more comes, a rush of pictures and smells and sounds that gather themselves, once again, into a single memory.

We stand outside McDougal's and I shield him from the wind as he lights a cigarette.

"Let's go, I want to show you something, Doc."

I follow him and we get in his van and drive.

Los Angeles at night, speeding by my window like a movie in fast forward. We float above the low buildings with their bright signs and the mercury vapor street lights that turn the sky a dirty orange. ZZ Top plays on the van's stereo as we fly above the streets in the neon space between the city and the starless sky. Over the streets we ride, on the freeway, then down the California Incline and up Pacific Coast Highway and past Will Rogers Beach and I have a bottle of Jack in my hand as I ride shotgun.

"Where we goin'?" I ask, turning from the dizzying show outside my window.

"Almost there," he says, the coast highway unreeling in his glasses as we head north.

I suddenly realize I don't know who this guy is. I only met him tonight—or last night?

"Hey," I say. "I'm sorry…I'm not so good at names… An' I forget things… What's your name again?"

"That's alright, I never told you my name."

"Oh," I say. "What is it?"

"Dave," he says.

And then we turn into the gravel parking lot at Temescal Canyon Park.

CHAPTER THIRTY-ONE

———

"Hey."

My face against something cold and hard. Something pushes on my shoulder.

"HEY."

I look up into the face of a bald giant who is shaking me with a piece of paper in his hand.

"Pay up and get the fuck out. You can't sleep here," the Giant says.

I look around. I am in the Midtown bar where Nicki left me and it is dark outside now and the bar is crowded and I am drunk—

"Let's go, this id'na fuckin' hotel," the Bald Giant won't wait for my shame bath. I lift my face from the cold copper bar and fumble in my back pocket for my wallet, unfamiliar with my new pants—*Don't thank me,* Nicki had said, *Thank Barney's for opening at nine-thirty on a weekday.*

I pull open my back pocket, popping the button off, and I take out my wallet and hand my Amex to the glaring Bald Giant across the bar.

"Need a driver's license," he says.

I give it to him and he scrutinizes it under some kind of magnifying scope *like he's fucking Louis Pasteur,* then he goes to the cash register. I feel people crowding around me, looking at me with contempt, with impatience, with fear—*there but for the grace of God...*

I wipe the saliva from my face and look in the mirror across the bar. I am a fucking slobbering, slit-eyed drunk, and I know it's no dream this time because I am *still* drunk, despite my little nap. I look at my watch: 5:22 pm.

The Giant comes back and gives me a piece of paper and I squint to focus on my bar tab: $126 dollars.

That's fucking respectable, even for New York, I think to myself, with the stupid gallows humor and perverse, self-destructive pride that only other drunks find amusing. I sign the damned thing and slide off the stool and walk out into the cold, which slams me a little more sober.

I nearly walk into two women who are smoking, the smell bringing me back yet again to a memory…

Heading up the trail behind him…behind DAVE…up the railroad tie steps, toward the small plateau in the shallow moonlight…

And then it's gone.

I move away from the women, who glare at me as I weave down the street. I straighten my stride, the wind sobering me more, feeling the cold and welcoming it now.

Have to think, have to remember…

But I can't.

I walk until I see the *Mirabelle Hotel* sign down the street, and I head toward it like a lost mariner toward a lighthouse and I reach it and nod at the doorman, who opens the door for me.

I go inside the warm lobby and I am heading to the elevators when a voice calls to me.

"Mr. Rhodes?" she says. I turn and see a stunning young woman at the front desk looking at me.

"You've got a lot of people looking for you," she says, flashing a dazzling smile full of impossibly white teeth. She reaches under the counter and takes out a packet of messages.

I go to her.

"Somebody sure wants to get a hold of you," she says, with her brilliant, friendly smile.

"Thanks," I say, and take the pink message slips from her. I look down at them—a dozen phone calls—from Nicki, Joel, Arnie—and from others, whose names I don't recognize. Some of the phone numbers have 213 area codes. Parker Center.

Fuck.

"D'you have an ATM?" I ask her.

"Yes, right down there, just past the elevators," she points the way for me. I wish I could stay and chat with her. I wish I could get to know her and find out what time she gets off work and buy her dinner and meet her daddy but I can't. I will be arrested tomorrow. If I stay.

I go to the ATM and withdraw all the cash I can: $900 bucks in three whacks of $300. The machine won't let me withdraw any more. I look into the tiny camera lens over the ATM machine's screen and I know that my face—from this camera—will be scrutinized in a matter of hours by FBI and LAPD and God knows who else.

I turn around and head back out the front doors, where I fumble with my wallet and find my parking slip and a twenty dollar bill and give them to the doorman. He whistles and a kid runs up and he gives him the parking slip and I wait, letting the fresh, cold air sober me further, and soon my truck appears at the curb and the kid gets out and holds my door open and I get in and he slams the door after me and I drive away, flattening my hand against the buttons on the armrest, opening the windows to keep me awake and alert. I drive carefully through the Manhattan streets, looking for a sign for the bridge, the bridge, which bridge? *Where's the confounded bridge?* Then I find it, and pull carefully into the flow of traffic and look for a sign that will take me west, out of the city. I don't know how long it will take me to get to West Virginia, but I know where I have to go.

THINGS PAST

When he arrived in Kansas City with the Angel from West Virginia, the fat old trucker who gave him a ride offered him a job. The old guy owned a small company—three rigs, one of which he drove himself on short hauls to Chicago and back to KC.

At first the job entailed the young man doing the heavy lifting that they picked up and delivered at the loading docks—machine parts, mostly. The old trucker suffered from emphysema, which was getting worse as he chain-smoked his Camels day and night. But soon the old man came to trust him enough to let him drive for long stretches at night, while the old guy stretched out, wheezing, in the back of the cab.

The commercial trucking license was easy to procure. The Mexicans in Chicago could get pretty much any document you wanted. But his endless hours of communion with the Angel in almost total darkness had left him extremely near-sighted, so he had to get glasses in order to drive. He chose a rectangular wire-framed pair with lenses so thick that his small eyes could barely be seen behind them.

The old trucker, a devout Baptist, was impressed with his knowledge of the Bible. So when the wheezy old man lit up a Camel after a steak-and-egg breakfast, then turned as red as their Naugahyde booth and dropped dead of a heart attack, his widow sold the rig to the quiet young man with the glasses who knew his Bible so well, and was clearly such a good Christian boy.

So, in his new rig, his phony commercial truck driver's license in his wallet, he took over the short hauls from Chicago, through Davenport, Peoria, Des Moines, St. Stephen, and back to Kansas City, carrying machine parts to appliance repair shops, car dealerships, and factories.

He lived in the rig, sleeping in the cramped rear of the cab where the old man had installed a mattress and a small TV. He bought window blinds for the truck's cab, and at night he was with his Angel, when he wasn't driving. He showered and shaved and ate at the truck stops along the way, and for a year or so he was content.

But the restlessness eventually returned. His embalming work on the West Virginia Angel had held up well, although he occasionally had to work on her with cosmetics. But this time it was his desire to have his story told again that drove him to the irritable, anxious state. He looked at the yellowing West Virginia newspaper articles about the girl Caitlin over and over, and he felt the urgent need to have due attention paid once more.

He had almost told the old trucker about his Angel once, but stopped himself, of course. So he talked about the Bible, in the rare moments when they talked at all. He speculated with the old man about Jesus—what if Jesus hadn't had Paul to travel the known world and spread His story? Would we ever have known His story, His gospel? But the old trucker was thick and slow, and just shook his head and wheezed, "Lord only knows, son, Lord only knows..."

CHAPTER THIRTY-TWO

It is 12:51 a.m. when I cross the border into West Virginia. I'm no longer drunk but I am still driving with the windows open and the heater going full blast to keep the alcohol smell out of the truck, just in case I get pulled over.

I have driven for seven hours and I am on the cusp of a hangover and almost out of gas but I don't want to stop. I am heading toward a place I made up in my last book, an unincorporated area in Morgan County, in the eastern panhandle of West Virginia, where I killed young Katie Stubens in *Killer Unbound*.

Once again, I don't know where I am going and yet I do. I have never been here—*at least I think I haven't*—but the details of *Killer Unbound* are still clear to me. I finished writing it less than a year ago.

I drive on, through the rolling foothills of the Appalachian mountains, passing a sign which reads "MARTINSBURG GHOST TOURS – *Tour Haunted Graveyards Fridays.*"

This is it, I know, and suddenly I can hear the voice of *Dave* once again, from the booth in the back of McDougal's…

"Tonight we're gonna talk about a little piece named Caitlin," he says.

Caitlin. Whom I had named Katie…

"You'll find her out in Morgan County, West Virginia…just off the interstate, past the billboard for the haunted graveyard there's a county road…"

…and here it is. I signal and carefully pull off the interstate and onto the county road.

"There are signs leading to the graveyard, you just follow the signs," he says, cupping his hands around his drink and making that low sound that passes for a laugh.

But what is this? A roadblock. Police lights.

Shit.

As I come nearer I see a *lot* of flashing lights. Cops everywhere. I see the West Virginia State Police logo on the side of one of the cars, and then a couple of black SUV's that I know are FBI vehicles. I slow down behind a row of cars waiting to be allowed through the roadblock ahead.

And then I see it—up ahead, along the side of the county road—the banks of brilliant lights that illuminate a crime scene. A backhoe is pulling off of a tractor-trailer, which is backed up to a large group of men and women—most of them in uniform—as they look down at what I know is the grave of a young woman I had named Kate Stubens.

I stop.

The cars ahead of me lurch forward, as each driver is allowed through the roadblock.

I have to get out of here.

But I can't. Traffic coming the other way is crawling past me as drivers gawk at the display of law enforcement, the multiple flashing lights dazzling them into a collective trance.

The driver behind me honks his horn. I ease forward, toward the state trooper standing with his boots on the double yellow line, checking everyone as they pass.

I am trapped.

A man in a dark blue Gore-Tex jacket is walking along the shoulder of the road, down my row of cars toward me, holding a flashlight. He walks quickly, shining his heavy black Magna-light over each car, into the windows. There is something about him that's familiar. Then he approaches my truck and I see his face—smooth and hairless, with a preternatural tan and those small gray eyes.

Detective Marsh, LAPD.

As I look at his face he looks at mine and instantly I know he recognizes me. He raises his light and blinds me with it and yells something to a nearby state trooper, who hurries up next to Marsh from the gulley, pulling at his sidearm—

I spin the steering wheel hard to the right and stomp the accelerator to the floor, ripping a u-turn on the shoulder of the county road, slamming into the guard rail and spraying Marsh and the trooper with gravel and grit as I tear back the way I came, along the shoulder, against the traffic that was backed up behind me. I don't even look in my rearview mirror as I reach the end of the line of cars behind me and then I skid back onto the road, cutting off traffic headed the other direction to a chorus of car horns.

Don't go back the way you came, they'll set up roadblocks and radio ahead…they know where you were coming from.

I get back to the interstate and continue west.

CHAPTER THIRTY-THREE

I get off the interstate two exits west, then pull over at a truck stop because I am about to run out of gas. I sit for a moment, my brief drunk now OFFICIALLY a hangover, and try to think through the fog.

Have to think.

I turn on my phone and see that I have sixteen messages. I flip through the caller ID list and recognize them as the same numbers from the pink message slips I was given by the beautiful girl at the front desk of the Mirabelle.

I slip the phone in my back pocket and open the glove box and grab Sallie Fun's Ruger. I check the magazine. Three rounds, plus one in the chamber. I remove the chambered round and slide it into the magazine and slap the clip back into the gun and click the safety on. I tuck the Ruger into the back of my waistband and get out of the truck. I go to the back of the truck and open the tailgate and climb inside and fumble with my keys to open the toolbox near the cab. I take out a tire iron and a crescent wrench and wire cutters and a hand sledge and I go wandering through the thicket of big rigs that are idling in the parking lot of the truck stop.

This guy Marsh is no dummy, Nicki had said. *He's got a real bug up his ass about you. He's reading all your books...*

Marsh had done the same thing I had done, only he got there first. *If I knew those things about Temescal, what about the other things, from the following books?*

I wonder if the police have been to St. Stephen, but I don't wonder long because I have to dodge behind a rig when I see a West Virginia State Police cruiser idling ahead, at the end of the long row of resting trucks.

I wait there for five minutes or so, pressed against the side of a rig, in the shadows, until the West Virginia State Police cruiser pulls away. I wind back the way I came, like a rat lost in a maze. I come out on the other side of the cluster of trucks and watch the State Police cruiser pull out of the truck stop and drive off toward the ramp leading to the interstate. I turn back to the parking lot and see a kid get out of a new Mustang. The kid heads toward the truck stop restaurant with his hand on his girlfriend's backside.

The kid enters the restaurant with his girlfriend and the moment the restaurant doors close I walk up to his Mustang and look around and then jam the bladed end of the tire iron against the lock in the Mustang's door and whack the other end of the tire iron with the hand sledge, instantly setting off the alarm. I whack it a second time, then a third time, as hard as I can, and the blade of the tire iron punches the lock in and I open the door. I lean inside and pop the hood release lever under the dash. I lean back out and go to the front of the car and lift the hood. I can't stop the alarm but I can silence the horn. I find the horn mounted against the firewall and yank the wires from it and the noise stops. But the parking lights on the front and rear of the car are still flashing. I circle the car, bashing each parking light out with the hand sledge.

Back inside the car and under the dash, wedging the blade of the tire iron up under the plastic sleeve around the steering column and popping it off and sorting through wires, remembering a young uniform cop telling me, after three beers, *"Your older vehicles were easier, there was a black ignition wire and a red hotwire and you just had to connect them but now they've changed the wire colors; they keep changing them and moving them into solid state circuitry but the good thieves, the pro's, they keep up..."*

I find a black wire and a red one and connect them and nothing happens and then I try a green wire against the black one and nothing and then I find a yellow one that leads to a circuit board and I brush the black wire across the soldered circuits and sparks shoot into my eyes. I strip the plastic sheath off the end of the black wire with my fingernails and press it against the circuit board and close my eyes this time as the sparks burn my fingers and I push on the accelerator with my hand and the Mustang's engine fires to life. I wrap the unsheathed black wire around the circuit board in a tight knot then I get in and drive off.

I look around and no one seems to have noticed or cared.

"Who cares about a car alarm?" The young cop had laughed as he drank the fourth beer I bought him.

CHAPTER THIRTY-FOUR

I head east in my stolen Mustang. I open the glove compartment and look through the owner's manual and the paperwork from the dealer as I drive. No LoJack manuals or logos on the windows. Good. The car is nice. It smells brand new and the odometer shows 988 miles. The kid must have impressed his girl-friend with his new car. Maybe it got him laid—

Flashing police lights in my mirror. I pull over and let them pass. State troopers, in a hurry to catch up with a Ford F-150 pickup truck that is behind them, parked between two big rigs.

I notice a semi with Michigan plates that has pulled aside, in the westbound lane across from me, to let the troopers pass. The trailer of the truck has an open top and I can see a load of oranges under a gray tarp. I grab my phone and dial Nicki's cell. She answers on the first ring.

"Jack! Where the hell are you?"

"I'm okay but I can't talk," I say. "I'm not going to stay on the phone, but leave the line open. Don't hang up. I'll call you in a couple of hours from another phone."

I open the driver's side window and lob the phone across the highway and into the back of the Michigan-bound semi as I hear Nicki's voice, pleading, "Jack! Just tell me where—"

The phone lands perfectly on top of the tarp. I drive away, watching the semi in my rearview mirror as it lurches back into traffic, headed the opposite direction from me.

THINGS PAST

Sharon Belton worked as a cashier at a truck stop outside of St. Stephen, Missouri. He had seen her many times, when he stopped to buy supplies. She, too, had the oval face of the Angel, and she, too, had completely ignored him, even when she rang up his purchases, week after week. She never spoke to him, never made eye contact, and would count out his change without letting her hand touch his, as though he were a leper.

He didn't try to talk to her. He knew she wouldn't respond and it wasn't what he sought, anyway. It wasn't her indifference or even her resemblance to the Angel that drove him to transform her. What finally drove him to act was the thought of her picture on the cover of the paper, just like his West Virginia Angel. He bought copies of the St. Stephen News and purchased a small digital camera and snapped Sharon Belton's picture with a zoom lens as she left work one afternoon, walking right past his rig. He printed her picture at a Kinko's in Kansas City and carefully pasted it onto the cover of the St. Stephen News. For a time it excited him, but it was a fleeting, counterfeit thrill. It wasn't real.

So once again, he began to plan.

He began by building a tiny room inside the truck's trailer—deep inside, right up against the cab. He built a false front for the little room, covering the seams of the fake wall by riveting strips of aluminum flashing over them. He scraped the flashing with a wire brush and pounded a few dents in it to match the worn aluminum flashing in the rest of the trailer, so it couldn't be recognized by even the most careful inspection. He did the same with the two four-by-eight sections of plywood that made up the wall. He installed hinges on one of the sections of plywood, on the side that faced the room.

Inside the tiny, secret room he installed a four-by-six foot stainless steel drain pan he stole from a delivery load to an industrial refrigeration factory. The pan was big enough to hold a body, and it sloped gently toward a drain at the center, designed to collect the condensation from the coiled copper Freon tubes in the enormous air conditioners the refrigeration factory built. Under the drain, he installed a flexible stainless steel tube to collect the body fluids that would sluice into a plastic bucket underneath.

He bought a hunting knife at a truck stop in Davenport—rubber-handled, with a serrated edge. He dug a grave in the woods near an abandoned church in St. Stephen. This time he didn't remove a layer of topsoil to conceal the grave. With head and hands missing, a positive identification of the body would take a while. And he wanted the body to be found this time.

Then he waited for the next new moon.

And so it came to pass that on one warm, moonless July night, he struck Sharon Belton in the back of the head with a tire iron wrapped in a towel, and took her to the tiny room in the truck's trailer and began his work. He dumped the fluids into a storm drain at the edge of the truck stop's parking lot, embalmed the head and hands—stitching the hands together carefully, as he had learned from the embalming book—and placed the china blue porcelain ovals under the eyelids.

He put the West Virginia Angel Caitlin in a heavy steel footlocker with two padlocks, and kept it in the small room in the trailer. Then he buried the rest of Sharon Belton in the woods by the old abandoned church cemetery. His new Angel from St. Stephen satisfied him quite well as he waited for the picture—the picture he knew would come.

And come it did. And this time it was even better.

The St. Stephen News printed several front-page articles, featuring his new Angel's yearbook picture, and eventually, after the grave was discovered, a haunting, spectacular photo of the gravesite with the church in the background. He pinned the pictures up in the tiny room in the trailer, along with the pictures from the newspaper in West Virginia, and he felt his power even more intensely. He would look at the pictures over and over, at times scarcely even looking at his new Angel from St. Stephen. The newspaper pictures and articles were becoming his greater source of pleasure now.

But it didn't last as long as he had hoped. Soon he began to fantasize about the walls of the tiny room becoming covered with his Angels, his story, his gospel. Angels, blossoming like the lilies of the field. Consider how they grow; they toil not, neither do they spin. And yet I say unto you that even Solomon in all his glory was not arrayed like one of these.

He waited until the stream of stories about Sharon Belton trickled to a halt, then he left Kansas City. He found a new route advertised in the back of a trucking magazine— delivering precision grinding plates from a small plant in San Bernardino that reconditioned disc brakes. The hauls were short: from San Bernardino to Oxnard, Burbank, and Pasadena.

But the short hauls through the heavy Southern California traffic were hard on him. He no longer had long, dark stretches of highway to be alone with his thoughts. He had to deal with more people, more traffic, and then the migraines started.

He was one of many now, lost in the mass of drivers, workers, drug dealers and hookers at the enormous truck stops. He began to feel powerless and anonymous. Common. He was losing his special feeling in the nights he spent with his pictures and his new Angel from St. Stephen. He needed more. He needed to be known. He needed his story to be told, and told right. The whole story.

He worked the problem over and over in his throbbing head. He got pain pills and Valium from truckers in San Bernardino. They sold meth for the long-haul drivers and Valium and various painkillers to come down from the amphetamines. The Valium helped, but not for long. It was not enough. He grew more restless, and he began to drink. He hated losing control, and the drink and the Valium gave him brief blackouts.

After six months he gave up his route and bought a used van from a kid in Oxnard. He installed a ramp so he could drive the van right up into the trailer of his rig and hide it there. He had saved plenty of money—he was often paid in cash—and since he had no Social Security number, no DMV or police records, no bank account or address, he paid no taxes. So he stopped working entirely and spent his time driving the streets of Los Angeles, Pasadena, and Burbank in his van. But it only increased his sense of being small and ordinary, when all about him were garish monuments to power and celebrity.

He had to find a way to have his story told. He needed his gospel spread, but he wasn't going to die for it. But how to tell his story without giving himself away? He needed his Paul, but he would have no Golgotha, no Calvary, no cross. He was no martyr. He was better—bigger—smarter than that. He was a man and not divine. But that was the point. What man could perform the miracles of transubstantiation as he had? He had the power to transform these course, vulgar young women into Angels. And the world would soon know it. He would find a way.

He spent sunny, empty afternoons perusing bookstores. He controlled his headaches with more Valium and painkillers and eased his restlessness by reading. He found he now *had much more interest in the true-crime stories than the fiction he read before. Especially if they were authentic and not shallow and sensationalistic like most of them were.*

And it was then that he came across a book—a pocket-sized true-crime collection about famous serial killers. It was well researched and well written. He found it fascinating and he read it over and over, and noted the author's name.

CHAPTER THIRTY-FIVE

Two hours later and by now the kid has no doubt gotten the cops all over his missing Mustang and I have to assume they've found my truck. I see a car dealership off the interstate as I enter the suburbs of Baltimore. I pull over and drive around to the rear of the lot where it isn't as brightly lit. I pull up close behind a row of *Certified Pre-Owned* cars and get out of the Mustang with my crescent wrench. I remove the rear license plate frames from two of the closest cars. The frames don't have tags, just the name of the dealership on a flimsy rectangle of plastic. I toss them in the Mustang, then yank a sign that reads *Low Mileage!* from under the wiper blade of a third car and toss it in the Mustang as well. Then I drive off, looking for an all-night gas station, preferably in a very bad part of town.

I find one as I approach downtown Baltimore just before dawn. There is a lone customer, an elderly man in a burnt-orange double-knit suit, pumping gas into his late-model Chrysler. The gas tank is on the passenger side of the Chrysler.

Perfect.

I pull in and circle the pump, looking for security cameras. I see one camera over the cashier's window and that's it. I pull around to an alley on the other side of the gas station where I can't be seen by the camera. I get out of the Mustang with my dealer plates and tools and *Low Mileage* sign and leave the doors unlocked and the windows down. I would write *STEAL ME* across the Mustang's windshield but I don't have anything to write with.

I watch the old man fill his Chrysler's tank, and the instant as I see him remove the nozzle from the car I walk toward him quickly with my head down. I walk right up to the driver's side of the Chrysler and open the door and see the keys in the ignition and I get in and start the car and drive off while the old man is still untangling the hose to replace the nozzle back in the gas pump.

A mile later I pull onto a dark side street and replace the Chrysler's tags with the dealer frames and I stick the *Low Mileage* sign under the wiper blade and drive off. I figure I am safe for at least three or four hours in my certified pre-owned Chrysler. It has a full tank and factory tinted windows and it'll get me where I'm headed in comfort, safety, and style.

And it has *Low Mileage.*

CHAPTER THIRTY-SIX

I hit New Jersey just in time for rush hour and the morning news. The old man had really tricked his Chrysler out. I listen to CNN on the satellite radio and learn that I am now the most famous writer in America. I am "horror-writer Jack Rhodes, author of the notorious *Killer* series." *Notorious?* I hear about Beverly Grace and Sharon Belton and I learn that I was last spotted near the shallow grave of Caitlin Stubbs. And if I hear the phrase "life imitating art" one more time I may actually *start* killing people, beginning with the guy on Fox who said I was "on an apparent rampage."

I may not be on a rampage but I'm definitely on a crime spree. Two counts grand theft auto, evading arrest, interstate flight... I am roaming the quiet countryside, preying on the young and the elderly.

Guilty with an excuse, Your Honor. That might just work, as long as I don't have to add kidnapping to the list. I don't want to but if I have to…

Unless I'm too late, I think as I take the bypass to Trenton.

I have racked my brain for more memories of *Dave* as I have driven along the back roads and state highways, and I have come up with nothing. As much as the booze helped me remember, the resulting hangover has blotted everything out again. But I know where I am going and what I have to do next and that is enough for now.

And here we are, the 53rd Street exit off 295. This is it. There is a little red brick house here. With a white trellis. I drive around, looking for the house that Laurie Vaughn lives in—Laurie Vaughn, from the fourth book, *Killer Unmasked.*

Marsh can't follow me here because he hasn't read *Killer Unmasked*. No one has. It isn't finished. It exists only on my hard drive, back at the cabin.

And then I see it: red brick, white trellis, and the name *VONN* on the mailbox.

Vonn to Vaughn.

And as I look at the house I remember a flicker of an image—*the house, in a picture Dave showed me: "This is where a little piece named Laurie Vonn lives with her mom…"*

And then the memory flickers out, like film breaking in a projector.

"Lives," he had said, not *"lived."*

I park the car and get out and head toward the house.

Please be alive, and please listen to me. Please, God.

I knock on the battered screen door. I have thought for hours about what to say to her, and what *not* to say. *Sorry to bother you, but I'm pretty damned sure there's a serial killer who's planning to murder you so you should get in my stolen car and get the hell out of here…*

She'll never come with me, of course. I have to warn her without scaring her too much…

I knock again.

Please be at home, please be alive. Please…

I lean around the stoop to look in the front window but the curtains are closed. I hear a TV. I knock again, harder.

"Who is it?" A young woman's voice.

"Laurie? Is that you, Laurie?" I yell through the door.

The door opens a crack and here she is, looking at me suspiciously over the chain. She doesn't look like the picture in my head, exactly, but she looks a hell of a lot closer than the other girls had by the time I got to them.

"Who are you?" she asks.

"I'm Sam Blevins, I'm your neighbor, from down the street," I say. I can hear her TV in the background but it doesn't sound like a news channel.

Her eyes move up and down me quickly.

"Did the police ever show up here last night?" I ask her.

"What?"

"The police, I called them last night. Didn't they get here?"

"I don't know what you're talking about," she says, fear in her eyes now.

"Shoot. I was afraid of that," I say. "There's been a bunch of break-ins in the neighborhood and last night when I was coming home off the late shift I saw this guy looking in your windows. I called the police but I guess they never showed up here, huh?"

"Oh my God," she says.

"You should call 'em," I say. "He was definitely checking your place out."

She looks at her watch. "I can't right now, I'm late for work. But when I get home I will. What did you say your name was?"

"Sam. I live down at the end of the block, next to the Stevens?"

She nods vaguely, glancing down the street. She is dressed in an orange waitress outfit, her nametag *"Laurie"* pinned to her blouse.

"Okay, well, thanks," she says.

"Okay, take care," I turn and head back to the car.

I get back in the Chrysler. *Now what?* I wasn't prepared for this. I should have told her more, but what the hell could I have said? I wait in the car for a couple of minutes, until she comes out of her house and walks down the sidewalk and gets in her dirty red Honda Civic and drives off. I follow her onto the interstate, heading back the way I came.

I follow Laurie Vonn's Honda through the late-morning traffic until her turn signal blinks and she takes the exit. She makes a right onto a bypass road and I follow her until she turns left, into the broad driveway of a gigantic truck stop.

Another truck stop, I think as I watch her park behind the sprawling building that houses the diner and the arcade and the shops within.

I pull around, among the trucks now, and stop where I can see her get out of her car and enter the service entrance at the back. I nose the Chrysler out from between the trucks and pull around to the side of the diner and I wait. After a minute or two I see her inside, through the big windows that wall the spacious diner. I watch as she tucks her order slips into the pocket of her uniform and begins her shift, taking orders from the truck drivers in the diner.

How long can I sit here? I see a pay phone next to the garage bay doors. I have to assume Nicki's phones are already tapped, so I decide against calling her.

I watch the truckers come and go in the diner.

I can't just sit here in my stolen car and watch her all day. I let the motor run, leaving the heater on against the cold. I lean my head back against the headrest and realize how exhausted I am. In half a minute my eyelids are closed. I catch myself and sit up straight. Can't fall asleep. Not in this car, not now. I watch a trucker climb from his cab next to me and light a cigarette with a silver Zippo lighter. He has a chain on his hip—a long, heavy chain swinging from his belt loop to his wallet in his back pocket. I watch him tuck the Zippo into his jacket and head inside the diner.

I stare at the chain on the guy's hip, trying to think about why this means anything to me... But the warmth of the heater and my exhaustion overcome me and I decide it's okay if I just close my eyes for a moment and I turn off the engine but leave the key in the accessory position so I can listen to the news. That should keep me awake.

CNN says Michigan State Police have set up a roadblock for me. *Great. They followed the cell phone. Marsh and the FBI are closing in on a truckload of oranges.*

Then I fall asleep.

THINGS PAST

It was at a bookstore in Pasadena where he met Beverly Grace. She had the Angel's face, and when he asked her for more information about the author of the serial killer collection he found so fascinating, she looked right through him and shook her head and walked away without so much as a word or even a glance back at him.

So, yet again, he began to plan. He was always more at ease when he had a purpose, a direction, a goal. To the work, to the work…

He had become much more proficient with his skills and it only took a few weeks of observing the routine of Beverly Grace before he transformed her, and buried what was left at Temescal Canyon. This part of his work no longer held much of a rush. Even communing with her, with his new Angel—Angel de Los Angeles—was a secondary pleasure. It was the stories he waited for.

And this time he was overwhelmed.

He was not prepared for the full force of the Los Angeles media—TV, newspapers, radio, and now the internet, which he accessed on a notebook computer in the back of the rig's cab. The endless stream of news about the missing Beverly Grace drove his pleasure to extreme heights—but too much so. This time there was so much attention—too much attention—that he began to worry. And he was infuriated that his story was being told in the most hackneyed and haphazard way. There were all kinds of inaccuracies and lurid speculation. And, of course, there was nothing near the full understanding or real recognition of his special power. There was only stupid, titillating tabloid noise.

So he left Los Angeles just as the stories reached their frenzied peak, on the morning of May 16, 2001.

He drove his van up the ramp into the back of his trailer and kicked his rig's engine to a roar and clutched and shifted through the traffic until he was on the 10 freeway and he headed east with a nice tailwind and a full tank of diesel and his three Angels and all of his stories.

East, east, whence came the wise men.

East, whence rose the star.

CHAPTER THIRTY-SEVEN

"Know what I like about you, Doc?" he asks me.

I am sitting on a little mound of dirt in the small plateau above Temescal Canyon Park with Dave pacing slowly in front of me while I drink my bottle of Jack.

"You listen." He paces slowly around the mound, looking down at it, walking around behind me, then back around in front of me, his wallet chain swinging at my eye level. "People are so wrapped up in themselves they don't know how to listen. They don't pay attention. Most of the time I let it slide, but when some little cunt looks right through you like you don't fucking EXIST... Well, you can't let that stand. Beverly Grace learned that I EXIST. You can bet your ass on that." He gives the low sound of a laugh that isn't really a laugh as he walks around and around the small mound of dirt I am sitting on.

★★★

I wake suddenly to the rumble of a massive diesel engine as the truck next to me starts up and pulls out toward the driveway. I look at the clock on the dashboard: 3:35 in the afternoon and the sky has darkened and it looks like rain.

I look at the diner and I don't see Laurie Vonn. Shit. I turn the key to start the car and the engine cranks lazily. Damn it. The battery is low from sitting with the radio on for hours while I slept. I turn the key back to the off position and pray and then turn it again and finally the motor kicks to life. I rev it a few times, then pull out, toward the rear of the diner where Laurie Vonn parked her car. It's still there. I circle around, looking in the windows of the diner. I don't see her. The lunch crowd has thinned, leaving only the stragglers, the coffee-drinkers, and a couple of waitresses chatting with the short-order cook over the counter. The news on the radio has moved on to the weather report—a big storm headed toward the northeast. I let the motor run for a while to charge the battery, then I turn it off and get out and head toward the diner, worried that I haven't seen Laurie Vonn.

I enter the truck stop shop, a surprisingly large store with racks of clothing, drinks in refrigerated shelves, groceries, drugs, and souvenirs. I keep my head down and try on a stone-washed denim jacket with the words *"Keep On Truckin'"* across the back. Then I grab a black and white New Jersey Devils cap that has a blood red lightning bold across it and peruse a tall carousel with sunglasses. I try on a few, choosing a tobacco-brown-tinted pair that cover my bandaged brow.

I take them all to the counter, where a doughy, grandmotherly woman smiles at me from behind the register.

"Find everything okay?" she asks.

"Fine," I say, smiling but keeping my head low. I glance up at the TV high up in the corner of the store and see my face on CNN—my old California driver's license photo, followed by my mug shot from my arrest for Richard Bell's murder. I run my hand over my face, to cover it. The nice, grandmotherly woman behind the register apparently hasn't mastered the scanner or doesn't trust it. She methodically types in every number from the bar codes on the hat, the jacket, and the sunglasses, and finally comes up with a total.

"Ninety-one seventeen," she says to me.

I hand her five twenties and as she counts out my change I pull the tags off the merchandise, trying not to seem in too much of a hurry. I pull on the cap, slip on the sunglasses, and take the change she hands me.

"Thank you," I say.

"You have a great day," she beams at me. She may be the happiest person I have ever met.

I put the jacket on and walk into the diner. I catch a glimpse of my reflection in the tall windows. I look like a guy who is trying to hide who he really is.

I look around at the restaurant patrons. *Everyone here looks like that.* The only difference is I am standing at the entrance to the diner conspicuously. I see the sign for the restrooms and head toward it as an excuse to walk all the way through the place and look around for Laurie Vonn. I don't see her. I get to the restroom and use it and wash up and adjust my bandages so they're not visible under my new sunglasses. *Has the ER in Burlington contacted the police about me?* I don't remember hearing anything about it on the radio. No description of me having any injuries. I was just a random bum that everyone in the ER forgot about. Funny where you take comfort sometimes.

I stop and think before I head back out. I decide I'll sit in the diner, order something to go, then return to the car. Beyond that, I don't know what the hell I'm going to do.

I walk back into the restaurant. Laurie Vonn had worked the section by the front window, so I take a booth on the opposite side of the dining area. It wouldn't do to have her come up to take my order and recognize me. I take one of the menus from the metal rack that holds the condiments at my table and open it and look over the top of it, watching for Laurie. After a couple of minutes a young woman hurries up to me with her order pad in hand. She is slightly heavy but cute and she wears the same orange uniform as Laurie. Her nametag says *Orlanda.*

"What can I get you?" she asks. She barely glances at me.

"Coffee and a grilled cheese to go."

She writes it down. "You want fries or cole slaw?"

"Fries, please."

She writes it down and turns my upside-down coffee cup over so it can be filled. "Be right back with your coffee," she says, and hurries off.

I put the menu down—now that I've ordered it might seem odd if I keep reading it. Or am I being paranoid?

Can you be called paranoid if people really *are* after you?

A New Jersey State Police car pulls up and parks right outside the window. Two beefy state troopers get out of the car and head toward the restaurant.

Call me paranoid, I think as I raise my menu to hide my face again.

Orlanda returns with the coffee pot as the troopers walk in the front door and head right for my booth, looking right at me.

Shit. I look away, then look back at them. There is no question they are headed right for my booth—for *me.*

I raise the menu higher. I can see only their Smokey the Bear hats approaching over the top of the laminated plastic.

No, no, not here, not now, not like this...

Orlanda starts pouring my coffee as they come up behind her. They stop and look down at me.

Fuck.

They stand there, behind Orlanda, waiting for her to finish with my coffee. In the time it takes her to fill the cup, dozens of frantic thoughts ricochet around in my head—

They'll wait for her to finish and then they'll start asking me questions: "Would you mind stepping out of the booth, please?"

Run.

No. Just get up and walk the other way as soon as she fills the cup. There's another exit, by the restrooms...

NO. Stay put, you jackass. Don't make eye contact. If they question you be casual but remember that cops expect a certain amount of fear when they confront civilians... What the hell's that on his hip? A .357? No way that's State Police issue. I'm Sam Blevins, I live at 6130 N. 53rd Terrace. "Hang on, I left my wallet in the car, I'll go get it..."

Shit shit shit—

The big trooper suddenly winks at me over Orlanda's shoulder, then he grins broadly at me.

What the FUCK?

Then, as she finishes pouring, the big Trooper wraps his arms around Orlanda and gives her a big hug, startling her.

"Ah!" she yells.

"Hey, Orlanda!" The bear-hugging Trooper says.

"Jeez— God! Don't do that!" she says, laughing. She knows them. "You nearly made me spill coffee all over this nice man."

"Aw, we wouldn't do that," says Smokey the Bear Hug, and he looks down at me and grins again. I grin back, adjusting the brim of my hat so that my hand moves in front of my face. I laugh a little, pretending to enjoy this light moment, but all I can think is *you fucking asshole, you should be out looking for people like me, not harassing waitresses.*

The troopers flirt with Orlanda all the way up to the counter, where they each take a stool and order coffee and turn their backs on America's most infamous rampaging serial author.

THINGS PAST

After leaving Los Angeles, he meandered across the country in his rig for two months, taking a rambling route that eventually led him to Trenton, New Jersey, where he ordered breakfast at a truck stop from a waitress whose nametag read Laurie. *She had a perfect oval face, with clear, clean skin that was flawed only by a splash of tiny freckles across her nose and high cheekbones. She even wore her hair the same as the Angel—long ochre locks that piled around her shoulders in silky coils. Physically, she was nearly identical to his original porcelain Angel.*

She took his breakfast order without looking up from her pad. She forgot his coffee. And after she brought his food she didn't come by his table again, except to slap his check down on the table as she hurried by without a word or a glance. It was late morning and he was the only diner in her section. She wasn't busy. She was in a hurry to go laugh and flirt with the short order cook.

He lingered over breakfast—over the empty plate she never came to clear away. He watched her.

It was too soon, though. The news about Beverly Grace was still on the cable channels. Laurie *would have to wait.*

He slept in the cab that night, his rig parked near the restaurant, and snapped a picture of Laurie as she arrived at work the next morning. He waited in his cab all day, reading his true-crime paperback and watching the news and checking online for stories about Beverly Grace. Then, just before Laurie's shift ended, he dropped the ramp from the rear of his trailer, backed his van out, and followed her home. He couldn't transform her yet—not for a long time. But he could prepare. He hadn't made any mistakes yet, and he wasn't about to start.

But when he pulled up to Laurie's house to snap a photo, he made his first.

He had followed her at a prudent distance, at least five cars behind her on the highway, at least a block away on surface streets, until he saw her red Honda pull into a driveway beside a little red brick house. He slowed, from two blocks behind her, giving her ample time to go in the house. He couldn't see her car, since the white trellis alongside the driveway obstructed his view, so he pulled over and waited for a full minute before driving up to the house and lowering his window to snap a photograph of the little red brick house, parking just close enough to record the address in the picture, as well as the name VONN on the mailbox—a stroke of luck. He wouldn't have to search online for her last name as he normally did when laying his careful plans.

But just as he took the picture, she got out of her car and looked right at him, his camera raised, pointed directly at her. He had assumed she had gone into the house, but she hadn't. She had stayed in her car, gathering shopping bags and her purse from the back seat.

She stood there, looking right at him. Time froze for a breathless eternity. Then, keeping the camera held up to hide his face, he reached down and pressed the button to raise his window. She locked her car, clicking her key fob twice to make sure the alarm was activated, then glanced quickly back at him and walked into the house with her things. He pulled away the instant the front door closed behind her—driving fast enough so that she couldn't read his license plate from her front window. But not too fast.

He left New Jersey that night.

CHAPTER THIRTY-EIGHT

Five minutes after ordering my food from Orlanda, I glance out the window and see Laurie Vonn outside, her coat on, filling her Honda with gas at the truck stop pump. I start to get up, then stop. My food hasn't come yet, and I wonder for a moment if I should wait for it. *She said she would call the cops when she got home. Maybe I should just let her go.*

But what if she doesn't call them?

An image of Laurie Vonn's body, decapitated in a shallow grave, suddenly comes to me.

I get up and leave a twenty on the table and walk out the front door. It's ten degrees colder outside than it was before and the sky is leaden with clouds and I can smell the rain coming—or will it be snow? I reach the Chrysler and get in and drive around the gas pumps just in time to see Laurie Vonn's dirty red Honda Civic pull out of the driveway and onto the bypass road.

I catch up to her and then slow to allow a few cars between us. It is getting dark so I turn my headlights on, but Laurie doesn't turn hers on and I almost lose her.

What will I say when she gets home? The story about the burglar won't fly. I may have to come clean and just tell her the truth. *But what is that?*

Think. *You're an imaginative fellow, a writer...*

I'll follow her home, knock on her door—no, I'll stop her before she gets inside the house and tell her who I am— No, need more lead time to get away.

I'll tell her to go inside and turn on her TV and watch the news and when she sees my picture there will be a tip line or some kind of number to call. I'll tell her to call that number and then tell them exactly what happened. *Tell them that I told you to place yourself in protective custody. Ask to speak with Detective Marsh from the LAPD. Tell him I said you were in danger.*

That might do it. If I scare her. She *should* be scared. And if she waits to see a story about me on TV it could give me enough time to steal another car. And by the time she gets through to the police and gets them to believe her and actually gets Marsh on the line I will have enough time to put some miles between me and Trenton, New Jersey. I start looking around for a gas station or supermarket where I can lift another car as I follow her. *Think ahead. Anticipate.* This could work, this could work. I could warn her *and* steer clear of the police.

If a lot of things break my way.

I follow her back to the interstate but she doesn't take the entrance. She drives right by it. I follow her for three more miles until she turns into a parking structure at a mall. I follow her into the structure, taking my ticket from the machine and keeping my head low. I am now automatically scanning for security cameras everywhere. *Paranoia is progressive, like alcoholism.*

I stop suddenly, as she stops in front of me. Then she turns right and drives slowly down the rows of parked cars, looking for a space. She turns and heads back down another row. Slowly. I take a long, deep breath to fend off my impatience, then follow her car down yet another row of cars.

What the hell am I doing here?

Saving someone's life.

At last she finds a space. Her backup lights come on and for an alarming moment I think she'll back right into me but she stops short, then turns the wheel and eases into a tight spot between two SUV's. I glance around quickly for a parking space nearby and I realize how enormous the parking structure is. Not a space in sight—

A car horn blares at me from behind. I look in the rearview and see the silhouette of a woman behind me in a Mercedes. I pull forward, trying to find a space and keep an eye in the mirror for Laurie Vonn at the same time.

Finally I find a space, at the end of the long row that Laurie parked in. I get out and I don't see her. I look around and see the word *Escalators* painted on a round concrete column. I follow the arrow to the escalators and ride up, straining to catch a glimpse of her.

The escalator deposits me on the ground floor of the mall and I see Laurie heading down the broad walkway between the food court and the stationery store and the Brookstone and the Verizon store and countless other shops. I follow her.

I'm weighing whether I should catch up to her and give her my speech when she disappears inside Nordstrom. I go to the store and follow her inside, past the make-up counter and into the lingerie. She stops and looks at a rack of bras.

If I approach her now she could find a cop or a security guard. But maybe she wouldn't. Maybe she would wait, feeling more secure in public… No, bad idea…

She moves on to a rack of nightgowns. A saleswoman has noticed me. I slow down, pretending to be interested in a row of panties—but not *too* interested. I look up and can't see Laurie. I head toward the nightgowns and look around. I stand on my tiptoes and see the top of Laurie Vonn's head as she heads into a dressing room with some clothes in her hand.

"Can I help you?" I turn to find the saleswoman behind me, a middle-aged woman with short gray hair and big glasses with bright red plastic frames.

"Ah, no, that's okay, I'm just waiting for my girlfriend," I say, easing down from my tiptoes.

"Oh, she's trying something on," she looks in the direction Laurie went.

Shit. Can't let her think I'm waiting for Laurie. She may say something to her.

"Oh no, she's—she's in another part of the store," I say lamely. *Damn it.*

The saleswoman looks at me for a second longer than I'm comfortable with, then she forces a little smile and turns and walks back to the register.

I move as far from the lingerie as I can and feign interest in some earrings, keeping an eye on the dressing rooms and the register. The saleswoman says something to the girl at the register and the girl turns and looks at me. I pick up a pair of gold hoops and read the tag. *14 Carat, 49.95.* I put them back and glance at the women at the register, who are both looking at me now. I move on, down the jewelry counter, and stop behind a circular rack of nightgowns where they can't see me. There is a mirror on the opposite wall and I go to it and pretend to look at a row of bathrobes next to it while I watch the women and the dressing rooms reflected in it. I glance at myself in the mirror. I am an unshaven stranger wearing sunglasses at night with my cap pulled low as I linger among lingerie, fingering panties and following a lone girl.

Smooth.

The saleswoman is on the phone. Shit. I look at the dressing rooms and see no sign of Laurie. She could be a while. I try to remember how many things she brought into the dressing room but I didn't get a good look.

I walk off, toward another part of the store—out of view of the saleswomen at the register. I walk all the way through the store and wind my way back through the sweaters and the jeans and the Junior Miss outfits. I pass a row of sweatpants with suggestive things stitched in sequins across the backsides. I keep moving and it just gets worse—*Girls Eight And Under.*

I turn and walk straight back out the way I came, not looking at the saleswomen.

I walk out of Nordstrom and down the broad indoor boulevard and out of sight from the store. I smell warm pretzels from a stand nearby and my stomach churns eagerly. The last time I ate was last night, with Nicki, at the Mirabelle. *No wonder I'm screwing up, I can't think straight because I haven't eaten.* I watch a man buy a pretzel for his toddler son. I turn and look in the window of an electronics store, waiting for the kid at the pretzel stand to ring up the man's purchase. The entrance to Nordstrom is reflected in the electronics store window. I can see Laurie at the register, talking to the saleswoman and handing her credit card to her. The man at the stand gives the pretzel to his little son and they leave. I go to the stand.

"Three pretzels, please."

"Onion garlic or original?" the pimply kid asks me.

"Original."

The kid picks up a pair of metal tongs and selects three big pretzels off a rack under a heat lamp and folds each of them into a piece of waxed paper and then reaches for a bag. I glance up and see a mall security guard entering Nordstrom. The kid puts the pretzels in the bag and hands them to me.

"Three-forty-five," he says. I take out my wallet and give him a five dollar bill and look at the window of the electronics store and see my face on six different big screen televisions—the same pictures I saw before: my driver's license photo and the ragged mug shot from the Richard Bell murder. Then I see Detective Marsh in his blue Gore-Tex, talking into a forest of microphones. I strain to hear what he's saying but the televisions are muted inside the store. The picture cuts to videotape of a roadblock and I see the truckload of Michigan-bound oranges swarmed by cops. *They found the phone.*

The mall security guard, a thickset Latino kid, walks out of Nordstrom. I take off my Devils cap and move behind the pretzel stand where he can't see me. He walks by the stand without looking back. He is armed only with a bulky black walkie-talkie. I take my change from the pretzel kid and walk back toward Nordstrom for a quick look and see Laurie signing her credit card receipt at the register.

I head for the escalators, devouring the pretzels. I don't see the guard around, so I take the escalator down. I get to the parking level and wander among the parked cars and suddenly I get the feeling I'm being followed. I turn around and see no one. I walk past Laurie's car quickly. I hear a shuffling noise. I look around again as I walk and again I see nothing. The parking lot is dark and quiet. It sounded close.

Footsteps?

I strain to listen but hear only the distant sound of car doors slamming and kids' voices far off, laughing. I wind around between the parked cars, beating a circuitous path back toward my car. *Have they found the Mustang at the gas station and connected it to the Chrysler?*

I approach the Chrysler cautiously, half-expecting to get jumped by a SWAT team. But the car is unmolested. No SWAT team. I get in and start the engine and look at my watch. I'll give her five minutes and then I'm gone. If I keep this up I will be caught.

THINGS PAST

He headed south from New Jersey in his rig, making sure to take a different route back west. He never drove the same highway twice. He drove and drove, down the eastern seaboard and across Georgia. The long stretches of lonely highway gave him time to think, to plan. He would have to get a new van, of course, since Laurie Vonn had seen him in his current one. But his cash reserves were getting low, given how much fuel the rig required. He thought briefly about finding a route and going back to work, but even that seemed dicey. At least for right now. He needed time. He needed to find a place to park and rest for a long stretch, where he could lay low and save money on fuel. He spent a night at an enormous truck stop outside Atlanta and considered staying there for a while. No, a rig lingering at a busy truck stop like that would raise attention. So he kept moving, through Georgia, Alabama, Mississippi, Louisiana…waiting, chain-smoking, burning fuel and money and heading nowhere.

He had printed the photo of Laurie Vonn at the business center in the Atlanta truck stop. He pinned it up, over the front page of the Atlanta Journal Constitution, and spent nights in his secret room with his Los Angeles Angel and the photos of all of his Angels. But as much as Laurie's picture excited him, it also reminded him of his mistake, and he couldn't find release with her image above him, taunting him.

The migraines came back, worse than before, as well as the restless anxiety and irritability that now bordered on rage. The only thing he could do to satisfy himself was read the paperback true-crime book about serial killers. He pictured himself in a book like that; he imagined thousands, maybe millions of people reading about him.

But the fantasies were just that—fantasies. Fleeting and false. He knew he would have to do something to stem the tide of restless rage that was rising in him daily…but what? He had encountered a few potential Angels on his long drive through the South, but that was unthinkably stupid. More than ever now, his desperation to have his story told was urgent to the point that he could hardly bear. He had to find a way…

And then, on a broiling August day in west Texas—a breakthrough. Another miracle. A vision. A plan. At last.

He had driven across Texas all day with the air conditioner off to save fuel, and the suffocating heat had stoked his mounting frustration and rage to a new and dangerous level. He was taking Valium and painkillers daily, with little effect. He needed relief. So after he pulled into a truck stop to gas up, he parked his rig at the stop and walked across the highway to a redneck bar and proceeded to get drunk. He took seven five-milligram Valium and ordered drink after drink, and the next thing he knew, he awoke in his secret room the afternoon of the following day, and all around him were the destroyed remnants of his embalming equipment. He had apparently returned to his rig and, in a blind, drugged, drunken fury, he had smashed everything. He had no memory of it, but his hands were scraped and bloody from beating and tossing around the heavy stainless steel equipment. The only things left intact were the Los Angeles Angel and the photos on the walls. He hadn't opened either of the two padlocked footlockers that contained his St. Stephen Angel and his West Virginia Angel. Thank God.

At first he was furious with himself for losing control. Who knows what he could have done while he was drunk and drugged like that? Try as he might, he could not remember a thing from the night before. He could have said things, told people things…

The thought of suicide came to him, and he was suddenly overcome with nausea and he vomited into the bucket where he collected body fluids.

He could have said things, told people things…told them about his Angels…

And in that moment, on his hands and knees in the stifling little room, trembling with nausea, tortured with self-loathing, he was suddenly struck with an idea—a brilliant revelation which, merely by thinking of it, calmed him completely, and glimmered with promise.

He dumped the bucket out from the back of the trailer, then hurried to the cab and turned on his notebook computer and began searching for medical articles on the combined effects of Valium and alcohol. He also read several articles about memory and brain function. He read for eight hours. The articles were very encouraging.

Then he entered a name into a search engine—an illegal site he had used to find information about his Angels as part of his careful preparation.

The name he entered he knew well—he had seen it a thousand times. And in half and hour he had an address, a brief biography, and various other bits of information.

He memorized all of it—never writing anything down—then he started his rig and headed west, brimming with hope and driving with purpose now. He figured he could reach San Gabriel, California in two days, maybe three if he took a less direct route.

Three days.

Three days of driving, a few weeks of watching and following, and he could be face to face with him—the man he could tell his stories to, and maybe, just maybe—the man who could become his St. Paul.

CHAPTER THIRTY-NINE

I spend five minutes in the parking lot of the shopping mall, behind the wheel of the Chrysler, trying to think up a way to warn Laurie Vonn. I could call the police hotline myself and tell *them* to watch out for her. Would they believe me? They would if I gave them information only I would know...

No, the minute I do that my location can be pinpointed instantly. Right now I could be anywhere, unless I've been spotted somewhere I don't know about. By someone I didn't see. Unlikely. But I have to call Nicki at some point. It will be helpful to find out what the police know, beyond the news reports.

I could leave a note on Laurie Vonn's car. *You are in danger. Call the police immediately. Someone wants to kill you.*

Jesus. And I'm a *writer.*

But what could I write? *Call Detective Marsh and tell him...*

Tell him what? How would I say it? What could I write that would convince her? *Come on, think—you routinely write two thousand words a day and now you can't come up with twelve?*

I look at my watch. Five minutes are up. I start the car. *Give her one more minute. Think for one more minute. At least come up with something or this girl could wind up—*

I see the security guard riding down the escalator and I drive off immediately.

Damn it.

I drive to the exit and pay for my parking and get back on the bypass road. It is dark now and sleeting, the tiny ice particles melting as they hit my windshield. I finish the last pretzel and my stomach growls so loudly I can hear it over the hiss of the tires on the wet pavement. Now I'm hungry *and* thirsty. I need to eat. I need to find another car. I need a shower and a shave and a new identity and five million in an offshore account.

I stop at a red light and glance at my rearview mirror and see Laurie Vonn's dirty red Honda pull out of the parking structure and head away from me, in the opposite direction.

I take the next right, onto a dark street, and make a u-turn, scanning wildly around for police, and then back onto the bypass road and after the Honda.

I will follow her home and warn her and then get the hell out of here.

I follow her back to the interstate. She merges with the evening rush hour and I pull up two cars behind her, watching the passing signs for a gas station or supermarket where I can pick off a car. I turn on the radio and I am once again the lead item in the news. They talk about the FBI's dead end in Michigan. They mention the stolen Mustang and give its license number, and I hear about them finding my truck. Several "experts" are summoned to talk about me. They speculate about my alcoholism and my "obsession" with the three dead women and my "wife's tragic suicide" and my previous arrest for the murder of Richard Bell. I am a *loner, a recluse who has withdrawn into his bizarre world of fantasy.* Maybe these sages will figure out what the fuck is happening and let me know. They congratulate each other on their insights and joke and laugh as they discuss the murder and mutilation of young women. *You can opine about my "twisted psyche" all you want, but you don't know about my Chrysler.* I am still "at large," and the anchor reads the police tip line three times. Good. The more I hear that tip line number the more I am assured they don't have any idea where I am. I look at the cars surrounding me and wonder how many people are listening to this. Millions of people will come home tonight and hear about me and see my picture and look at the phone number. Maybe they will write it down. Maybe I look like their cousin or their ex-husband and they will remember my face.

We come to the 53rd street exit off the interstate and I get in the right lane, anticipating that Laurie will take the exit to go home but she doesn't.

"Where to now, girl?" I say aloud, exasperated.

She passes the exit and continues north on the highway. I nudge the Chrysler up alongside her and catch a glimpse of her behind the wheel but the car ahead of me slows and I back off and blend in with the herd of commuters.

God knows where she is going. Dinner? Market? Boyfriend? I have done what I can and risked capture doing it and now I have to get another car. But the traffic is too thick to get off right away so I follow her through the stop-and-go all the way to the New Jersey Turnpike which she takes north out of Trenton.

Where the hell is she going?

THINGS PAST

It was easy to track the author Rhodes. He had a simple routine: head from his little place in San Gabriel to a dive bar in Pasadena around two in the afternoon and stay there until closing. The guy was a drunk—another stroke of unexpected good fortune.

He followed Rhodes for a couple of weeks, then one night he entered the dark, dingy bar, and watched as the writer drank his Jack Daniel's on the rocks until his shoulders slumped and his head began to bob and weave.

He waited until Rhodes was drunk enough—but not too drunk—then ordered a bottle of Jack and two glasses. He dropped three Valium into one of the glasses and stirred them until they dissolved in the brown whiskey. Then he approached the booth where the writer sat hunched over his drink.

"Mind if I join you?"

The guy just looked up and gave a vague shrug. So he slid into the booth across from the writer and poured himself a drink, then pushed the one with the Valium across the booth to him. He made some small talk, asked some innocuous questions, and then he listened to the writer. He wanted to get a sense of the guy before he told him anything.

After his third Valium cocktail, the writer's eyelids were nearly closed and he began talking about his fiancé's suicide. He let the writer go on about her until he was just about to pass out, and then he took out his yellowed clippings from the West Virginia papers about Caitlin Stubbs, and he began to tell his story. He was careful never to refer to the killer as "I." Rather, he told the story as if it were just that—a story. He didn't tell the writer his name, didn't mention where he was from or what he did. That could come later. He had picked up the crude vernacular of the truckers and loading dock workers and he *had begun to speak like them, to blend in. He spoke like that to Rhodes, in a quiet, low voice, affecting a slight Midwestern drawl peppered with ignorant blue-collar idiom. He sat with his back to the lighted bar so his face was in shadow. He wanted the writer's memory of him—if any—to be a version of him that could be disputed by another version of himself.*

And the writer listened.

CHAPTER FORTY

An hour north of Trenton I click the Chrysler's defroster fan up to its highest notch. The Outside Temp gauge reads 8 degrees and the windshield keeps fogging up. The tiny defroster vents on top of the driver's side door are plugged with tissues I found in the old man's glove compartment, leaving my window obscured with fog while the windshield stays clear enough for me to see Laurie Vonn ahead as she takes the New York State Thruway through the heavy sleet that is driven horizontal by the fierce wind.

In the past hour a hundred different worries have gnawed at me. *What if the saleswoman at Nordstrom told Laurie about me and Laurie called the police and they told her to go someplace safe, out of town? Would they tail her? Are they on me right now? What if she saw my picture or heard a description of me on the radio and connected the dots?*

A lot of *what if's*, but still… I realize I am chewing on a tissue and stop. *Calm down. If that were the case I would be in cuffs by now. They wouldn't use a young woman like that as bait, anyway…*

Would they?

We have traveled a couple of stretches where the traffic was sparse—no one behind us for a quarter mile or so. Outside of town the bad weather has kept people off the road. This is reassuring. And as I drive, I realize Laurie Vonn may have done me a big favor. It was stupid to think of stealing a car in Trenton. In fact, it was stupid to stay there any longer at all. Trenton P.D. will be looking for the Chrysler, but the police in New York won't be looking for it…unless FBI has connected the Chrysler to the Mustang. But with any luck, the Mustang is already in pieces in a chop shop in a Baltimore slum. God bless bad neighborhoods. As reliable as dawn.

I have kept a scan going 360 around me as I drive, looking for anything that resembles a police car, and the constant vigilance and hunger and dehydration are wearing me down. What if it never stops? What if this is it? Running… I think of Melvin "Cowboy" Beauchamp, whom I occasionally called at FBI to pester with questions. Over drinks just a few months ago he had leaned his huge frame back in the booth and said, *"I dig your books, Jackie, but I don't know how long your Killer can stay at large and still be realistic. In real life, at some point, they all make mistakes. At some point their luck runs out. They get tired or lazy and they let their guard down or take an unnecessary risk, and that's when we're there to welcome them."* He had grinned broadly when he said it. Melvin got the nickname "Cowboy" because he had gunned down a whopping total of 6 fugitives in his career so far, and after the third beer he described each killing with a smile of satisfaction.

I wonder what Melvin thinks of me now? Hell, he's probably leading the investigation, right there with Marsh. I wonder if Melvin would shoot me dead and smile about it later over beers…

This is not positive thinking.

I turn up the radio to drown out my thoughts. The news channels have been repeating the same information hours, which is a relief but also a nagging worry. The more they talk about me the more people will be looking out for me.

Laurie Vonn passes the exit for the Newark Bay Bridge, the first exit to New York City. Then she passes the next one, and the next.

Okay, so we're not going to the city.

She stays in the middle lane, keeping at a steady sixty-five miles an hour.

A family emergency? A sudden hankering to see upstate New York?

I watch the exits for New York City passing by. I could get off right here. I can't call Nicki but I could waylay her somewhere— No, they'll have surveillance on her. Besides, what could she tell me? That they're after me? What could she do for me now?

I drive on, following Laurie Vonn. If I stop following her and she turns up dead and they connect her to me…

I went to her house. I was seen following her at the mall. I have to keep on her. Have to protect her.

I have to save her.

★★★

Three hours later, in rural upstate New York, Laurie Vonn takes the VT-22A exit.

Vermont.

THINGS PAST

It took him three nights of careful conversation to tell his stories to the drugged, drunken writer—including his plans for Laurie Vonn. And on the third night, he doubled the dose of Valium in the booze—a recipe for a complete blackout—and drove him to Temescal and showed him the grave of Beverly Grace, and the hair clip he had placed in the tree.

He knew there was little chance the writer would remember any of it. And anyway, the guy was a world-class lush and no one would believe him even if he did. But he had laid the groundwork. He had planted the seed. Most important, he had relieved himself of the burden of his stories. He luxuriated in un-spooling the details of his adventures, and the writer was listening—REALLY listening to him. And even though Rhodes' eyes were barely open and his speech slurred almost to the point of incoherence, he was delighted when the writer asked the occasional question. Here was a man who could fathom a mind like his. A man who had written so clearly about others like him. Here was a man who understood.

He didn't know where it would lead, but he knew where Rhodes lived, knew where he drank, and if he ever wanted to tell more of his stories to someone, he had found him. Maybe he could even take the chance one day to return to Pasadena and tell him more without drugging him. And maybe—just maybe—Rhodes would one day write his story for the world to read. Just like the stories in the dog-eared paperback on the seat next to him; the collection of killers, which Rhodes had written, and which he read daily.

But when he brought Rhodes back to the bar after Temescal, it was just before closing time. After last call he left the writer, unconscious, slumped in the booth. And as he got in his van, he saw the bartender half-carry the staggering writer out to the alley and slam the door behind him. The writer slumped to the gritty pavement of the alley and slept.

He watched from the van, debating whether to go and help him—to take him home—when he saw a rough-looking fellow slip into the alley and pull the writer's wallet and keys from his pocket. When the writer stirred, the robber began to beat him, and that's when he got out of the van.

★★★

Richard Bell never saw the knife. The serrated edge sliced completely through the front of his throat and into his spinal cord and he was dead when he hit the ground.

He dragged Bell to the writer's car—too much blood to put the body in the van without the heavy plastic tarps he normally placed there before a transformation. And he couldn't leave Bell where he lay. Police would come, and they would find Rhodes and question him. He couldn't run the risk that Rhodes' fresh memories might surface under pressure from the police. So he drove Bell to Highland Park in the writer's car and heaved the body into a dumpster in a dark alley behind a hardware store. He quickly wiped down the car for prints—usually he wore latex surgical gloves, just as a precaution, even though he knew his prints weren't on file anywhere. Nonetheless, he had never murdered on impulse before and he was careful to clean up. He took the writer's keys and left the car next to the dumpster and walked all the way back to his van, reaching it by morning.

He drove to his rig, pulled the van inside, and left the city. His New Jersey Angel would have to wait even longer now. He had never killed without careful planning and he wasn't about to take any more chances. He had told someone his stories and he had murdered on impulse. He would have to get out of the state—possibly out of the country—and lay low for a long, long time.

He headed north.

CHAPTER FORTY-ONE

The horizontal sleet has turned to horizontal snow in the Chrysler's headlights and I can no longer see or think clearly. The Outside Temp gauge reads 2 degrees. I have followed Laurie Vonn for an hour into Vermont, giving her a long lead. I am able to keep her in sight through the heavy snow and the foggy windshield because we are the only cars on the miserable road, and because the red plastic lens of her left rear tail light is broken and I can pick her car out from a long way off by looking for that bright point of white light.

But there is no such beacon for my mind. I can't think straight, and the treacherous driving conditions have added yet another vexation to my overflowing pot of confusion and fear.

Where the hell is this girl going? I think for the thousandth time. And for the thousandth time I have no answer. Nevertheless I think it again, stuck on the thought, stupid with exhaustion.

Ping! The LOW FUEL light blinks on, bright orange. I look down at the fuel gauge, which shows empty. I look around the dashboard controls to see if the onboard computer will tell me how many miles I have left—

The Chrysler suddenly loses traction and goes into a slide, which I steer into and straighten out when I take my foot off the gas. *Keep your eyes on the road.* I slow to twenty miles an hour and then ease back up to forty just in time to see Laurie's turn signal blinking as she gets in the right lane and slows down and I suddenly know exactly where I am.

"No… *No…*" I say as I see the reflective white letters come into view through the thick snow, forming the word FEATHERTON on the exit sign. I take my foot off the gas and watch as Laurie Vonn takes the exit and heads down the ramp toward the county road that leads to my cabin, three miles from here.

What in God's name is she doing here?

I am far enough behind her to take a full minute to decide whether to follow. I leave my foot off the gas and let the inertia of the heavy Chrysler guide me closer to the exit.

Take it or not?

If I take it and the police are there…?

If I don't take it…

…What? Keep going until I run out of gas? Pull over and wait for the weather to clear? How long? What if I fall asleep? I would wind up face to face with police, who will be out checking the roads for accidents and stranded motorists. There is nothing around for miles and the weather has gone from worse to God-awful. *I* could wind up stranded. I wince at the thought—trapped in my stolen car and rescued by Vermont's finest…

The closest gas station is in Featherton. I guide the car to the exit ramp and roll down it slowly, my decision borne more from a lack of imagination than anything else. I can't see the Honda but I turn right, toward town, toward my cabin. I can drive right by the cabin on the way to town and get gas…

The police will be at the cabin. They will have searched the place and—

—and then it hits me: FBI would have already searched my cabin and taken my computer. They *HAVE* read the fourth book, the unfinished manuscript on my hard drive.

They know about Laurie Vonn. They know where she lives. They contacted her and warned her and this is a trap.

I curse myself for not realizing this earlier. *In real life, at some point, they all make mistakes.*

No, they wouldn't use Laurie Vonn as bait. They would have contacted her and instructed her to drive to the police where I would have been arrested. They would never let her lead me all the way back here, especially not in this weather…

The Chrysler slides on the snow-packed road again. I slow down to fifteen miles an hour.

Maybe the police aren't at the cabin. In this weather…

But then what the hell is she doing here?

The snow is coming down so heavily I can only see a few feet ahead of the car. There is a turnout ahead. I could turn around and get back on the interstate and keep going north. I could be in Canada in two hours. They'll be watching for me at the border, of course, but maybe I could get close enough and cross on foot somewhere... But I need gas and food and a heavy coat... If I turn around and get back on the interstate, the next gas station is at least ten miles away. The one in Featherton is closer. Five or six miles. But I'll have to pass my cabin. *Shit.* How much gas do I have left? Five miles? Ten? I have no idea and I can't risk running out.

I will drive on, passing the cabin like any other slow-moving motorist caught in the blizzard. There is a mini-mart at the Featherton gas station and I can get food and supplies. If it isn't open I can pull right up to the pump and wait until morning— *No, the owner, old Virgil, will recognize me if I go inside to buy food. Virgil takes the night shift himself at the gas station; he's too damned cheap to hire someone. And if I use my credit card to pay at the pump there will be a record of it and they'll know I was here.*

It would be smarter to steal a car in Featherton. No one is out tonight. Hell, you can barely *see.* I could be a little choosy. Get a four-wheeler, maybe, something that can handle the roads...

I crest the last hill before the cabin. I strain to see my driveway, a hundred yards ahead, but it's impossible. I creep ahead until the Chrysler's headlights illuminate the numbers on my mailbox. I keep at a steady fifteen miles an hour as I get closer. There's the driveway. Almost on it now. I slow to ten miles an hour and watch as I approach the entrance to my rutted drive.

I lower my window two inches and peer out at the cabin.

Nothing. I would be able to see if any lights were on. But I see only a void of thick snow near my car in the ambient glow of the headlights, and beyond that there is only darkness. The lights are off in the cabin, then. And I see no headlights or tail lights along the driveway. I ease to a stop in front of my driveway, staring as hard as I can into the snowy darkness toward my home.

Nothing.

I look all around me and see only the dim forms of trees surrounding the road through the dense snow in the headlights. The wind is blowing so hard the heavy Chrysler is buffeted to and fro and my face is pelted with stinging snow from the two-inch opening in the window. I close the window and press my foot gently on the gas pedal and the rear tires spin but the car doesn't move. I ease up on the gas, then try again. The Chrysler's motor revs and the tires spin to a high whine in the packed snow but the car doesn't move. I curse, then drop the shift lever to the lowest gear and touch the gas pedal again, pumping it gently to rock the car into traction. The car rocks slightly forward, then back, then forward and I let the momentum carry me for a second, and the car slides ahead. I ease up to fifteen miles an hour in this herky-jerky way, feeling the car drift around on the icy, snow-covered road.

"Come on…" I urge the car along.

I push the gas pedal down a little further, but it only sends the rear of the car careening around and for an awful moment I am about to slide into the ditch, but I let up off the gas and the car stops sliding and I try again. *Easy, easy…*pressing the pedal gently and pulling the car straight and inching forward. I breathe a sigh of relief but then the rear of the car comes around again and I let off the gas and sit there.

This is madness.

I pump the gas again and crawl forward but it's slow going and I am wasting precious fuel to gain paltry inches.

GODDAMNIT.

Have to keep it together. Breathe and try again. Pushing gently on the accelerator, letting up, then pushing again, then sliding. I step on the brake to stop the slide but the brake has no effect and I slide up to the edge of the ditch on the left shoulder. I touch the accelerator with my foot as lightly as I can… *touch touch touch*…and the car slowly spins in a circle until I am facing the opposite direction.

Jesus God how did I wind up here like this? What did I do?

I pump the car around, sliding until I straighten out again and head once more toward my imagined four-wheeler I will steal in Featherton.

But the Chrysler won't cooperate. I keep slipping and sliding, at ten miles an hour, wasting gas and risking a dive into the deep ditches that shoulder the county road.

I am sweating and my breath is short. I stop and breathe. I will never make it like this.

Think.

There is a driveway, about twenty yards ahead. I can see it in the headlights—the overgrown, vestigial driveway that led to the 18th century farmhouse that was razed long ago. Motorists now use the driveway as a turnout. I could pull off onto the useless old drive and hide the car and…

…and what? Freeze to death?

I roll ahead and the Chrysler decides for me—the nose of the car sliding inexorably toward the old driveway and off the county road. The driveway slopes down and the car toboggans in slow motion down the path and into the woods. I touch the brakes but they have no effect. The car drifts sideways and comes to a stop. I pump the gas but the rear tires spin in place. I pump a little harder, spinning the tires and wasting gas.

I am stuck.

I tuck the Ruger in my waistband and get out of the car and the vicious cold assaults me. I shiver and the inside of my nose freezes instantly. I button my denim *Keep On Truckin'* jacket up to the collar and start looking for a rock or a chunk of wood that I could wedge under the back tires to get traction. The floor of the woods is carpeted with deep snow. I kick through the drifts, looking for wood or rock and find nothing. My teeth start chattering. I turn and look back—the car can't be seen from the road here. I peer through the trees toward my cabin, fifty yards away.

No lights on in the cabin, no headlights in the driveway. Maybe it's empty. Maybe there's no one there. I could get a couple of two-by-fours from the woodshed and bring them back and put them under the rear tires. There is even a shovel in the shed; I could clear a path for the car, back to the road and get back on my way into town—

Can I risk going near the cabin? If I don't…if I get back in the car and run the motor to keep the heater going I will run out of gas in a matter of minutes. If I stay in the car with the motor off I could fall asleep and freeze to death or be discovered…*which would be worse?*

I stand there for a moment, frozen, hatless, stuck. I take a step toward the cabin, moving slowly, lifting my feet high through the deep snow. *I'll get closer and see if there are any cars in the drive. I can see it from the woods if I get close enough. Surely there won't be police standing around outside in this arctic storm. I can watch the place for a while and see if it might be safe to approach the shed, which is right by the edge of the woods…*

I continue down the driveway to the small clearing where the 18th century farmhouse once stood. There is a footpath from the ruins of the farmhouse that leads to my cabin. I created the path on my daily walks through these woods. The path is invisible to anyone else in the deep snow, but I know exactly where it is after trekking it hundreds of times.

I tramp across the snow-covered ruins of the farmhouse. There is no structure left, only the heavy stones that once formed the hearth, and a few bits and pieces of the old house. I go to the footpath and proceed through the deep snow, shivering uncontrollably now, keeping watch all around me as I walk. The heavy snow in the air and on the ground makes my progress silent, but it also would cover the sound of anyone near me. I wipe my nose on my sleeve and continue. I should be able to see the shed by now, only twenty yards ahead or so. I can see the end of the thick woods and I come to it and stand behind the largest tree, beside the entrance to the path, and peer around it.

I can see the dim outline of the woodshed, but not the cabin or anything beyond it. I wait, standing stock still in the freeze, letting two full minutes pass before I venture out toward the shed, keeping myself hidden behind it.

I reach the shed and press against it, using it as a windbreak. I wipe the snow from my eyes and brush it out of my hair, relieved to be sheltered from the onslaught of the stinging blizzard. I breathe in and out through my nose, then lean carefully around the corner of the shed to look at the cabin.

I can see the outline of the cabin. Is that a car in the drive? Pulled up to the front? I can't tell. I close my eyes for a minute, letting my pupils dilate, then I open them again and squint into the dark—a large vehicle, an SUV— Sheriff Claire Boyle's. I can't make out any markings on it but I can see the outline of the lights on its roof. I can't see inside the vehicle, but I can tell the engine isn't running. I would see exhaust coming from the tailpipe in the frigid air. And I hear nothing but my own teeth chattering beneath the roaring wind. I look around at the cabin. Not a light or sign of life anywhere. I think of my heavy coat hanging on a peg by the front door, in the living room. I think of the thick wool cap in the pocket of that coat, and the gloves and ski mask in my dresser drawer in my bedroom and the food in my pantry, thirty yards from me.

I wait another minute, watching the cabin for any sign of movement, then I slip around the side of the shed and go to the shed door and pull, but it is stuck— three feet of snow have drifted up against it. I pull harder and the wooden door makes a loud CRACK. I turn and look at the cabin. *Shit.* If I force the door open it will make a hell of a racket, even with the soundproofing blanket of snow. And I can't stand out here digging the snow away, exposed to the SUV and the cabin.

I decide to make a dash for the cabin and I reach it in thirty rushing, head-long strides and press against the wall of logs, my chest heaving from my short sprint, the freeze crawling down my throat and into my lungs.

I let my breathing return to normal, then sidle along the cabin to the front and get a closer look at Claire Boyle's SUV. I still can't see inside it but I can't believe she would be sitting inside with the motor off. Would they have left the SUV here, empty, just to ward off the curious? Maybe they worked in shifts, and she is getting coffee with a deputy someplace and they will return any minute…

And then I see something else—another car, parked beside the SUV. I can only see the front of it, the rest is hidden behind the SUV. A deputy? FBI?

I move around the cabin, in the other direction, through the silent snow. I creep all the way around the cabin, keeping low and quiet. The windows are well above my head, but I remain hunched over as I pass under them and approach the front of my cabin from the other side now.

There is not one other car, but *two*, parked beside Claire's SUV. The car next to Claire's is Laurie Vonn's Honda. The other car is a white Toyota Camry I've never seen before.

What the hell?

I still can't see inside Claire's SUV, but from here I can tell there is no one in the Honda or the Toyota. I hunch over and creep along the front of the cabin, under the windows and up to the Toyota, where I squat down between the side of my front porch and the front bumper of the car. The Toyota has Vermont tags and the license plate frame reads *Enterprise Rent-A-Car* in raised white lettering.

I crawl around the Toyota and rise up slowly and peer inside the driver's side window. I brush the snow off the glass and strain to see inside. Nothing—

Then I see an object in the back seat. I crawl back to the rear window and brush off a small space to look inside and I see the object clearly.

A little black Kate Spade handbag.

Nicki.

CHAPTER FORTY-TWO

I crawl back through the snow and duck behind the side of the cabin and huddle there, squatting in the deep drift, shuddering violently, my mind racing.

Why would Nicki have come here? Certainly not to look for me...

Would she have come to supervise the search of the cabin? The computer... I try to remember if I told Nicki about the fourth novel but in my frozen state of confused exhaustion I can't remember.

If I did tell Nicki about the fourth book maybe she came to get it—before the police— maybe she read it and contacted Laurie Vonn and that's why they both came here—

Deep inside it feels like wishful thinking but what else would make sense? Why else would both Nicki and Laurie Vonn be here? What would she possibly—

A sound. Inside the cabin.

Shrrick...shrrick...

I hold my breath, listening. *I know this sound...*

Shrrick...shrrick...shrrick...

The short, sharp sound, barely audible from inside the cabin.

A chill that is not from the cold spreads up my spine.

Shrrick...shrrick...shrrick...

Relentless, methodical... Like fingernails on a chalkboard only sharper, quicker...deadlier.

Despite the cold I feel drops of sweat trickle down the small of my back, which freeze instantly into a tissue of ice over my goosepimpled flesh.

Then another sound—

Nicki's voice.

Muffled, pleading—

—and then screaming.

Then her scream is cut short and there is only silence. I listen so hard I can hear snowflakes falling onto my face.

And then I get up and run to the front of the cabin and jump onto the porch and twist the knob on the front door—locked. I throw myself against the heavy, solid oak door, against the four heavy gauge steel hinges and the three titanium deadbolts, pushing and kicking at it, not caring if Claire Boyle sees me from her SUV—not caring if the door will be opened by Detective Marsh or Melvin "Cowboy" Beauchamp or anyone else—

I turn and look at Claire's SUV. She hasn't seen me, if she's inside. I jump off the porch and run to the SUV and see Claire inside, behind the wheel.

I pound on her window. *She's fallen asleep with the heater off and she is freezing—*

I open the SUV door and Claire's head falls off her shoulders and lands hard on my right foot and rolls off and her face turns over and her pale blue eyes stare up at me from the insouciant serenity of death.

And then something explodes inside my head and there is only blackness.

THINGS PAST

He was ten miles south of Portland when he heard on the radio about the murder of Richard Bell. He lit a cigarette and turned up the volume and learned that the writer Rhodes had been charged.

He listened to the news until he pulled into a truck stop just south of town. It was a big stop, and he tucked his rig carefully into the middle of the pack of parked semi's. He crawled into the cab and watched the news on television and scoured the internet all night, without leaving the rig.

The next morning he risked a trip into the truck stop's store to buy supplies: food, a large bottle of water to drink, and then urinate into when empty, eliminating the need to use the truck stop's restroom. He also bought clothes and a pair of barber shears.

He returned to his cab and cut his hair short, then pulled on the new clothes. Then he waited and watched for three days and three nights before leaving the cab again. He learned that the charges were dropped against Rhodes, and he was released. There was no mention of his Angels—nothing at all about West Virginia, St. Stephen, or Pasadena. Nothing at all. Rhodes had been released because the bartender at the dive vouched for his whereabouts. And Rhodes had either forgotten about Temescal and the Angels or he had kept quiet about them.

He moved on, still heading north. He wanted to get as close as possible to the border.

Two weeks later, in Seattle, he bought two fake passports from a Mexican forger—one U.S., the other Canadian—and two new commercial truck driver's licenses to match the passports. They were good forgeries and they weren't cheap. His savings were almost gone. He had to pay a thousand dollars for the documents' fresh fingerprints alone—provided unwillingly and unknowingly by a crackhead the Mexican inducted when he found him passed out in a doorway on Seattle's skid row.

The business with the fingerprints reminded him about wiping down the writer's car, and it worried him. What if he had missed a print? He had no fingerprints on record, but if someone in the bar remembered him and the police matched a print to a glass in the bar...

He consulted the medical journals online. While researching the side effects of various drugs on memory, he had come across a drug called Capacetabine, used in chemotherapy, which had the unusual side effect of causing the skin of the fingertips to peel away, eventually leaving the patient with no fingerprints at all. He found the drug, available on a Russian pharmaceutical site, and had a large supply sent to a post office box he rented in Tacoma. He began taking the drug, titrating the dose carefully, taking it with the synthetic steroid Dexamethasone to combat the nausea, and when he noticed the skin on his fingertips beginning to peel, he started looking for work. The Capacetabine also thinned his hair, but that was a bonus. No prints, no hair. He was being born anew.

It took him six weeks to find work. There were jobs available but he avoided any routes that would take him to California. Eventually he got a route—short hauls around the Northwest—delivering tool and die equipment to lumber mills.

After a few months, his worries began to ease. He kept constant vigilance on the news reports from Los Angeles, Missouri, West Virginia, and New Jersey. There was nothing to concern him. He settled into a routine, driving his route, sleeping in his cab. The more time passed, the more he began to feel at ease. The gray, wet Northwestern weather had a calming effect on him. The steady rains and the low, leaden clouds were like a cloak. He felt secure, as if a blanket were pulled over him, providing cover.

The memories of his conversations with Rhodes had also eased the pressure, and the migraines stopped. He no longer needed painkillers or booze, and he was able to find release once more as he lay in his secret room with his pictures and his Angels. He sold his van and waited before buying a new one. The time would come, but he felt no urgency, even when he encountered women who would be fine candidates for transformation. The time would come. He drove his rig, kept his head down, and waited.

And then, in a bookstore one drizzly afternoon in Seattle, he was perusing the true-crime section and he wandered into the mystery titles and he saw it.

Featured on a cardboard stand, was the book called **Killer**.

From the author Jack Rhodes.

His heart leapt. His first impulse was to leave the store, the city, the country.... But he couldn't resist it. Hands trembling with fear and anticipation, he picked up a copy and began to read.

★★★

He lay in his secret room that night, reading and re-reading the book. After his fourth reading he closed the book and held it to his chest and closed his eyes.

Dizzy, reeling, ineffable bliss. More than a miracle. More than he had ever dreamed, even in his grandest fantasies.

He had found his St. Paul.

And the more he read it, the more he was pleased. Rhodes, the drunken writer, the damaged, beaten, grief-wallowing burnout; Rhodes, drugged and half-conscious, had risen from his anesthetized torpor—risen above it, like Saul had risen above his sinful life of persecution, and told his story. And in the most clever twist, he had done so as if it were fiction. He had changed just enough of the facts to protect him—he changed names, places—meaningless details, for the most part. But he got the story right; he captured its essence, and kept his killer nameless, faceless, and without identity. He had protected him even as he exalted him to millions. A number one bestseller. Millions.

Best of all, on the back cover, was the promise of another book, another story about him.

He lay there in the dark, in the secret room, and he let the waves of blissful grandeur wash over him. He could not imagine any other human being had ever felt more powerful, or more fulfilled.

He took out all three of his Angels and they sang to him all night, they sang in his dreams, and took him beyond any of the special places he had missed for so long, the places he had longed for for so very long.

CHAPTER FORTY-THREE

Jesus just left Chicago and he's bound for New Orleans,
Well now Jesus just left Chicago and he's bound for New Orleans.
Workin' from one end to the other and all points in between...

The slow thrum of the bass and the smoky blues guitar.
Shrrick...shrrick...
The sharp sound keeping time with the throbbing Texas shuffle...
Dave and I are both sitting on the little mound of dirt in the small plateau overlooking Temescal Canyon Park.
Shrrick...shrrick...
Dave slides the blade of the knife against the small whetstone in his hand, in time with the music...
How can I hear the music up here, in the canyon? It is loud, thumping in my chest...
"So what do you think of Dave's Hit List?," _Dave says._
"Wat list?" _I ask, stupid with drink._
He gives his low, mirthless laugh.
"See, that's another thing I like about you, Doc. You listen, you pay attention. But you don't remember a goddamned thing."
Shrrick...shrrick... I watch him sharpen the knife as I take another pull from the bottle of Jack.
"Those four pretty little pieces I told you about. Dave's Greatest Hits."
Shrrick...shrrick...

I don't remember, but I listen.

"Three of those four pretty little pieces are already in pieces—and they aren't very pretty pieces," he says, and I can hear the smile without seeing it.

Shrrick…shrrick… He sharpens the ten-inch knife with a serrated top and black rubber handle.

I drink again—and suddenly flash on a memory of his pictures as he laid them on the table at McDougal's…that's where the music is from…the jukebox…?

And now somehow we are back in the booth at McDougal's. He lays the pictures out and I hear him smile.

"It's been fun telling you my stories, Doc. I'm gonna have to leave soon. What do you think? Good stuff, huh?"

"Yeah. Good stories," I mumble around my glass, barely able to keep my head up or my eyes open.

"Yeah, good stories," he looks down at the pictures. "Good times," he takes the picture of Beverly Grace off the table.

"Three down, one to go," he says.

Shrrick…shrrick…to the beat of the music.

★★★

You might not see him in person but he'll see you just the same,
You might not see him in person but he'll see you just the same.
You don't have to worry 'cause takin' care of business is his name.

The dream about *Dave* goes away but the music continues. And the sound of the knife on the whetstone…*shrrick…shrrick*…in time with the slow Texas shuffle is still loud in my ears.

This is no dream, I realize as my head begins to throb and I smell the stale cigarette smoke and feel something cold and hard against my left wrist and I open my eyes and there he is.

Dave.

Standing over me, sharpening the knife casually, the long chain swaying from his hip.

"What's up, Doc?" he says in his low, sonorous voice, the sound of a smile behind it.

Jesus God…what is happening…? I blink my eyes, trying to clear my head, and I feel something warm running down the back of my neck and realize I am sitting on the floor of my bedroom and I move to touch the back of my throbbing head but my left hand is handcuffed to a steel conduit behind me.

"I'm sorry I had to put you down there on the floor but it got a little more crowded in here than I planned on," Dave says, moving aside so I can see, behind him in the dim light, Nicki and Laurie Vonn, tied to my kitchen chairs with nylon rope, back to back, each with a swatch of duct tape over their mouths. Nicki's eyes flash wide with panic at me. The front of Laurie Vonn's blouse is covered with blood from a cut at her throat, but she is alive. She looks at me with the mindless terror of a dying animal in her eyes.

Dave leans over and looks into my eyes and I smell his stale cigarette smoke and see myself reflected in his rectangular glasses, reversed, twice.

"Do you know that Paul never met Jesus?" he asks me.

I stare at him, still trying to gather my wits.

"Never met him. Paul spent half his life persecuting Christians, and the other half spreading the gospel to the world," he says. "How does it feel?" he asks me.

"How does what feel?" I say.

"To see me again," he says. "To meet the man you've immortalized."

A hundred responses ping-pong around in my throbbing head, but none of them are right.

"Kind of overwhelming, isn't it?" he says.

"Yes."

He smiles at me. He looks—and sounds—different from my distorted memories. He is slight and pale, his hair thinner, and he speaks with quiet confidence and intelligence, rather than a trucker's swaggering drawl, as I remember.

"I found my favorite song in your CD collection," Dave says, tucking the whetstone into his jacket pocket. He waits for the end of the verse, then arches his back and throws his head back and bellows along with the song, suddenly transforming back into the redneck trucker I met in Pasadena so long ago.

"AHH TAKE ME WITH YOU, JESUS!"

He looks back down at me, grinning now, his eyes alight, and I see the full madness of the man—madness in full bloom before me. In an instant he had changed his voice, his expression, everything. I look up at him, astonished; afraid to move or respond.

"We have a lot of catching up to do, but first we have some business to take care of. You really made me proud. Or, I should say, I'm proud of you. The way you told my stories to the world. Very clever. You didn't get every little detail right, but hey, you were completely fucked up at the time. I'm surprised you remembered as much as you did. Guess I made an impression on you, huh?"

I nod.

"I liked you for that, I really did," Dave says to me. "You were happy just to listen to somebody else so you didn't have to think about *her*, weren't you?"

I nod, watching the knife in his hand. I feel around the back of my waistband but the Ruger is gone. *Think...*

"Did you believe me when I told you my stories and showed you my pictures?"

I shake my head. "No. I thought they were just...stories..."

"Really? Even with all those details....the way you described the pictures... everything you put in your books?"

I nod, feeling the cuff around my wrist. It's just loose enough to move my wrist around and slide it down to the knuckle of my thumb. I look around me—*a weapon...a tool...anything...*

"What about the presents I left you, Jack?" he asks.

"I don't know what you're talking about," I say.

He looks at me with that penetrating look, and again I hold his gaze.

Then he straightens up and looks around the cabin. "You did pretty good for yourself, remembering my stories."

"I didn't think I was remembering. I thought I was making it all up."

"Really?" He looks at me for a long time, standing stock still, his eyes invisible in the darkness behind his rectangular glasses. "You never lied to me before," he says.

He waits, watching to see my reaction. I hold his gaze steadily.

"But now it's all fucked up," he says. "Now they're saying YOU did those things, which cuts me out of the picture. And you DON'T CUT ME OUT OF THE PICTURE, JACK."

"I know that now." My eyes darting around the room. *Think think think...*

He reaches for a book that is on the top of my dresser. When he leans past Laurie she closes her eyes and makes a terrified noise. He turns the book over— the most recent paperback of *Killer Unbound*. He reads the promotional copy aloud from the back of the book.

"Coming soon—the exciting fourth book in the bestselling *KILLER* series—*Killer Unmasked*—in which author Jack Rhodes will reveal the true identity of Killer once and for all." He looks at me. "Is that what you were planning to do? Tell the world who I am?"

"No, I thought I made you up…I didn't think you were real."

"You know I'm real now, don't you?"

I nod, watching him tap the blade of the knife against his thigh. I can see my bookcase in the office, through the doorway and across the hall…*The Dangerous Summer is still there…did they search and find the gun? How thoroughly did they search?* I can see into the bathroom. The plumber's tape is still intact around the drain trap under the sink…*FBI didn't take the traps apart yet…maybe they only had time to do a cursory search—*

"I'm as real as rain, Jack. I EXIST. At the very *least* you're guilty of plagiarism."

He pulls a pack of Marlboros from his jacket pocket and flicks open the top on his Zippo.

"Do you mind if I smoke in here?"

I look at him. He's serious, holding the lighter and waiting for my response. *The nicotine may calm him.*

"No… Go ahead."

He lights the Marlboro with his silver Zippo.

They didn't search the drain traps…they didn't pull the books off the shelves…they were in too much of a hurry, on their way to Michigan after the phone in the oranges…

He lights the cigarette and inhales, then exhales, talking around it.

"All the great men had their biographers. Presidents. Emperors. Old Jesus sure had his. But now everyone thinks *YOU* did those things you wrote. And that cuts me out. You didn't *DO* those things, you were *TOLD* those things, and we need to set the record straight. That's why I came here. We have some things to sort out, and quick, before any other cops or feds show up."

I sit on the floor, watching him smoke, trying to think through the fear, to sort through the meaning of his words. I try to think of things to say, anything, and I think of a hostage negotiator for NYPD who once told me, *"Best thing to do is keep your mouth shut. When in doubt, say nothing. Do nothing."*

The music fades out, leaving only the sound of the howling blizzard outside the bedroom window.

"They're gonna write books about both of us now, Jack," the smile back in his voice as he looks down at me.

There must be backup—someone to relieve Claire—how long before—?

"After you went to the cops in L.A. I kept on you. I knew once they dug up Temescal they'd be asking a lot of questions. I paid you a visit here when you got back. You had the book about Sharon Belton on your nightstand and I knew you'd be going to St. Stephen."

He stands there with a strange smile, looking down at me over his cigarette, dangling from his lips, which are curled in a superior half-smile. Master to apprentice.

"I wasn't sure if I should kill you or not in St. Stephen," he says. "On the one hand, I didn't know if you had told the police about me, so I figured I should. On the other hand, how could I kill my St. Paul? So I decided, since we were at Calvary Assembly of God, I'd put you in the grave and see if you rose like Jesus did at Calvary. And sure as hell, you did. You're a bulldog, Jack. Once you get a bone between your teeth you don't let go, do you?"

"No," I say.

"Then when I saw you went fugitive I knew where you'd be headed," he says, cocking his head back toward Laurie Vonn.

"You were right," I say.

"Yes. Well, we can catch up later. Right now we've got work to do," he takes one last drag off the cigarette, then grinds it out casually against Laurie Vonn's neck. She screams in agony behind her taped mouth, and her red-rimmed eyes brim with fresh tears.

Dave turns and looks at her with mild interest. Then he looks at Nicki.

"This one here says she's your lawyer. Is that true?"

"Yes," I say.

"Are you fucking her, Jack?" he smiles at me.

Which is better, yes or no? Which will keep her alive?

"Come on, tell the truth," Dave says to me.

"No," I say.

"I wasn't expecting her, but now that she's here we have to take care of business and be on our way. The little headless horsewoman out front is bound to have somebody out here soon to check on her, so let's get to it. I took a big risk leading you here and I don't like to take risks, as you know. So we have to get to it. To the work."

He grips the black rubber handle of the knife and walks over to Laurie Vonn and grabs the high back of the chair and Laurie screams behind her gag—

"Please—don't—" I say.

"Oh, I'm not gonna kill her," he says, then drags Laurie's chair over beside me and tips the chair back so that Laurie's head is right near my lap as she lies on her back.

Dave throws the knife at me suddenly. It sticks in the floorboards, an inch from my right foot.

"You are," he says. "That's why I left your right hand free. You're right-handed," he says, as if he had shown me a great courtesy.

"You do that one and the other one gets to live another day to sue somebody," Dave says, and then he slides back into his trucker's drawl. "If you're not up to it then I do 'em both, Doc."

He looks at me, waiting.

Think, think, think…

"Do it and get it done and we're outta here in that Sheriff's four-wheeler outside," he looks at his watch. "Pick up the knife, Doc."

I look at the knife stuck in the floor by my leg. I can see Laurie Vonn's terrified eyes beyond it, looking up at me, pleading.

Stall, talk, anything…

"How? How do you want me to—" I begin.

"You know exactly how, Jack," he says, impatient, dropping the trucker drawl. He points at Laurie Vonn's neck. "You wrote about in perfect detail. Decapitation between the sixth and seventh cervical vertebrae, amputation of the hands at the radiocarpal joint."

He waits, watching me. Then he reverts to the low, deep drawl again. "Or, as Killer would say, you just cut between the big bone and the little bone at the back of the neck. You'll feel a snap when the blade cuts through and then it'll lie still and the rest is easy. Like carvin' off a drumstick."

Laurie begins to sob, her chest heaving uncontrollably, tears from her eyes and her nose running as the blood runs down her front.

"Time's a wastin', Doc."

"I—"

"Shut up and cut, Jack, or I'll carve up both little Thanksgiving turkeys. Breasts and thighs," he says. Then he pulls Sallie Fun's Ruger from the back of his waistband. "It would be a shame for all those fans of yours to hear that the bestselling author Jack Rhodes was found with two dead women and a bullet hole in his head, self-inflicted, his prints on the knife. It would be a neat out for me, but I'd prefer to keep you alive, to tell you more stories. But *c'est la vie*," he drawls out the French: "Say law vee."

"Now, cut."

Anything, talk about anything to stall…

"You've read all the books," I say.

"Oh yeah. I'm your number one fan," he husks a short laugh.

"I never mentioned your name," I say. "I didn't remember…talking to you."

"Yeah. Pretty fucking clever how you did it," he says. Then he looks at me funny. "You really didn't remember those three nights we spent. Talking. Hearing all about my Angels?"

"No, I didn't. I didn't know what was going on."

The low, mirthless laugh. "I guess it's been a long, strange trip for you, then," he says. "A little mind-fuck for the big shot writer."

"It was."

"Cut, Jack. You can't stall or placate me with talk."

"How long have you been following me?"

"Oh, I came out here after I read the first book. Paid you a few visits right here in this room, just to keep tabs. I'll say one thing for you, Jack. You know how to keep 'em guessing."

"So do you," I say.

"Enough. Cut, Jack. Cut *now.*"

He stands still as a statue, coiled, waiting for me to make a move.

I lean forward and stretch my right hand out and grab the handle of the knife, pulling my left wrist against the cuff behind me. The steel handcuff cuts into my wrist and I feel blood drip down my hand. Pain from the cut makes me wince and tears come to my eyes. I grip the knife and look down at Laurie Vonn, who stares at me with such terror that I have to look away. She is making horrible little sounds with every breath—short, sharp little whines, muted pleading and crying. The knife is heavy in my hand and my other hand is wrenched in a way that cuts the steel cuffs deeper into my skin and I feel the blood flow around my wrist, making it slippery.

"*CUT,*" Dave says.

I twist around to move the knife toward Laurie Vonn's neck. I avoid looking in her eyes and pull my left wrist harder, behind my back, the pain ravaging but the blood pouring over my hidden hand is making it slippery and I can slide the cuff another half-inch down, over my thumb joint.

If I can just…

I lower the knife toward Laurie Vonn's neck and pull my cuffed hand harder, pulling and wrenching hard—and with a sudden, muted SNAP and a shot of *PAIN* I feel the chrome and polyurethane joint come apart inside my wrist and it is all I can do to keep from screaming. Tears course down my face.

"Get it over with," Dave says, impatient with my tears.

If I can just… If I can take it…if I can take the pain I can…

I slide the knife under Laurie Vonn's neck as I pull my left hand with all my strength against the cuff, tearing into my skin, peeling it back, peeling off muscle and digging into bone—

Oh Dear Sweet Jesus God the PAIN…please let me go…please let me…

Dave comes over me and leans forward, his hands on his knees.

"Last chance," he says. *"Cut."*

I press the knife along the back of Laurie Vonn's neck and she screams behind her gag and I pull my left hand one last time, breaking the knuckle between my second and third fingers—

THE PAIN—! Almost…almost…

"How do I—" my voice shaking from the raging pain, "How do I know you won't kill me and my lawyer if I do it?"

He jacks a round into the chamber of the Ruger.

"Have I ever lied to you, Doc?"

Pulling—PAIN! PAIN!! Jesus PLEASE Jesus if I can—if I can—if I can keep my head while all about me are—

And then I rip my left hand free and lunge up at him with the knife, aiming at his chest and plunging the knife into him, just above his collarbone—

He staggers back, more from surprise than anything else, and then roaring. "FUCKING—SHIT!" Twisting the knife out of him and away from my grasp. I throw a wild right cross at him and connect with his chin, but I'm off balance and I don't have my weight behind it. Dave staggers back and waves the Ruger in my direction. I dive out the doorway of the bedroom as he fires and I hear the sharp whistle of the slug past my left ear.

I scramble across the hallway and into the office and grab *The Dangerous Summer* off the shelf as Dave fires again from the bedroom doorway. I duck behind my desk and take my .45 from the wooden box—my hand shaking violently as Dave appears at the doorway and fires again, right over my head. *Three rounds fired, he's got one left.* I suddenly rise up from behind the desk and fire at Dave, grazing his shoulder. He fires back as I dive back behind the desk. He pulls the trigger again and I hear the empty click of the firing pin. He's out. He ducks behind the doorway as I rise up and fire again, blowing apart the door jamb. I hear him running down the hall and I follow and fire again, blowing out the window by my front door as he opens the lock on the door I aim carefully—*aim at the center of mass*—and I fire and he yells as he opens the door and grabs his right leg and I see blood on his leg and he is out the door and I fire again, too high, over his head, and I fire again, running, as he gets in the SUV and I run after him, firing, shattering the back window of the truck and it starts and pulls away, spinning and careening through the snow covering my rutted drive.

I run out onto the porch and aim at the left rear tire carefully and pull the trigger but I have emptied the cylinder and the hammer clicks uselessly and the SUV bounces and slides away down my drive and onto the county road and the headlights disappear in the snow and the darkness.

CHAPTER FORTY-FOUR

Thirty-six hours later I wake up in a hospital room from a long, dreamless, narcotic sleep, and I see Melvin Beauchamp standing over me. I know it is Melvin before I can see clearly. Melvin is hard to mistake—a 6'5" African American man in a Hugo Boss suit that fits him like a coat of paint.

"Morning," he grins at me.

"Nice suit," I say, my voice dry and rasping, my mind foggy from medication. Melvin opens a bottle of water and hands it to me. I take it in my right hand—after discovering my left arm is hanging from traction wires in a bulky plastic cast.

"If I have to wear a suit to work, it might as well be a *good* suit," Melvin says.

"So you're here on official FBI business," I say, slurring the words slightly.

"I am."

I look at him for a moment, waiting for my mind to clear.

"You gonna tell what that official business is?" I ask.

"You mean, am I here to arrest you?"

"Something like that," I say.

"Nah, we don't want you any more."

"You here to recruit me?"

"Like I said, we don't want you," he laughs.

Then the fog clears and I recall the events at the cabin.

"Nicki and Laurie—?"

"They're okay," he says. "Nicki's here, she just stepped out to take a call, and Laurie Vonn is right down the hall, in her own room. She's shook up and pumped full of meds, but physically she's okay. How about you?"

"I'm alright," I look at my arm, hanging in the air in its bulky plastic cast.

"Nicki gave us a full statement about the cabin, and Laurie corroborated it."

"Have you found him?"

Melvin shakes his head. "Found Sheriff Boyle's car—and Sheriff Boyle—in Manwalk, New York. A mile from the Canadian border. Sheriff's shotgun and service revolver were gone, along with the first aid kit. RCMP is here and we need to know everything you know about this guy. Nicki and Ms. Vonn's descriptions of him only went so far. Doc says you're probably not gonna be awake for long so we need everything you can give us and we need it quick, before you fade on us."

Nicki enters. She is wearing jeans and a pink cashmere turtleneck sweater. Her face is pale and there are red marks around her wrists from the nylon rope. She comes to me and leans forward and kisses the corner of my mouth.

"Thank you," she says.

"For what? Getting you into a situation where you nearly got killed?"

"No. For getting me out of it," she says. "How are you feeling?"

"Alright. Little foggy."

Nicki straightens up and looks at Melvin and says, "Okay, let's talk while he's alert and see if we can't catch this crazy fucker."

I talk for the next hour, telling everything I know to Melvin and Nicki and an officer from the Royal Canadian Mounted Police, who is even taller than Melvin. A stenographer records every word I say. After an hour my hand is throbbing and I am pressing the button on the PCA pump at my bedside for the pain injections almost constantly. My eyelids are drooping and the fog is creeping back.

"Alright, that's enough for now," Melvin says. "We'll pick this up after you get some rest."

I nod, trying to think if there's anything I left out.

"The women—the other victims," I say. "Were any of them waitresses?"

"Two of them had been," Melvin says.

"Truck stops?" I ask.

"Caitlin Stubbs and Sharon Belton worked at truck stops."

"He's a truck driver—or was. Said he used to haul machine parts out of Chicago."

Melvin nods. "That's good. Helps a lot," he says. He turns to make sure the stenographer makes note of it. I can't keep my eyes open any longer and I begin to drift off. Melvin gives me a tap on the shoulder and a nod.

"Good work, Jack," he says. Then he and the RCMP officer and stenographer leave, and Nicki comes to the side of the bed and I open my eyes and see her watching me.

"Why did you go to the cabin?" I ask.

"To oversee the search. I wanted to get there before the FBI. See if there was anything I could find that might lead me to you. And I wanted to make sure their search warrant was as limited as possible. I was really scared. And I was furious with you."

"Still mad?" I am fighting to stay awake.

"No," she says. "You've suffered enough. Laurie asked me to tell you something."

"What?"

"She wanted me to tell you 'Thank you.' "

She smiles at me, then goes to the window and closes the blinds and I am asleep before she turns back.

CHAPTER FORTY-FIVE

Three days later, I have just arrived at LAX with Nicki and Melvin Beauchamp when Melvin's cell rings and he stops and says "Hold up," to Nicki and me. Melvin listens to his phone, then points to a television near the gate, and the three of us walk over to it and I see the face of David Doyle Harris, as he was identified from the forged license in his wallet—*Dave*, as I knew him—staring back at me from his commercial truck driver's license photo on CNN.

David Doyle Harris pulled a stolen Cadillac into the parking lot at Belvedere Hospital in Franklin, Oklahoma last night, propped Claire Boyle's shotgun under his chin, and blew his head through the roof of the car.

I feel Nicki stiffen beside me when she sees his face. We watch the coverage as Melvin talks to his boss in Washington. CNN doesn't know much, but we see Dave's body on a stretcher, the blood-soaked wallet chain dangling from under a bloody sheet, and a quick shot of the blood-spattered car interior. Dave's body is loaded into the Franklin County Coroner's van and Melvin gets off his call.

"Looks like he knew he was about to bleed out from that shot you gave him in the leg. They think he drove to the hospital, then decided he'd rather die right there than turn himself in." We watch CNN as the news breaks, and I see more about me, and about Nicki and Laurie Vonn.

Did he go out like that…like Sara…as some kind of message to me?

Like a lot of things, the answer died with David Doyle Harris.

Nicki looks at Melvin. "What now?" she says. The three of us have come to L.A. to talk to Detective Marsh, to see if there's anything more I can help them with. Nicki worked out a deal with LAPD, West Virginia, and Maryland to drop all of the pending charges against me—grand theft auto and felony evasion, and a string of other things—in return for my compliance in helping to find Dave.

But now Dave is found. David Doyle Harris is dead, and Melvin calls LAPD and it is decided that we should go ahead to Parker Center so I can tell them what I know and make a statement for the record.

"Might as well get to see Marsh squirm a little," Melvin says. I know Melvin takes satisfaction from this. Marsh got a lot of TV time in pursuit of me, and Melvin hates showboating as much as he loves shooting bad guys.

Melvin calls for our ride to pull up, and while we wait we watch the CNN coverage, as more information about David Doyle Harris comes in. He had owned and operated his own truck, hauling machine parts on different routes all around the country. He had no police record, and no known address. "We know the license was forged. He had half a dozen documents with different names. Who knows what his real name was. He was as off the grid as you can get. Probably lived in his rig," Melvin says.

I wonder how long Dave had followed me. I think of my kitchen door standing open, and the noise that woke me that night—the floorboard that cracked—

How many times had he been in my home? How many times had he watched me sleep?

I think of things—a spare set of keys that I thought I had lost…

"Jesus," I say under my breath, and a slight shudder moves through me. Nicki looks at me and touches my shoulder.

"Come on," she says, and she and Melvin and I leave the terminal. The last thing I watch of the TV coverage is a shaky handheld shot of Dave's rectangular wire-framed glasses, lying on the pavement outside the car, shattered and covered with blood.

We go out to the curb and get in the black Chevrolet that pulls up for us, a young FBI field agent at the wheel. Melvin gets in the passenger seat and Nicki and I get in back. The young agent hands Melvin a large manila envelope.

"What's this?" Melvin says.

"Security video from the parking structure at the mall in Trenton." The young agent's eyes flick up at me in the rearview mirror. "You might find it interesting," he says to me. Melvin and the young agent talk about coordinating agents and flights to and from Oklahoma, their conversation punctuated by Melvin's constant phone calls.

CHAPTER FORTY-SIX

The meeting at Parker Center was uneventful. Marsh was formal, as his supervisors and the District Attorney looked on, and he expressed "regret about the course of the investigation" without looking at me. My old pal Detective Larson was there, sporting a black necktie a mortician would be proud of. I don't think he looked at me once during the hour that I spoke, on the record.

After I finished, Melvin played the time-stamped security video from the mall parking structure in Trenton. The video showed Dave, about to break into Laurie Vonn's Honda, then moving into the shadows when I walked past. *The footsteps I heard.* Then, once I was gone, Dave broke into the Honda with a Slim Jim and climbed into the back. A few minutes later, Laurie Vonn got in her car and drove off. Dave then forced her—with the point of the knife in her neck—to drive to my cabin.

But the most striking part of the video was at the beginning. Just before Dave broke into the Honda, he punched out the lens of the left rear tail light with the handle of his knife. He wanted to make sure the Honda could be seen in the dark, through the storm. He knew I was following her. He was probably following me since I went to her place. He was waiting there for me to show up. And I had done exactly as he planned. I had been so preoccupied with keeping a step ahead of the police I didn't realize he was ten steps ahead of me. Just like Killer—smart, meticulous, leaving nothing to chance.

"Marsh has some serious egg on his face," Melvin says happily to Nicki and me in the car as we pull away from Parker Center. "Not only did he NOT catch the guy, he wasted a lot of time and money chasing the wrong guy. He was adamant about you, Jackie boy—one hundred percent convinced you killed those girls."

"How about you?" I ask him.

Melvin shakes his head. "Always let the facts lead my judgment, not the other way around."

"And where did the facts lead you?"

"To a damned truck full of oranges," Melvin says, and turns and shoots me a glare in the backseat. I can't keep the grin off my face. Melvin turns back and looks out the window.

"We would have caught you, you know," Melvin says after a moment. "Eventually you would have fucked up."

"I know," I say.

The car is quiet for a moment.

"Hey, Melvin?" I say.

"Yeah?" He turns and looks back at me again.

"If you had caught up with me but I ran from you...?"

A slight smile from Melvin.

"I wouldn't have killed you," he says. "Unless you shot at us."

"I wouldn't have done that."

"Then I'd have put you down but I wouldn't have killed you," he says casually. He points a long finger at my knee like a gun. "Woulda gone for that left knee you favor, unless I had to go higher." He grins at me and I smile back, but I know he means it and I know he knows.

"Tell you one thing," he adds. "If I'd have caught up with you right after I found that phone in that damned truck full of oranges I'da blown your head straight off." He looks at me and I smile and look over at Nicki next to me, who is resting her temple on the tip of her index finger and looking at us.

"Can we talk about something else?" She says.

CHAPTER FORTY-SEVEN

The city of Los Angeles had graciously offered to pick up the tab for our first-class airfare and two hotel rooms, and Nicki had graciously accepted. "Wouldn't want to appear ungrateful," she smirked at Melvin as the FBI car pulled up to the Bonaventure downtown.

Nicki and I get out. Melvin has to return to LAX to catch a flight to Oklahoma City, where he will oversee the autopsy and the forensic work on David Doyle Harris and his stolen Cadillac.

Melvin gets out and gives Nicki a quick hug and shakes my hand and says, "Next time write a nice love story or something, okay, Jack?"

"Yeah," Nicki agrees, turning to me. "Something where nobody dies."

"People die in love stories," I say.

"Why do people have to die in love stories?" Melvin asks, with more outrage than I've ever seen from him.

"Because people die in all of the best stories," I say.

"Why?" Melvin says.

"Because that's what people do," I say.

Melvin and Nicki exchange a glance.

"You're a grim motherfucker, you know that?" Melvin says.

I smile pleasantly.

"I wouldn't want to live in your head," Melvin says.

"There are times I'm not crazy about it myself," I say. "But what's the alternative?"

"You need to get out more," Melvin says, and then he gets in his car and it drives away.

★★★

Nicki and I have a nice meal at the hotel, sitting side by side in a corner booth. We chat about the weather in Los Angeles, earthquakes, Malibu mudslides, our favorite movies—about anything and everything except David Doyle Harris and the last few days. And over dessert, a crème brulee we were supposed to share—of which Nicki ate a total of two microscopic bites—I ask her a question that I've been wondering about. It is late and we are the last diners in the dim, elegant room.

"That night," I say. "At the Mirabelle. When you got mad at me for tracking down Sallie Fun..."

She looks at me and says nothing.

"I told you I thought there was something else—something more that was bothering you than just having a reckless client," I say. "What was it?"

She is quiet for a moment. She takes a sip of her wine. I wait.

Then she speaks, softly.

"My childhood sweetheart was a boy named Michael Furie," she says, finally. Her words come slowly, carefully. "We started dating in the ninth grade, and we went to Brown together. We were...he was everything to me," she says, and takes another drink, then a long, deep breath.

"He asked me to marry him the day we graduated. The wedding was a month away when he was mugged one night, just a few blocks from where we were living. The guy took his money, then shot him. He died three days later."

She is quiet again for yet another long moment. I keep my mouth shut, and wait some more.

"I sat in court and watched the state's case fall apart. Watched them make mistake after mistake. When they asked the guy why he shot Michael after he'd already given him his money, the guy just shrugged. 'No reason,' was all he said. He got six years for it," she says, her voice edged with bitterness. "That's when I decided to become a prosecutor."

I say nothing. We sit there and let the long silence play out again.

"It's just that I couldn't—I can't stand the thought of losing someone again that I care about," she says so softly I can hardly hear her.

"You said you weren't sure if you trusted me."

"Yes."

"Still not sure?" I ask.

"No, I'm sure," she says. "You've earned it."

The light from the candle in the center of our table catches the fine, narrow band of downy blonde at her hairline and makes it shimmer bright gold.

"What did you think about what Melvin said?" she asks me.

"What, about shooting me in the knee?"

"No," she smiles. "About how you need to get out more. Get out of that head of yours."

"I think he's right," I say. "I think I've always known the time would come, but I didn't feel like I was ready. Until recently."

She takes another tiny sip of wine.

"You never talk about her," she says.

I know what she's talking about, but I pretend like I don't and give her a blank look.

"About Sara," she says.

"What do you want to know?"

"Who she was. Why you loved her. Why…" she begins, then chooses to let me complete the question.

"Why she killed herself?"

"Yes," she says. "I don't expect you to talk about it, but it's part of your past and part of who you are now…so I thought I'd ask."

"I don't know why," I say.

She looks at me. There is a deep, pure empathy in her eyes that raises my heart into my throat. I push the painful feeling away, out of long habit.

"I don't know why," I say again.

I don't want to talk about this. Not now, not yet.

I look away, lost in myself. The deep feeling I was sharing with Nicki only a moment ago dissolves into something else—different feelings. Pain. Regret. I was completely focused on this lovely, brilliant, vibrant woman just seconds ago, and now it's gone. Just…gone.

Did something in me die along with Sara? When you have ached for one, how can you ache for another? Smarter people than me have lost their way in this tangle of thorns. I have no guide, no map, because there is none.

Nicki gives my hand a little squeeze, bringing me back to her, to this booth, to this moment.

"We're both exhausted," she says. "We've been through a hell of a lot these last few weeks. Last few years, for that matter."

She squeezes my hand tighter and waits until I turn to her and meet her steady gaze.

"Why don't you do us all a favor and join the living," she says.

CHAPTER FORTY-EIGHT

The wake-up call from the front desk rings at seven-thirty a.m. I have a nine o'clock appointment with a specialist in Beverly Hills who is going to rebuild my wrist and hand. I dress and think about calling Nicki but decide to let her sleep. Her plans are to have breakfast in bed, then lie around the pool all day. After that we will head back to the airport for an eleven p.m. flight back home.

The lobby of the hand specialist's office is white, with a black slate floor and a soaring ceiling peaked by a massive domed skylight webbed with ribbons of shredded copper. The lobby is dominated by an enormous sculpture of what is obviously intended to be a penis.

I give my name to the receptionist, whose physical beauty seems so perfect it's almost inhuman. I turn from the desk and go sit in a molded plastic pink neo-revival bullshit incredibly uncomfortable copy of an Eames chair and stare at the bronze penis, which is about the size of an adult tiger shark. *I guess I could see it in a urologist's office, but...*

I look around and notice I am the only male patient waiting in the lobby, and then the sculpture makes a little more sense. I pick up a brochure and learn that hands are the new frontier in cosmetic surgery. Apparently people are lining up in Los Angeles to have surgery to make their hands look younger. I wonder if my hand will wind up looking younger. Will they have to do the other one too, just for symmetry?

I am called by a nurse—another young woman who looks like she just leapt from the cover of *Glamour.* My wrist and hand are x-rayed and examined by the movie-star-handsome Beverly Hills surgeon, who has discarded the traditional white coat for a pinstriped Savile Row suit. His hands are so youthful and perfectly manicured that I actually feel shame when he looks at my mangled wrist and hand. He tells me I will need one "procedure," which means surgery, and after physical therapy I will be good as new. Typing won't be a problem, although I will need a specially designed ergonomic keyboard.

"But will I ever play the violin?" I ask.

★★★

The hotel car takes me back to the Bonaventure and I find Nicki out at the pool, sunning herself. I pause for a few seconds, just to look at her. She is lying on her stomach on a chaise, the straps open on the top of her bright yellow bikini to avoid tan lines. After all the tailored suits, after the jeans and sweaters and the fitted leather jacket, she is now another revelation entirely— delicate shoulders, narrow waist, the gentle arc of her naked back, her legs toned and tanned. I could stand here for the rest of the afternoon, cataloguing her fine qualities, but I go to her and I am disappointed when she fastens the straps on her top and slips into her hotel bathrobe.

We order lunch at a table near the pool, under a bright yellow umbrella. We talk about my doctor visit, about cosmetic surgery and Los Angeles, and about the last time I was here, when I fled the interview with Marsh. We talk about her plans for the afternoon, which include a massage and a nap. She asks me what I'm going to do and I tell her I have no plans.

"You said you were going to get Sara's things when you were here before," she says as she nibbles on a cold shrimp.

"Yes," I say.

"But you never did," she says.

"No, they're still here."

She looks at me for a moment but doesn't say anything. Then she puts down her shrimp and says, "After my fiancé Michael died, I kept his things— pictures, gifts we'd given each other and stuff—kept them out, all over my apartment, everywhere. And little by little I took them down and put them away over the years, until they were all put away. But I left the engagement ring he gave me in my everyday jewelry drawer. It's still there. I see it every morning. I didn't know why I left it in there at the time, but I just couldn't bring myself to stick it in a box somewhere I'd never see it. And now I think I did it because it doesn't hurt so much anymore to see things that remind me of him. It's part of the past, that's all. It doesn't make it any less meaningful to me, it's just a little reminder of something in my life that will always be with me, and it's a comfort to always have it nearby, but in the back of the drawer."

★★★

Nicki heads off for her massage and I go back to my room for a nap, but I don't sleep. At four o'clock I finally get up and sit on the edge of the bed and look out the window at the San Gabriel Mountains. After a long time I pick up the phone and call the storage place where Sara's things are, and once again I arrange for some boxes to be placed there for me. Then I call the front desk to have a hotel car take me there and wait while I box up her things.

Two hours later I am riding in the back of the hotel's Town Car as we pull into the parking lot at the storage space. I tell the driver I will need an hour to pack up everything and he goes off to get a bite to eat.

I walk down the row of doors, to the storage unit I have been paying for for five years. I put my key in the lock and turn it and enter the little room, which has a musty, mildewy smell, and I reach for the light switch and flip it on and the single, bare light bulb in the ceiling illuminates my past.

The room is about the size of an average bedroom, the floor is concrete, the walls cinderblock. The bare bulb overhead, caged in steel, casts a dim yellow light over the boxes and items scattered haphazardly around the space. I stand at the doorway and take it all in. Some of Sara's things are already boxed up, some are stacked sloppily—a pile of clothes in one corner, a pile of books in the other. The stack of corrugated boxes I ordered is leaning next to the door, flattened, with a plastic strap around them. I find the box-cutter the manager left for me, as well as a thick roll of brown packing tape in a plastic dispenser.

I pick up the box cutter and slice open the plastic band around the boxes. I build the first box, bending and folding the stiff cardboard, then leaving the top open. I turn to Sara's things and, finally, pick a place to start. I begin with her clothes piled in the corner, folding each item carefully, then placing it in the box. I fill the first box, then close it and tape it up, then build the next box and look around the room for what to pack next: more clothes, some papers, files, magazines, and I look at the massive wooden trunk that she bought at a junk store before we met.

I kneel at the huge, oak trunk—*her hope chest,* I had called it, teasing her. I open the heavy lid and see the bright red wool scarf she wore when it was cold, and in the corner is the shoebox with her jewelry and photographs. I pick up the shoebox and tape it shut without looking at it—I don't want to look at the photos. But I fumble with the tape roller and the box falls from my hands and the contents spill out and I see the pictures: *Sara and me at Santa Monica pier, the two of us at dinner, at a New Year's eve party*—and I can smell her scent now, coming from the clothes inside the chest, and my heart hurts and my eyes burn and I start to cry.

Don't do this, I think, and I collect the photographs and put them back in the box but it doesn't stop my crying and the tears fall over the pictures and the clothes and the jewelry and I don't fight it because I don't remember crying over her, although I'm sure I did when I was drinking. But this is the first time I have cried over her when I was sober and it hurts and I let it hurt and I sit in the corner behind the enormous hope chest and let the tears come and they don't stop for a long time.

Finally I wipe my face on my shoulder and I sit up straight and I begin to sort the things from the hope chest into the box I have put together and as I do I notice a small packet of letters at the bottom of the chest. There are a dozen or so. Five of them are from me—love letters I quickly put aside. There are two letters from her mother, four from her best friend Susan, who had moved to London, and one envelope with a return address I don't recognize. *Dr. Evelyn Stillman, M.D.*

Sara's doctor was a woman whose last name was Frank. I remember this because Sara and I had begun to try and have a child a year or so before we planned to marry. Sara was an only child, like me, and we both wanted to start a family right away—possibly a large one if we had the means. And I remember Dr. Frank because Sara hadn't gotten pregnant after months of trying. And, after visiting a clinic to eliminate myself as the cause, I finally persuaded Sara to see Dr. Frank in her Pasadena office for fertility treatments.

But this is a doctor I've never heard of, with a Santa Monica address. I open the letter and read the letterhead. *Dr. Evelyn Stillman, M.D., Obstetrics and Gynecology.*

The letter is handwritten, and brief.

Dear Sara,

Please return my calls right away. I know how painful and upsetting your last visit was, but you must understand, there IS hope—even for stage four patients. But only if you begin aggressive treatment immediately. As I mentioned, there is no way to know how long you have had the condition, since routine PAP tests do not detect it. I know you feel hopeless, but you have to fight, and start right away. I have given your information to Dr. Linman, the oncologist at Cedars we spoke about. He is an expert at treating ovarian cancer, and his patients have a higher survival rate than almost any other doctor in the state. I urge you to see him right away, and to begin counseling as well, Sara. Please don't give up, I beg you. You do have a chance, but only if you fight!

Evelyn

The letter is dated three weeks before Sara's suicide.

★★★

I sit back against the concrete wall of the storage room and stare at nothing. Numb, spent from crying and now this...

An answer. But an answer birthing new questions. Sara was outspoken and independent, but she could be passive about certain things. She hated doctors and she could be feckless about her health. She smoked too much. She wouldn't complain if she was sick or in pain. She had a reluctance to talk about herself, or to admit she was having a problem. At first I mistook this for stoicism, but I came to realize it was fear. Of the unknown, the unfamiliar, or appearing weak or incapacitated or sick... In times she was troubled, she turned her attention to others—to her students, to me, to her friends.

Some puzzle pieces came together. The visits to her doctor, supposedly for fertility treatments, were probably visits to Stillman that she kept hidden from me. Even if she had survived the cancer, she wouldn't have been able to have children. She had gone off her antidepressants around the time of Dr. Stillman's letter. She must have simply given up.

But the missing pieces. How could she have kept this from me? How could she go on planning a wedding, a life with me, and maintained a contented demeanor when she must have been terrified? No matter how tough and stoic she liked to appear, how? Was she afraid I would abandon her, as her father had? Was I so absorbed in my struggle to build a career that she found me unreachable? Was she protecting me? And why no note? The letter I hold in my hand is the closest thing to an explanation that she left behind. Is that why she kept it? *Why didn't she fight? Why did she do it?*

Why?

I sit with this question. I have lived with it for years, but in a more abstract form. I will have to live with this new form of it now, and it will never go away.

But now, as I sit here holding this terrible letter, feeling nothing; numb, spent, I think of Nicki's words. Now, even though this question will always be there, someday, maybe, I can put it in the back of the drawer.

★★★

I sit against the rough cinderblock wall for a time, then get up and fold the letter into my back pocket and return to my packing. I move away from the trunk, to a pile of books, and I notice three banker's boxes along the wall next to them. I don't recognize the boxes so I pull the first one out from against the wall and look at it. I don't remember it but that doesn't mean anything. I was mad with grief and booze when I put her things in here. I lift the box and I'm surprised at its weight. I slice open the packing tape on the box with the box cutter and lift the lid and find several layers of plastic wrap across the top.

What the hell...?

I slice open the plastic wrap and then, suddenly, I know what I will find—

I rip open the plastic and there is Beverly Grace's head, rotted, smelling of death, her hands in front of her face in a praying position.

I knew what it was before I saw it.

I stand alone in the dim little room, stunned, nauseated, my mind reeling, the dingy gray walls spinning around me—

I look at the other two boxes and I know what they contain.

Did I put them here?

No, that's impossible...

I rip open the next box, tearing through the corrugated cardboard and plastic wrap and find the head of Sharon Belton—her dark brown almond eyes open and shriveled and staring at nothing, covered with a milky, mildewed film.

I hold the head in my hands and then drop it into the box and move to the next box, choking and retching and desperate to remember, but memories don't always obey—

"Merry Christmas, Jack."

I whirl around and see David Doyle Harris standing in the doorway, holding Claire Boyle's service revolver. I step back, falling over Sara's hope chest and upending it and dropping the box cutter. I sprawl amid Sara's clothes and jewelry and photographs as Dave closes the door behind him and picks up the box cutter and pockets it.

"You look like you've seen a ghost," he says, holding Claire Boyle's .38 on me. He is pale and disheveled, and I can tell from the tilt of his body that he is favoring his right leg. His thinning hair is dyed blonde and he wears a short, scruffy beard and new glasses with large, black, horn-rimmed frames. It takes me a moment to really believe it's him. I slide down, as if hiding behind the hope chest will protect me.

"I'm as real as rain," he says. "You told me you couldn't find Sara's face after she blew it off. You talked about that a lot. That information came in handy. It was an inspiration." He waves the gun toward the door. "Come on now, let's go. We've only got a couple hours before they print that poor headless fool with the Cadillac and figure out it's not me."

"You followed me here?" I say. *Talk to him…*

"Just get up."

I look at the banker's boxes.

"Did I—? Did I put those boxes here?

"You really don't remember?"

"No. Tell me," I shout at him.

"That's for me to know and you to find out, Jack."

"Tell me."

He laughs his low laugh. "All in due time, my friend. If you want to know more you're going to have to come with me." He raises the gun. "Let's go. We've got a lot more to talk about. I've got more stories for you. Some things you're really going to like. So move," he waves Claire Boyle's gun toward the door. "We've history to make."

"Not until you tell me what happened," I say.

"I'm not gonna fuck around with you, Doc," he drawls.

"I'm not going anywhere with you until you tell me what happened."

"No, turn that around: you're not gonna know what happened *unless* you come with me," he says.

"Come with you where?"

"A journey of self-discovery," he says. "Now get up or I'll shoot you dead right where you're sitting. I let you dig yourself out of one grave but you won't be digging out of the next one."

"If you kill me you won't have anyone—no one to tell your story," I say.

"That's a chance I'm willing to take. Now get up right now or your story ends here," he says, and points Claire Boyle's service revolver at my face.

A thought occurs to me.

Is it loaded?

"Move," he says, tightening his grip on the gun.

Think, think, remember...is it loaded?

He looks over the sights of Claire's gun, pointing it at my face.

Check the safety...the safety is off...but WILL IT FIRE?

"One more second and my patience is out, Doc. You fucked me before but this is *it*."

Please God...

"Alright, then. So long, Doc. Been real," he says.

His fingernail whitens slightly as he squeezes the trigger—

And I lift the shotgun inside the hope chest and Sara's 12 gauge Mossberg in matte black blows open the end of the wooden chest and a red hole explodes in the middle of Dave's throat and he is dead before he slams against the cinderblock wall.

I watch Claire's .38 bounce from his hand as his body flops down to the concrete floor and I sit very, very still and my eyes don't leave him for a long, long time.

CHAPTER FORTY-NINE

"So," Dr. Benjamin Abrams says to me.

I am sitting across from him, in a leather chair that tilts back. If I lean all the way back I can see the rooftops of the fancy buildings on the upper east side through the large window beside me.

"So," I say back to him.

It has been four weeks since I killed the man known as David Doyle Harris. Yesterday I called Abrams to talk, but now I suddenly don't feel like talking.

Abrams looks at the small cast on my arm.

"Your wrist healing up okay?" he asks.

"Yeah."

Abrams sits like a Buddha in a cardigan, watching me passively. We could spend all afternoon like this and I'm certain he would never seem ill at ease or impatient. I look over his shoulder, at the shelves behind him. The late afternoon sun slants into the room, bathing the pre-Columbian statuettes behind him in a lazy glow. We have gone through the pleasantries, talked briefly about the conclusion of things in Los Angeles, including my discovery of Sara's letter from her doctor. And now the silence is piling up.

"I'm seeing Nicki tonight," I say finally. "She's not representing me anymore, now that the case is all settled."

Abrams nods. "Okay," he says.

"She's making me dinner," I say. "I'm supposed to be at her place an hour after we're done."

"Sounds nice," he says.

I rub my hand through my hair. Why is this so goddamned hard?

"I like her," I say.

"Good," Abrams says. I search his eyes for something more, but he is opaque.

"Don't you think the impassive Freudian thing can be taken too far?" I say.

Abrams chuckles. "Why don't you tell me what's on your mind?" he says.

The light has moved imperceptibly up the shelves behind Abrams as the sun sets, illuminating a row of books. I can't make out the titles.

"I want to see her. I've thought a lot about her, about being with her. And I want that," I say. "To be honest, I don't really know why I wanted to see you."

"Did you make the date with her before you called me?" he asks.

"Yes."

"Would you rather talk at some other time?"

"No."

"So why is it important that we talk before you see her?" Abrams asks.

"I don't know," I say. "There have been times when we were together and I wanted her so badly...I'm not sure why I'm hesitating now."

"What's changed since those times?" Abrams says.

I shake my head. "It was different. More spontaneous, I guess."

"Did you feel like she wanted the same thing, when you were with her before?"

"I think so," I say. "But it wasn't right—for her. She was my lawyer and she had...doubts about me."

"What kind of doubts?"

"She was angry with me for being reckless...for confronting the guy in Jersey City, and then running from the police."

"So you knew, at least unconsciously, that she wouldn't respond in kind."

"Yeah, I guess so."

"And how does she feel now?"

"I think maybe she wants the same thing now. I hope she does."

"So now that it's a real possibility—the two of you being together—you're hesitating."

"Yeah."

"Any thoughts as to why that might be?" Abrams asks.

"I don't know," I say. "Maybe I'm not as ready as I thought. Maybe that's why I wanted to talk to you."

"Well, the timing of your visit seems pretty significant to me," he says.

"What do you mean?"

"In that you felt the need to talk to me before seeing her."

I look out the window as last moments of sunlight skim the tops of only the tallest buildings.

"Maybe I want permission," I say.

"That's not my job."

"Okay," I say. "Maybe I'm afraid."

"Ah," Abrams says. "Now you're talking. What are you afraid of?"

"I don't know," I say.

"You stood up to two men with guns pointed at you and now you're afraid of dinner?"

"You got it," I say.

"So, what is it about dinner with Nicki?" Abrams says. "What are you afraid of?"

"Somebody getting hurt."

"Somebody?"

"Me or her."

"You told me before that you haven't been with anyone since Sara's death," Abrams says.

"That's right."

"So," he says.

"So…maybe I feel responsible for Sara. Maybe I did something wrong, or maybe I should have done something and didn't do it. Why the fuck does someone do that? She didn't even leave a fucking note," I say. "She found out she was sick and she just…checked out. So it's just guilt, I guess."

Abrams the Buddha just looks at me.

"I'm tired of feeling guilty," I say. "Will you please fucking say something, Doc?"

"I'm not sure guilt is the big deal here," Abrams says. "You told me before that you don't like being bullied and you don't like being afraid. Who's making you afraid? Who's bullying you now?"

I lean back. Look out at the rooftops again.

"She is," I say, finally. "Sara. I'm afraid to be with someone because of what she did."

Far away, below us, I hear a doorman whistle for a cab.

"I guess I'm really mad at her," I say.

Abrams raises an eyebrow.

CHAPTER FIFTY

An hour later I knock on Nicki's door. She opens it and gives me a brief kiss on the cheek. I have a bottle of Chateau Montelena for her and a bottle of Martinelli's sparkling cider for me. She puts them on her kitchen counter while I close the door. She opens the wine and I open my Martinelli's and we fill two wine glasses and then clink them together and drink. Then she puts her glass down and darts around her kitchen, steaming Littleneck clams and boiling linguini and sautéing spinach and opening the oven door every ten seconds to check on the lyonnaise potatoes she's making for the first time.

When dinner is ready we carry it out to her small balcony and eat, surrounded by the lights of the city and bathed in the warm glow from the candle she has placed in the center of the table. She is radiant in the light. I eat hungrily and it's good. She talks about her day and I talk about mine, including my visit with Abrams. Nicki listens to me talk about my session with Abrams and says nothing.

When we're finished we clear the table on the balcony and bring the dishes inside and move close around each other in her small kitchen, cleaning up. When the kitchen is spotless we settle down on her sofa. She is wearing a bright Pucci summer dress that clings around her waist and hips. Her legs are bare and tanned and she slips off her turquoise slingback sandals and curls her legs under herself in a way that I find astonishingly intimate and sexual. We talk about the weather, then we talk about politics and her family. And then we're quiet for a while.

"So can you forgive her?" she asks, after half a minute of silence.

"Yeah," I say. "As soon as I realized how angry I was I knew I had to let go of it. So I let go of it."

"You make it sound easy," she says.

"I can be pretty disciplined when I know what I have to do," I say.

"Have you forgiven yourself?" "Pretty much," I say. "That may take a little longer, but I'm making progress."

She brushes her fingers across the back of my hand and looks at me. I touch her thigh, just below her hemline, and then I lean forward and kiss her. She is very still and she opens her mouth slightly. After a long moment she takes my face in her soft hands and takes her lips from mine.

"Sure this is a good idea?" she says, her mouth so close to mine I can feel every word.

"No, but I'm sure that I want it," I say.

"That doesn't necessarily mean it's a good idea," she says.

"Well," I say. "You have to start somewhere."

I slide my fingers down a little, following the curve of her leg beneath her knee, making lazy little circles over the back of her silky calf.

"And since the charges are dropped, you're no longer representing me," I say.

"There are still a couple of loose ends," she says. "Paperwork isn't done on the grand theft deal with Maryland yet. There are a few more billable hours." The corners of her mouth turn up in a slight, sly smile. On any other woman that smile would seem like a practiced, coquettish look, deliberately chosen from a repertoire of flirting. But on Nicki it's genuine and spontaneous and maddeningly attractive.

"You're fired," I say. She laughs, cocking her head to the side, then tucking an errant lock behind her ear.

"You've been alone for a long time," she says.

"Yes."

She puts her hand on mine against her thigh and looks at me. I slide my hand further up her bare thigh and the talking stops and I kiss her again and we do that for a long time.

Later we make our way to her bedroom and I slip her summer dress off as I kiss her and shed my clothes and then we are naked in her bed and I can't get enough of her. We make a fine mess of her bed and we do all the things that teenaged lovers and lonely people do when they finally connect with someone, and it goes on for hours.

Finally we lie next to each other and recover ourselves.

"Been a long time for me," I say.

"Me, too," Nicki says.

"Tell me about that," I say.

She bites her lip and her eyes move back and forth they way they do when she is thinking deeply about something.

"I think I compare men to Michael. Actually, I compare them to the memory of him, which isn't fair, I know. It's hard to know where the difference lies between the memory of something real and the fantasy of how you'd like to remember it. And it's impossible for anyone to compete with a fantasy. But I'm working on it," she says, and moves closer to me and brushes her lips across my neck. "This is nice," she says.

"I agree," I say, and we lie there quietly, skin against skin, all up and down both of our bodies. She is warm and smooth and soft.

"I'm selling the cabin," I say.

"Good," she says. "You need a fresh start. Where will you move?"

"I was thinking of moving to the city," I say. "Near here."

"Yeah?" she says.

"Where else can I get steamed clams like that?" I say.

"Could you write here?" she says. "Away from your isolation?"

"I was thinking I could work for you," I say. "You said you need a new investigator."

She smiles. A sardonic half-smile that I haven't seen from her yet. I find it indescribably arousing.

"I think we make a pretty good team," I say. "What do you think? You and me going around, solving crimes?"

"Don't you have a job?" she says. "I seem to remember you've done pretty well for yourself writing books."

"Sure, but I can do both," I say. "I'll write books during the day and at night I'll fight crime with you."

"I don't work nights."

"I seem to remember you showing up at my hotel room at three in the morning to check on your client," I say.

"That was different."

"Okay then, I'll fight crime on my own. And then I'll come here and mess up your bed with you, late at night, after I've vanquished the bad guys."

"When will you sleep?"

"When does Batman sleep?" I say, and she laughs and I take her in my arms and kiss her deeply and we make love until the Roman shades on her bedroom windows turn iridescent blue with the pre-dawn light.

And then we sleep.

FINAL CHAPTER

———

"We see the past through tears, which render events into perfection. But our everyday lives assault us with the imperfect present—moment by moment, endless and indifferent—the only eternity we know. But in lonely moments we are haunted by what has passed, and helplessly beguiled toward a future perfect tense."

From *Killer Unmasked*

With these words, I concluded the *Killer* series. My publishers were graciously willing to let me off the hook for the fourth book, in light of the circumstances. But I knew I had to finish it, to put the final nail in the coffin. The chapter of my life that began with Sara's death, so long ago, had to be put to rest. I changed Laurie Vonn's name, changed her circumstances, and ended the series with the death of Killer—from a shotgun blast through his throat, fired by Katherine Kendall.

The publicity surrounding the events regarding David Doyle Harris catapulted sales of *Killer Unmasked* into the stratosphere. In three months, *Killer Unmasked* sold more copies than all three of the previous books combined. I instructed Joel to privately distribute all of my profit from the sales of the book among Laurie Vonn and the families of Caitlin Stubbs, Sharon Belton, and Beverly Grace.

I went to Sara's grave for the first time since her funeral, on one of my trips to Los Angeles to have my wrist and hand rebuilt. I left flowers and said goodbye. I sent her things to her mother, who never responded. It is just as well.

I sold the cabin and moved to the city—I'm not going to tell you where. But one of the many things that have changed in my life since I killed David

Doyle Harris ten months ago is that I no longer crave isolation. I enjoy the friends I am slowly coming to know, and Nicki and I are together pretty much all of the time. I even got a dog. A ragged terrier of dubious ancestry. And instead of trooping through the woods and ruminating over ruins, I walk my terrier, Joe, through the streets of the city—sometimes alone, sometimes with Nicki, but always with a pocketful of doggie treats and ridiculous plastic gloves people use to pick up dog droppings.

I attend writer's conferences and speak sometimes and give interviews and book signings. The initial fury of media attention about David Doyle Harris lasted until the next big scandal took over the cable news, and I have settled into a routine that begins with work each day, then a workout at the gym down the street, and ends with a meal with Nicki and occasionally friends.

My new apartment is large and full of windows and light. The view of the city is spectacular and I like my neighbors and they seem to like me. The apartment has a bedroom, a guest room, an office, a large living room with a fireplace, and a spacious, brand new kitchen where I am perfecting my culinary skills through trial and error and Nicki's unvarnished opinions. Melvin comes by whenever he's in town, and one night after dinner at my place he took a sip of his favorite single malt and sat on the couch across from Nicki and me and said, "So what are you gonna write about now, Jackie? Now that you've killed the killer." He gives me an arch smile.

"I'm working on an idea right now," I say. "In fact, I was planning to call you in the next week or so to pick your brain."

"Funny you should say that," Melvin says. "I was thinking of calling to ask you the same thing."

"Why would you want to pick my brain?" I ask, surprised.

Melvin tilts his head and lifts his eyebrows—his version of a shrug. He is not generous with compliments and he thinks for a while before he says, "Bureau's full of good guys. Smart, thorough...but they're Boy Scouts. Sometimes they're not the most imaginative people on earth. You're a good guy, but you've got that dark, crazy thing going on in that head of yours. I don't know anybody who knows how to think like a bad guy like you can. And there's a case we're working where you might have some insight."

"Wow," I say. "Do I get a badge and a gun?"

Nicki glares at me.

"No badge, no gun," Melvin says. "Maybe a library card, if you're good."

"Hell, I got one of those already," I say. "What's the case?"

"Three homicides, all women. Actresses…sort of. Actually, I thought of you because you might know something about one of them from your old days knocking around Hollywood—" Melvin is just warming to his subject and for a moment a trickle of memories from that time spill from somewhere in my head. But Melvin stops when he sees the look on Nicki's face.

"We can talk later," Melvin says, looking at the storm clouds gathering in Nicki's eyes. "I think I'm already in trouble."

"Yes, you are," Nicki says. "Don't encourage him. He thinks he's Batman."

Melvin laughs.

"I'm talking about reading books and briefs, not flying around like the caped crusader," he says.

"Stick to the library," Nicki says to Melvin with a level look. And even fearless Melvin seems smaller all of a sudden.

"I wouldn't dream of dragging him out into the real world of desperados," he says to her. "Sorry, crusader," he says to me.

"Your loss," I say to him. "Like you said, I did kill the killer."

"Yeah," Melvin admits. "You did."

"You don't know him," Nicki says to Melvin. "He's inclined to run off like an idiot, thinking he can solve crimes and catch bad guys single-handed."

"Yeah," Melvin says. "And run from the cops and the FBI and think he can actually get away with it."

"Who, me?" I say.

★★★

It is quiet in my apartment, but I can see plenty of life streaming outside my windows whenever I feel the need, which is frequent. My office is well-lighted and lined with books, and I will spend the next chapter of my life here, hopefully filling the shelves of fine bookstores everywhere. No one may yet confuse me with John Updike, but I have new ideas and new books to write. Always, always books to write. Because although my apartment is full of sunlight during the day and laughter and love come evening, when the moon rises and the friends go home, after Nicki falls asleep in my arms, my thoughts turn to the hole in my life, and what memories may come. Because memories don't always obey, and the demons are always, always just around the corner.

Killer in the Hills
by
Stephen Carpenter

In the thrilling sequel to _Killer_, Jack Rhodes's past comes back to haunt him when actress-turned-prostitute Penelope Fox is found murdered in a suite at the Chateau Marmont. As Jack uncovers brief memories of his drunken fling with Penelope, he revisits unsavory characters from his past to solve the puzzle of who killed Penelope—and whether he and Penelope shared more than just a brief tryst.

ABOUT THE AUTHOR

Stephen Carpenter created the NBC television series *Grimm* and wrote screenplays for *Ocean's Eleven*, *Blue Streak*, and other feature films. A graduate of the UCLA School of Theater, Film, and Television, Carpenter has also written and directed several thrillers, including *Soul Survivors*, starring Casey Affleck. His first novel, *Killer*, was an Amazon bestseller and dubbed a "blockbuster" by *Entertainment Weekly*. His latest book, *The Grimm Curse Trilogy*, was published in February 2013 by Amazon.

66333828R00133

Made in the USA
San Bernardino, CA
11 January 2018